ADVANCE PRAISE

"**A darkly comedic tale, superbly told**, *Compass* is a tour-de-force debut from an author whose name we should all remember. This is storytelling at its finest, featuring shape-shifting Arctic landscapes, a wryly laconic Inuit guide, an undersea sorceress, hockey stick harpoons, a chorus of seals and a disturbing finale. I read it wrapped in warm blankets, both grateful and envious at not having to face the same travails as the novel's hapless narrator."

> WILL FERGUSON, winner of the Giller Prize, the Leacock Medal and the Libris Award Fiction Book of the Year; author of *The Finder, Road Trip Rwanda* and *419*

"I could not put down Murray Lee's *Compass*. It's not only that it is a highly literate, intelligent novel or that the story is riveting, but also the unstrained, steady humor, the easy erudition about the history of and conditions in the high Arctic combine to make it such a compelling read. Most remarkable is the **stunningly good writing, an effortless flow of language, word choices of startling precision and beauty.** Such a rare gift Lee has, a writer we'll be hearing of. *Compass* is a joy."

> SHARON BUTALA, finalist for the Governor General's Award, winner of the W.O. Mitchell Book Prize; author of *Season of Fury and Wonder, Zara's Dead,* and *Where I Live Now*

"Start with long experience of the Arctic and its people. Add a deep knowledge of exploration history and a gift for telling tall tales. Sprinkle with dark humor and bare-faced fabrications – why did Franklin go back to sea again? – and you get **a phantasmagoric adventure, wildly original, from the land of the midnight sun.**"

> KEN MCGOOGAN, award-winning author of *Fatal Passage, Lady Franklin's Revenge,* and *Dead Reckoning*

"A bleakly comic cautionary tale. **The narrative is witty, honest, sardonic.** This is a man-against-nature novel in a grand tradition."

DOUG LOGAN, author of *Boatsense*

"Murray Lee's *Compass* flips the old-school hagiographies of European explorers lost in the High Arctic, and in their place offers up a hallucinatory, perilous voyage to The Edge, narrated by a less-than-stable outsider with **a suitcase full of stories of long-dead adventurers and a penchant for comic asides.**"

BRIAN PRESTON, author of *All the Romance a Man Can Stomach*

"A **powerful and visceral exploration** of one man's journey to the physical and psychological edge. *Compass* fuses the solitary struggle of *The Martian*, the magical realism of *Life of Pi*, and the twisted psychology of *Heart of Darkness*, layered on a stark northern landscape."

ARUN LAKRA, winner of the Woodward Newman Drama Prize and the Praxis Screenplay Competition; author of *Sequence*

"Murray Lee's debut novel *Compass* is a meditation on hubris that takes the reader to **the blinding white light of the Arctic** and the limits of a southern adventurer's endurance."

MONICA KIDD, author of *Chance Encounters with Wild Animals*

COMPASS

A NOVEL

MURRAY LEE

PUBLERATI

Cover painting reproduced with permission of Dorset Fine Arts:

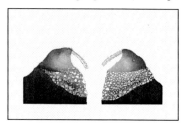

Ningiukulu Teevee
Glittering Walrus, 2019
Etching, Aquatint and Hand Colouring
78 x 121 cm

Cover design by William Oleszczuk

Publerati donates a portion of all sales to help spread literacy.
Please learn more at www.publerati.com

For Marla

"In a bleak land is not the place to enjoy solitude."

Joshua Slocum

PROLOGUE

Today's delivery was the most difficult yet. I didn't bother to count my steps — the double load and my gammy leg would have made the measure unreliable. Still, I am certain new ice is forming. The floe's edge feels farther away than it has for months. If any ships were searching for us they surely would be well on their way home by now. The birds, too, have departed. For the first time since we set sail from Portsmouth, I am alone.

It is sad to part company with Coombs and McClintock. Though I cannot say either man paid me much heed during the voyage or over the course of our troubles, they have both been most generous since their deaths. What a surprise it was to have survived them. It was Coombs, after all, who most obsessed on the "Custom of the Sea." He first made mention of it when our larder was still half-full. Alas, when it came time, Coombs could not muster much of an appetite and McClintock had no remaining teeth. If not for the sustenance they so gamely provided, I would never have had the strength to deliver them to the sea.

What a relief it is to be finally free of this chore. The little fortitude I gained from the summer sun is waning as fast as the light. The extra time it took to sink Coombs (for some reason the Welshman bobbed like a cork in the slush) almost scuppered me. Tonight I will burn the toboggan, a celebratory bonfire to retire it from its funebrial duty. Tomorrow, if the weather is fair, I will walk back to the water without it. Thirty-nine men I have delivered off the edge. With the fortieth my work will be done.

Last recorded entry in the journal
of Jedediah Briggs, Midshipman
on the HMS *Corinthian*

October 18, 1848

PART ONE

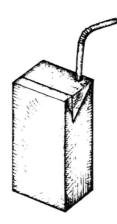

4

CHAPTER 1

I trade in the tales of adventurers. Men, mostly white, all long-since dead. Ideally they are men who had the good form to die *in extremis*, after a suitably heroic battle between their indomitable will and nature's merciless fury. An Arctic whaler locked in the ice. An ocean rower eaten by a shark. The Captain Ahabs. The Major Toms. Braggarts and boors, good riddance to them all. They can't be trusted to tell their own tales.

As a general rule, survivors make shitty storytellers.

To be sure, I am capable of constructing a story out of a man's full biography. I find, however, that those who have gone to great personal pain to escape society do not tend to function well when confined back to it. Sorting through the late-life misadventure typical of such characters—the marital discord, the mental breakdown, the bankruptcy—is more the job of the researcher I once was and not the storyteller I have become. Death in a whorehouse is a decent postscript for the hero of one of my tales. The years of despondency and alcoholism that preceded the climactic coronary are not.

Lawrence Oates' suicidal walk into an Antarctic blizzard on gangrenous feet is the archetype of the stories I tell. His final words—*I'm just going out and may be some time*—are almost certainly a fiction first told by his boss, Robert Scott, shortly before he and the rest of his party also died. I have read each of their journals and am familiar with

5

all of their lies. My professional opinion is that Scott likely told the dying Oates to leave, lest the others eat him. Regardless, with Oates out of the way, Scott gifted us with *a very gallant gentleman,* then set down his pen and died with every expectation we would say much the same of him. Both men were martyrs to the grand idea of sacrifice. To the nobility of exploration. To adventure and perseverance. As David Livingstone is said to have proclaimed, *I am prepared to go anywhere as long as it is forward.*

Dr. Livingstone spent the next decade wandering about in a daze, then died.

For years I trolled through the diaries of dead adventurers and reconstructed from their records tales of adversity and ingenuity. I assembled a cast of very gallant gentlemen. Then I traveled the world (or at least the pale, wealthy world where I was likely to find an audience) dressed up like Indiana Jones and convinced auditoriums full of soft, pasty people that somehow, miraculously, adventure is within us all. I am, I'm led to believe, a great storyteller. Until recently I was in the employ of a preeminent international geography magazine which, due to recent events, I am no longer permitted to name. Nevertheless, I earned a significant amount of money and a useful sort of fame after I abandoned academia to shill stories.

They are great stories. They are all lies.

To be clear, I have not been dishonest to the historical record. I have been faithful to the word set down by my subjects and am certain I have been telling their tales as they wished them to be told. But in being true to their word, I am complicit in their lies. I have seen the smudge marks in the margins of these men's journals. They are the fossilized tracks of the tears that once infused their emotionless text.

They are our secret. These men died believing no one wanted to know of the special sort of insanity that sets in when a man realizes he has just committed a very slow suicide.

My adventure, when it came, was of a different sort. I, too, kept a journal, but it adds nothing to my narrative. Unlike the articulate and even hand of Victorian explorers who documented each day's adventure with clinical precision (*Frederick lost his two remaining toes today, poor chap. Wind stiffening, NNE*), my notebook contains little more than the doodles of a madman. There are drawings of birds—robins I think—even though I saw no birds and have no particular affinity for the things. There is what I believe to be a map, although it too might be a bird, albeit unfinished. What text there is mostly appears in bursts of single words and short phrases, scattered throughout the journal with no regard to relative size or orientation, as random and informative as something sneezed onto the page. The overall effect is about as sensible as an envelope of cutout words, the ransom note of a glue-less psycho. In a moment of early lucidity, I took the time to carefully record an inventory of the contents of the sled: skin (caribou?); rifle; shell (1); fuel cans (2); knife; and so on. The food items I boxed off into a corner of the page, like in a larder, crossing each off in turn as the list became less a tool for rationing and more a countdown to what I assumed would be my eventual starvation. Of the scant legible prose contained in the journal, two pieces stand out. The first—a note to my wife—primarily comprised a bulleted list of things I thought she ought to do upon discovery of my body. It could charitably be described as stoic, if not for the fact that it was immediately followed by a much more effusive letter to a former and entirely estranged girlfriend. In my defense, I have a tendency to sentimentality when I'm hungry, something my wife will not bear. Remarkably, these were not among the several pages I ate.

There are, of course, no timestamps.

As a historian, I am satisfied that my failings as a diarist are unlikely to disappoint any future biographers, if for no other reason than my story no longer attracts the interest of anyone. The popular account of what happened has already been told. A stick of kindling fed into the fire of modern media—a brief flame of infamy, told rapturously once, before a couple of days when it was scrolled in type across the bottom of bigger, breaking stories. Besides, I survived, memory intact and much else in ruins. If anyone wants to know what really happened on the ice they can read my account here.

CHAPTER 2

In the early part of my career—the earnest, honest part—I was a marine archaeologist. My focus was the North: searching for the lost ships of the Franklin expedition; exhuming the corpses of dead whalers; scrabbling along beaches in search of trinkets, tin cans, or teeth in the sand. It was good work. The Arctic is chock full of such artifacts. The only problem is that for most of the year they are encased beneath ten feet of ice.

To get around this obstacle, I timed my trips north to coincide with the short window each summer when the land was thawed and the ice gone. I'd set up research camps on nameless islands, filled with graduate students who mucked about the mud in search of my treasure. Like migratory birds, we would drop in and flit around, with one eye always on the timing of our escape. Mangy icebergs lingered offshore, relics of the winter past. We would stay a few weeks, a month at most, and leave as snow flurries signaled winter's return.

Aside from that short spell each summer, the beaches and bays in which we worked are usually frozen solid. The windswept snow on the land slopes down and fuses to the flat, white plane of solid sea ice. In much of the Arctic, through most of the year, you can walk off the land and onto the ocean as easily and mindlessly as you step off your driveway and onto the street. The Inuit have been using the sea ice— the floe—for ages. They need it to get around, to hunt and to camp. It is a crucial piece of traditional Arctic infrastructure. But it has a limit. There is always a point some ways out where the sea's solid surface stops and the ocean becomes fluid again. They call that place The Edge.

For years, I have read my adventurers' accounts of The Edge. They were outsiders who bumped up against the thing in their boats, stymied in their attempts to sail onward by a great, white wall of impenetrable ice. Others, arriving from the opposite side, stopped and stared forlornly at an impassable expanse of extremely cold water. To those explorers, The Edge was a perilous place. It was the horizon made manifest in a single, straight line. It was the end from either side.

In those summer camps, however, I heard my Inuit colleagues speak of a different sort of place. To them, The Edge wasn't an obstacle or a dead end. It was a destination. A clean, crisp line marking the border between two worlds. On the dry side, man. On occasion, a bear. On the wet side, every other animal of the North. Beluga. Narwhal. Walrus. Seal. And everywhere birds, passing between the two worlds as freely as spirits. To the Inuit, The Edge is a market town, a place of wealth and renewal. Whether it was true to the stories as told or just my imagination I don't know, but in my mind I populated that place as densely as the Bronx Zoo. It was as though Noah himself had emptied his Ark right there on The Edge. Sitting in the cold gray drizzle on an empty Arctic beach while dining on tinned beef and weak tea, it sounded pretty good. It sounded like Shangri-La.

Years later, while sailing through the same waters on summer "adventure cruises," this was the story of The Edge I would tell. A place where all the animals of the North would gather, on the ice or in the ocean depending on their proclivity, to negotiate their peace or arrange for their next meal. A vivid, Arctic Eden. The description became so engorged and arousing that it seemed ridiculous I hadn't actually been there myself. So, like a teenage virgin recounting in breathless detail an imaginary conquest, I lied. In rooms that reeked of mosquito repellant and popcorn (the lecture theatres were invariably repurposed cinemas from the ships' earlier, more family-friendly, tours of duty) I painted a beautiful and intimate picture of a place I had never been.

Not that anyone really cared. The lecture series on those boats were about as academic as the passengers were adventurous. We were all pretenders. Some days I felt like I was part of an enrichment program on a busload of baboons. Besides, no one would ever know the accuracy of the floe edge I described. The voyages were so carefully timed and charted that we were pretty well guaranteed the only ice we would encounter would be in our drinks. If a ship named the *Titanic* could be taken down by a rogue iceberg in the mid-Atlantic, I didn't like the chances of the *Polar Princess* were she to come across a sheet of pack ice in the Northwest Passage. If all went well and we made good time, the same satellites that had guided us free of the islands would be tuned to find a lone iceberg in the open ocean towards the end of our voyage. There, while the ship idled safely nearby, the hardiest of the passengers would board Zodiacs for a short trip out to touch the thing, the little launches circling the berg like pilgrims at Hadj. In preparation for their supplication, each passenger would dress head to toe in a Gore-Tex outfit that cost more than the entire earnings of any member of the ship's bewildered Filipino staff. I was certain that within a week each of those jackets would be permanently stowed in some suburban closet, outgassing DEET and fraudulent memories for a lifetime.

The cruises were a side gig in what I thought was going to be the second half of my career. Usually I was part of a team of onboard experts that included an ornithologist (the bird guy) and a geologist (the rock girl—whether for gender equity purposes or in an attempt to make rocks more interesting, the geologist was pretty well always a young woman). I was the history guy. They were fun little teams, far more friendly than any group of colleagues I had ever associated with at a scientific conference. The collegiality was probably due to the fact that despite our disparate backgrounds we had one key thing in common. Nobody does the cruise ship circuit to advance an academic career.

Rachel was the rock girl who first called me out on my lie. She worked in a mine where Inuit laborers were gradually giving up their territory's gold in exchange for alcohol and gonorrhea, which when you think of it is a fairly ancient barter. A PhD thesis in invertebrate paleontology had already become trivia ("I'm the second most useless doctor in the world," she had said with a nod towards the ship's geriatric physician), and she was now working to retire her debts and support her travels. Rachel had been in the Arctic for five years. Already she had seen and done more in the North than I had in my entire career.

I saw her slip into the back row at the beginning of my talk on the Copper Inuit and their prolonged ice camps on Coronation Gulf. Rachel's presence was a welcome distraction from the man in the front row who was actually taking notes. I was happy to see her lingering by the bar with a beer during the inevitable post-talk meet and greet. I headed towards her as soon as I was free.

"The floe edge is truly amazing, isn't it?" she said.

"That it is," I said, keeping my attention on the bartender. There had been a look in her eye that had me worried and I was relieved when she said nothing more. I got my beer and turned to raise the bottle in a toast. She raised her own, then waited for me to take the first sip.

"You should see it sometime."

Any chance I had to cover my lie was betrayed by the beer I coughed out my nose. Fortunately, she was smiling as she handed me her napkin.

"What gave me away?" I asked after recovering use of my trachea.

"It was a pretty evocative description," she said. "You almost had me convinced."

Her emphasis was on the almost. I waited for her to finish.

"But you were missing the key bit."

"Yeah?" I said. I couldn't imagine what I might have been missing. I think The Edge I described even had penguins.

"It moves."

She drew out the 'ooh' like a long ocean swell.

If Rachel judged me on my fiction she didn't let on. She did, however, tell me about a professional guide in the town of Iviliiq who could take me out, a man by the name of Simeonie. She had done an extended trip with him the year before and thought he would be the ideal guide for a trip to The Edge. I demurred.

"You do want to go, don't you?"

"I do," I said. "But I also feel like it's too late. It seems like someplace I should have already been."

13

"And yet, here you are," she said. "Telling stories."

"They're good stories."

"They'd be better if they were your own," she said. "Just call Sim. You'll like him. And you'll finally get to experience what life is really like at The Edge."

"If you say so. Honestly, though, I've always felt that the most authentic experiences are those that aren't planned."

"Not everything has to be an expedition," Rachel said. "But sometimes you are going to have to make the first move."

CHAPTER 3

People used to ask me what I have against modern adventurers, why the subjects of my stories were always the wool-wearing relics of a bygone era. The short answer is simple: I'm a historian. I'm not sure how long some idiot's GoPro footage has to be up on YouTube before it becomes my business, but I can promise you that it hasn't happened yet.

There is another, longer answer and it isn't much more complicated: I disdain them. Modern adventurers are too transparently narcissistic—they are so fascinated by themselves that there isn't room for the rest of us. Their combination of self-promotion and shallowness leaves nothing to be discovered. I have always found it to be a safe bet that when someone on first glance appears to be an asshole, when you dig deep you will discover that they really, *really* are an asshole. There is an honesty to them that way. No doubt many of my Victorian gentlemen were also assholes—who else would not only be willing to leave a family behind for two years but, more tellingly, would also have a family that was happy to see them go? I know for a fact that my stable of adventurers also includes narcissists, pederasts, bigots, and bullies. But they at least had the class to pretend they were doing it for Queen and Country.

Worse, today's adventurers are too careful, too prepared. They live-blog their feat while engineering all the risk, both physical and psychic, out of it. There is something about sailing off the edge of the known world that just doesn't compare to jumping off a bridge with exactly the right amount of rope. It's not that I don't appreciate good planning or sound engineering, it's just that I don't find it all that exciting. Flying at 40,000 feet in a 787 may be amazing but it isn't an adventure and I don't need some blowhard in the seat next to me nattering on about it all the way across the Atlantic.

I had nine months between my encounter with Rachel and when I first stepped foot on the ice. I had a full three-quarters of a year to prepare. I think I only took two days to pack.

I wasn't rushed, nor was I unready. I just wanted to feel authentic.

CHAPTER 4

My journey to Iviliiq took me first to Winnipeg, a city that believes there is something special about being almost exactly in the center of the continent. Well, Winnipeg, there's not. If you don't believe me, ask Tashkent. Although there ought to be some poetry in starting an expedition to the edge of a continent from its center, there is as it turns out, absolutely nothing poetic about Winnipeg. It's the kind of city that prides itself on a list of famous people who have left, without acknowledging that other, longer, list of regular people who also managed to get out and aren't coming back. I used to have to travel through the city regularly—it, along with the dozen or so other self-proclaimed "Gateways to the North," was an important stop for both earlier research trips and later speaking tours. I've done my time in the Peg. I don't think they will be asking me back.

From Winnipeg I traveled more or less due north on a series of ever-smaller aircraft. The kind of planes where pimple-faced pilots—kids I wouldn't trust to drive my car—stoop part-way out of the cockpit to give the safety briefing. On one of the legs one of these child-pilots handed me a juice box.

By the second stop I noticed that the trees had grown thin and scraggly. By the third, they were gone.

At each landing strip the plane would taxi off the gravel runway and up to a terminal building that had the general dimensions and grace of a shipping container. There, my fellow passengers and I would mill about as the pilots rearranged cargo. "Gotta get the balance right," the juice-box pilot told me. It sounded like a delicate job, but the work on the apron looked about as methodical as when I rummage around the house searching for my keys.

I distracted myself by studying my fellow passengers. There was a young mother who was no doubt returning from giving birth in the South, carrying, as she was, a newborn baby and a large box of doughnuts. I could only hope that the latter was her own idea and not a request of the expectant father ("Oh hey, honey, while you're down there..."). They were in the company of an older woman who, despite her joy with the baby, did not look well. A hospital bracelet under her cuff suggested that she, too, was on medical travel. Then there were the two other southerners besides me. One was obvious—a tradesman, a Newfoundlander by the sounds of it, who had his toolbox as his carry-on. "If they're gonna lose anything, it ain't gonna be my tools," he said, looking out the window at the gong show beneath the plane. The other southerner was young and looked at ease with the delay. I would have thought she was a teacher, but it was the time of year when they migrate the other way. I lingered a little too long attempting to figure her out. She took this as an invitation to talk.

"I'm guessing this isn't your first time in the North?"

"How can you tell?" I asked.

"I dunno. You look like you belong up here," she said. "Maybe it's the beard?"

You don't know the half of it, my friend, I thought. I'm paid to look like the North. It's a cultivated ruggedness. The magazine I worked for hired a stylist who so filled my closet with flannel shirts and down vests that I could outfit a camp of lumberjacks. That was the closet I had looted when packing for this trip. And the beard? It was specifically designed to be longer and looser than what any professional might wear, but still shorter and less self-conscious than current hipster fashion. It could be nothing but the beard of an adventurer. And it cost me thirty bucks twice a month to have some hipster barber shape it that way.

"It's a disguise," I said. "Besides, I have a very weak chin. I'm actually from the States. How about yourself?"

"Flin Flon," she said, with apparent confidence that an American would know where that might be.

"You don't say," I said. "What brings you up here?"

"I travel around the territory digitizing the work of artists in the smaller communities."

"Neat. So like a virtual museum?"

"In part. But it functions more like an online community. And a marketplace. There are some exceptional people out here doing stuff that nobody ever sees."

"Is it still art if nobody sees it?"

"What else would it be?"

"I don't know. Craft? Like is a book a book if it's never read?"

"If it's any good it ought to be." She handed me her card. "Here. You can see for yourself."

The card had the beautiful but disturbing image of a man throttling a seal. I slipped it into my pocket.

"So what communities have you seen so far?" I asked.

"All of them. I've been at it for four years."

Everybody I had ever met in the Arctic had a specific reason for why they were there. In some cases it is entirely economic—the Newfoundland laborer looking for work, for instance. More often it is personal. Generally speaking, most of them were either drawn to the North or were pushed from the South. Either they wanted to experience life at the edge of civilization or civilization wanted to be rid of them. Aside from the Inuit, of course. For them it's just home. The artist seemed to be drawn north. At the time, I believed the same to be true of me. Still, I hadn't told many people what I was up to with my trip and was coy when she brought the conversation back to me.

"I'm an author," I said. "I'm doing research for my next book."

As it turned out this wasn't even a lie.

The artist and I parted ways in the town of Rankin Inlet. She headed off with the juice-box pilot on a flight to Baker Lake while I waited for my plane to Iviliiq to be cleared for departure. Apparently there was "weather" somewhere along the route. When I asked the guy manning the counter what sort of weather, he replied with a shrug. "Fog?" he suggested. He added a goofy smile to make it even more clear he had no clue. The pilot, sitting just behind him in a little side office, continued to play with his phone and said nothing.

With the other flight already gone and my delayed flight the only one left on the day's schedule, the airport had emptied out. It was just me, the dying elder, and the new mother and her baby. I wandered the small space looking for distraction, pacing out the perimeter of my enclosure like a confined bear. In one corner I found a machine selling

Coke for three dollars a can. Taped next to the coin slot was a hand-lettered sign reading *MIGHT NOT WORK*. Next to that was the kind of candy machine that offers everything from gum, to chips, to chocolate bars, except in this case every row of its display was bare. Without a sign suggesting otherwise, I assumed this machine was operational. I wondered whether it would be more frustrating to put money in a machine that harbored Coke but refused to deliver, or in a machine that would dutifully spin an empty rack in an honest effort to provide something it did not contain. My deliberation was interrupted by the sudden static of a PA system being turned on.

"For the attention of passengers travelling to Iviliiq."

The three of us turned to the desk where the agent, only a few feet away, leaned into a microphone.

"There are no current updates."

Again with the goofy smile.

After switching off the mic the man added something in Inuktitut, which garnered a laugh from the young mother and elder. As always when people laugh in a foreign language, I assumed they were laughing at me. I suspect it is one of the fundamental insecurities of the monoglot in a multilingual world. In my case the fear is further stoked by a particularly unsettling interview I once gave on a German TV talk show. I had been discussing the varying rates of cannibalism among explorers of different European nations. From the audience's mirthful reaction, I can only hope the interpreter was talking about something else.

"Any idea when there might be an update?" I asked, trying not to sound like an impatient prick. I find the gift of empty time is only of use when you know roughly how long it is going to last.

"There's a new weather report every hour," he said. "So maybe four-o-five?"

I looked at the clock. It was 3:20. For the next forty-five minutes I attempted to read my novel but was distracted by the constant effort of trying not to check the clock every five minutes. At 4:10, a similarly suspenseful announcement on the PA was made. Still delayed. I stowed the novel and pulled out a new biography of Shackleton. I already knew how the story went and figured it wouldn't need much concentration. At least it had pictures.

From 5:05 to 6:10, I wandered the room a couple more times, played Sudoku on my phone, and made an unsuccessful attempt to return to the novel and push my way to the end of a chapter.

At 6:10, I decided the adage *no news is good news* is garbage. I realized I was hungry. I gambled three dollars on a Coke and lost. Sitting back down next to my pack, I stared for a while at the new mother's box of doughnuts.

Sometime around 6:30 I must have fallen asleep.

I woke at 7:20 to the elder kicking my foot. She gestured to the door with her thumb. Through the window I saw the mother climbing up the steps to the plane. Years of travel stress, long lines, and nearly missed connections rose up in an angst that was entirely incommensurate with the current situation. I shoved my loose gear back into my bag, hurried to the door, then fumbled through my pockets for the boarding pass. I finally found one stashed in the pages of my novel. It was for an earlier flight on a different airline but that didn't matter. The door was open and the agent waved me through without any concern to see my credentials.

A few minutes later the little plane was airborne. I looked around the cabin—the mother and baby were now sitting a row ahead of me and to my left. The elder sat two rows directly behind. It occurred to me that for an entire day we had been playing some strange Kafkaesque game of musical chairs.

I am a seasoned traveler. I don't say that with any pride. I'm not some smug, card-waving snob who shows open contempt for the tourists clogging my airports. Although, in the interest of full disclosure, I do have a Trusted Traveler card. I used to recommend to everybody that they get one until I realized that everybody *was* getting one and as result our lines were growing as long as theirs. I am in no way offended by people who can't quite work out the rules in security lines—shoes off in the US, shoes on in Canada (the opposite of what you do in their homes, oddly). On the contrary, I envy the innocence of the novice traveler. I still remember a time when the smell of jet fuel provoked a sense of excitement in me. When I was a child, my father schlepped the bags and my mother managed the paperwork and food—all I had to do was stare out the airport window with my trusted travel companion (a ratty sock monkey whose name I'm ashamed to say was just Monkey) and inhale the fumes of adventure. Now all I get from the smell of an airport is the same sort of emotion triggered by milk that might be a little off. You know—the kind you decide not to put in your coffee but still put back in the fridge. Not revulsion. More like resignation.

By seasoned what I mean is that I'm experienced. I am a competent and generally efficient traveler. I have familiarity with airports and airplanes and can trudge through the routines of travel as brainlessly as you make your way through your morning ablutions. On occasion, fellow travelers—particularly worried travelers—read this dulling of emotion as a sign of great patience, as if through contemplation and repetition I have managed to achieve some sort of enlightenment that goes beyond my frequent-flyer status. I have not. If there is an ascetic aspect to my travelling, the monastic traditions I adhere to are much more Benedictine than Buddhist. More hair shirt, less Zen.

I think back to the untold hours I have spent in completely unintentional trance-like states and realize I have squandered a great opportunity. I have given months of my life to standing in lines and staring at the sky and have accomplished nothing for it. I have *spent* time. And in return I received nothing. Stoners coming out of a thirty-minute high have more life-changing insights than I have had in years of travel. I may be relatively patient and am a rockstar at Sudoku, but I don't think either of those attributes would impress my fellow friars after six months of contemplative silence.

Perhaps for my next career I'll start a chain of yoga studios and meditation centers in the departures areas of airports across the world. I could call it *A Higher Plane*. We would announce the flights with a gong. Someday when you find yourself wedged into a seat beside a blissed-out businessman who reeks of massage oil and incense you'll know that I've found success.

For much of the final flight to Iviliiq I drifted in and out of consciousness. It was the kind of airplane sleep that approximates the light sedation offered with a colonoscopy and it had the same effect of only partially relieving the suffering. The world beneath us was entirely white. Feature-filled but completely foreign, it was like a NASA image of that icy moon of Jupiter (Ganymede? Europa?). I knew that some of what I was looking at was sea ice and some was land, but it was difficult to tell one from the other. My focus was frustrated by swaths of low wispy clouds that moved in and obscured the defining bits every time I thought I knew what I was seeing. As with pixelated porn, I couldn't distinguish between a crack and a ridge. At one point I woke to see that the clouds had cleared, revealing a single dark line cleaving the world in two. Blue on the right, white on the left. The floe edge. Compared to the washed-out whiteness of everything else out the window, it was absolute. Then I fell back asleep.

I had one of those intense dreams that happens right at the onset of sleep, the kind that explode fully formed within the unconscious brain. I love those dreams. They're like a single, beautiful firework that wakes you with a bang and leaves you with only traces of smoke to hint at what just happened. I get night jerks too, sometimes at the same time as these dreams. It makes me wonder if the same neuronal discharge that fires off a wild spasm in my leg has also zapped the deep brain structures that house memory and love and fear. I've never much been fond of drugs, but these dreams make me want to experiment with electricity. In this one, I was lying stark naked on a metal gurney as a team of medical students dug around elbows-deep in my open abdomen. *It's got to be in here somewhere,* one of them said. She handed me my liver. *Here. Hold this.*

I woke, as they say, with a start. It's a nice little word to encapsulate a snort, a flail, a quick search for drool and the other various processes a man requires for a rapid return from reverie to reality. I had been asleep for only a minute but when I looked back out the window the floe edge was gone. I watched for a while longer in the hope I might see it again but the low clouds were gathering closer. A few minutes later I realized that everything I was staring at and trying to sort through was cloud. There was no land, no sea—just sky. The clouds carried on unbroken until we found our own way down through them, punching out the underside five hundred feet above ground and two minutes from target.

The small plane came back to earth like a windblown balloon, bouncing twice on the gravel runway before the pilot cut back on the throttle and the plane's full weight returned to it with a sigh. The magic of flight was over. Visibility was good, the sky was bright. I, however, was still in a fog.

CHAPTER 5

The terminal building at Iviliiq wasn't *like* a shipping container, it *was* a shipping container. A couple of rectangles cut to accommodate a door and a window and it had become a building. The building was bright blue and had a series of white shapes painted across it in sharp contrast. A triangle, a weird triangle, a Nike swoosh, and some squiggles.

ᐃᕕᓕᖅ

I assumed it said Iviliiq, although for all I knew it could have said Airport or Welcome. Maybe it said Property of the Hainan Shipping Corporation. The building stood by itself at the edge of the apron, a blue box alone on a flat white floor. I could hear snowmobiles idling on the far side. With no other barrier separating the tarmac from the town, we could easily have walked around. Instead we had to pass through. It was a metaphor of an airport.

Another agent, a man so much like the last that I was momentarily puzzled about how he got there so fast, held open the door to the terminal. It was the kind of door you see on an industrial freezer. I didn't know whether to take this as a sign of the ingenuity of the Inuit, who have been repurposing bits of southern flotsam for centuries (little gifts from the gods like a piece of driftwood or an

27

abandoned British frigate), or simply a sign that it gets really, really cold up there. As I climbed the steps I looked in through the window. The waiting room appeared to contain every single person in town. I've seen Mediterranean migrant ships on the evening news less crowded than the Iviliiq airport was that day. I entered the tiny room and squeezed my way to an open space on one side. The young mother with her baby and the elder took up separate positions towards the center of the room and began to receive the crowd. I watched as everybody present cycled past both women. The mother received a variety of nose-to-nose touches and handshakes. Her baby, hidden down the back within the folds of her parka, got a lot of coos from people peering down into the space with that universal expression we seem to save for new babies. The elder received handshakes, single soft-gripped pumps of respect. It was not the hand squeezing, elbow-pumping, arm-wrestle of the South. It was the handshake I had learned from my colleagues through years of polar research. The subtle, secret handshake of Arctic society.

There was one man standing in the back of the room who was waiting his turn to greet the returnees. He was a hunter by the looks of it: big boots, well-worn parka, rifle slung over his back (Nunavut transportation safety rules: keep your shoes and your safeties on). After greeting the elder—the handshake, a deferential nod—he moved to the mother. He nosed her a little more intimately than had the others (until that point I had no idea I could tell an intimate nosing from a platonic one), kissed the baby gently on the forehead, and then lifted it out of its nest. The father. I was happy to see that he ignored the doughnuts.

"It's like theatre, eh?"

I turned and saw that I was standing beside the only other non-Inuit person in the room. We were both on the outside looking in. He had a book in one hand and a carry-on bag by the opposite foot, a departing traveler heading back south.

"Weird thing is you're going to see this same group of people everywhere you go," he said. "Sometimes it feels like there are only thirty people in this town but they always cram themselves into whatever room I'm in. A million miles of empty space and you still can't be alone."

I didn't know this guy's story, but in my broad categorization of the two types of southerners one finds in the North, I suspected he was in the group that had been pushed. He didn't sound like someone who got along well with anybody, anywhere, but somehow still managed to convince himself that the problem was with *them*. There is not much point in engaging a guy like that in conversation, so I gave him a non-committal response, the sound halfway between *hmm* and *hah* that conveys nothing but the intention of saying nothing. He seemed to accept it.

"Your bag will be on the truck," he said, pointing out the town-side window. A pickup truck had driven around the building and was pulling up in front of the terminal. "The guy you're looking for is over there."

I turned to thank him just as the agent called the flight. He was already at the door. I wanted to ask him how he knew who I was looking for but before I could say anything he stepped outside the freezer door.

I looked for my bag on the back of the truck. It was, as you would expect, certifiably adventurous. A rugged canvas duffel bag, unadorned and indestructible. In the South, it read North. In the North, it sat alone and self-aware amid a bunch of giant Tupperware containers and cardboard boxes. I didn't even have to ask for it, being so obvious that it was mine. The man unloading the truck heaved the duffel bag at me like a farmhand tossing a bale of hay. I tried, with limited success, to catch it with the same insouciance. As I regained my balance, I swung the bag over my shoulder and turned from the truck towards town. I had no idea where I was supposed to go. One of the men in the group the southerner had pointed out flicked his cigarette into the snow and moved towards me.

"Simeonie?" I asked.

"Yep," he said. He pulled off a glove and offered his hand. I think I might have surprised him with my well-executed version of the secret handshake because he seemed to soften a bit. He almost smiled. We exchanged a few pleasantries, which included my name. He repeated it only once, presumably to confirm that he had heard it right, then called me Guy for the remainder of the time I knew him. Not the French *Guy*. Just guy. As in white guy. He led me to an idling snowmobile and gestured through a cloud of exhaust for me to climb onto the back.

"Do you know the man who is flying out?" I asked over his shoulder as he took his seat in front of me. It was a strangely intimate position to be in. I was practically spooning him.

"The qallunaaq?" he said.

"The what?" I couldn't quite hear him over the tubercular sound of his snowmobile.

"White guy. Qallunaaq," he said. "Gringo."

I knew the word from my earlier trips. Embraced it even. Nobody had ever been able to give me a literal translation, offering definitions such as "man with bushy eyebrows" or "person who is useless on the land." All of the variants seemed to fit me fine.

"Right. Do you know him?"

"Yep," Simeonie said. "He's an asshole."

That was the only explanation that was coming. No job. No name. No story as to why he was there, unless that single description was intended to cover it all.

"I figured as much," I said. "Anyhow, how'd he know what I'm doing?"

"Everyone knows everything here, Guy."

On the short ride to the hotel, Simeonie gave me a tour of the town. "That's the Co-op," he shouted over the clattering noise of the snowmobile's tread on the hard-packed snow. He was pointing at a building with Co-op written on the side in very large letters. "That's the church." "That's the school." "That's the health center." It wasn't the most informative tour. Like all northern towns, Iviliiq had one of everything so it was pretty easy to figure out what each of them was. I know small towns everywhere pride themselves on having a definable number of amenities that bigger places can't count—Walmarts, stoplights, high schools. Truly remote places, however, itemize things into much broader categories. One *store.* One *school.*

The tour continued. "That's the hamlet office." "That's the RCMP." "That's my mother's house." I spun my head to try to pick out which of the little pillbox houses he was referring to. Was it the one with the broken snowmobile and dead caribou at the front or was it the one with the two dead seals out front and the broken snowmobile off to the side? He turned a corner and both candidate houses slipped out of view. I turned forward just as Simeonie pulled to a stop in front of a homely two-story house without any clear markings.

"This is the hotel."

He shifted forward in his seat. I took it to be a sign that I was supposed to get off. I slipped out from under my bag and stood up. Simeonie stayed where he was. The machine was still idling.

"If you need anything check at the Co-op."

My intrepid Inuit guide led me as far as the hotel and took off. There was no arrangement as to when I would see him again, when we were going to set out for the floe edge, what I would need to do to prepare. I wasn't even entirely certain that the nondescript building I was standing in front of was the hotel. But from its steps I could see the blue on white of the airport in the near distance, framed between the RCMP and a house that might have been his mother's. So if worst came to worst, I had a few people I could turn to for help.

I walked up the stairs and through the makeshift porch that was attached to the outside of the building like an airlock, entering a vestibule whose primary purpose was announced with a large sign reading REMOVE ALL FOOTWEAR. Judging by the absence of empty boots and the stillness of the space, I was fairly certain I was the only one inside the building. Still, I called out two *Halloos*, the second slightly louder than the first, as one typically does when trying to disperse an empty space of spirits.

The vestibule led to a small dining room, the floor of which suggested the prohibition against indoor shoes was not universally followed. It was not a nice place to be wearing socks. In the middle of the room was a table with some papers and a single pen in a Styrofoam cup. Registration. On top of an invoice made out with a reasonable representation of my name, I found a key. The fob was stamped Room 202. The number seemed a bit grand for a hotel fashioned out of a four-bedroom house. I suppose the numbering system left room for expansion, like those prairie towns that are laid out on a grid with the center being defined as the corner of 50th Avenue and 50th Street—counting down to the south and east, up to the north and west. I find it remarkable that in all their excitement for a new world, those ever-optimistic neo-Cartesian immigrants of the American West could still take one look at the stubbly plain and say, "Nah. Fifty ought to be enough." I took a wild guess and headed upstairs with my key. Room 202 was the first door on the right.

The room was much the same as every other northern hotel room I'd ever been in. It looked like the set from a high school theater program's production of *Death of a Salesman*, constructed out of painted plywood and pieces of furniture scrounged out of the basements of the actors' parents. I dropped my duffel bag on one twin bed and myself on the other. In a reflex born out of too many years of mindless travel, I turned on the TV and did one full lap through the fifty-four channels. Finding nothing of interest, I cycled back through to the hockey game I had no desire to see. I thought I'd watch one period then go for a walk to check out the town. Instead I fell asleep.

When I awoke, the hockey was gone and in its place was a game of darts. I had that concussed feeling one gets when awaking from a nap that has accidentally evolved into a deep sleep. It was an ache of consciousness compounded by the fact that for a moment I had not a clue where I was. I checked my phone and discovered two things. One, it was 1:12 a.m.—I had slept for three-and-a-half hours. Two, my phone was on the verge of death after spending the entire time I had been asleep and much of the previous day's journey in a futile search for a signal. I find it interesting that we engineer our devices to be even more desperate to stay connected than we are ourselves. I had given up as we taxied across the tarmac in Winnipeg, but my phone never quit trying to find its friends. I don't think an unplugged toaster joneses for electricity in quite the same way. Phones are like little pocket parasites that feed off Wi-Fi and the caress of human thumbs. I tranquilized the thing by putting it in airplane mode, much like one might calm a parakeet by putting a sheet over its cage, and once again turned it into a combination really shitty camera and stupidly expensive watch. I'm sure it would be an affront to my former employer and its Swiss sponsors if they knew the Korean-made phone was my only camera, and my only watch.

I turned off the TV to silence the room. From outside came the sound of children laughing. Light leaked around the curtains like water over a dam. I went to the window and parted the blinds, dissolving the dimness in my little den. Outside was a group of kids, a few playing street hockey, a couple others deconstructing a crate. One kid menacingly pointed towards my window, at me, then bent over to select from a small stack of snowballs. It looked like recess. At one a.m. The sky was still as light as it had been when I arrived in town. It wasn't necessarily bright—the entire scene was cast in the dull gray of a once-white undershirt—but it was definitely light. There were no shadows, no sun. Just the thin gruel of light on a late-May night in the Arctic.

CHAPTER 6

Sometimes I think when people talk about the midnight sun they think of their own midday summer sun stuck high in the sky over an imagined scene of a Jack London Yukon. I'm sure it's a lovely vision, but it's a bit of a stretch. It neglects a couple of things. One—the weather: a cold maritime climate that more often than not laminates a shield of clouds from the stratosphere down to about your shoulders. Two—the latitude. The Arctic is pretty far north, the sun is not. Even in the height of summer the sun never gets very high in the sky. In fact, if you go far enough north it never even truly rises. It just circles around the horizon like a pathetic little plane struggling to get airborne.

Still, it is unusual to have midday light in the middle of the night. Dropping into it from the diurnal world has always been disorienting to me. It seems to cause a decoupling of the two parts of my brain—the outer thinking bit that can read time and process the idea of a midnight street-hockey game, from the inner working bit that is tasked with keeping my body alive. A circadian arrhythmia. It's like jet-lag but without an oncoming night and the opportunity to reboot.

Despite having spent years traveling to the Arctic on summer research trips, I've never totally been able to adapt to the loss of darkness. Like a lot of southerners, I tried to cope by imposing the idea of night on a world where there was none. In the evenings I'd use sleep masks, alcohol, and for a while a few too many pills. In the mornings I'd use caffeine, alarms and, during one gloriously productive summer, one of my grad students' Ritalin. I invested in a specially-designed fly for my tent, a distinctive black nylon shell that was a landmark of the camp. It didn't work. The only significant effect was to turn my tent into a dim little hothouse, a wind-rattled incubator of sweat and sleeplessness.

Occasionally when passing through communities on the way to or from a camp, I'd find myself in a hotel room where the windows had been blacked out by tin foil. The window treatment always looked like an attempt to stave off insanity, undertaken by someone in whom it was already a little too late. The foil was typically attached with reams of Scotch tape, an ineffective adherent, which I took as a sure sign that the materials for the renovation had all been scrounged from the hotel kitchen during one desperate night. Invariably on these blacked-out windows there would be a little piece of the foil scratched back, a fingernail-sized window revealing to the quieted but still crazy inhabitant that the sun was still there.

Yet outside every one of these tin-foiled rooms, each containing a single southerner as unhealthy and pale as a mealy potato, would be a town full of people who were getting on with their lives. Elementary school kids playing hockey, teenage loiterers looking for love or trouble, adults heading off hunting—all in the dead hours from midnight to five a.m. As best as I can surmise after years of watching them in sleepless study, I think they do it by giving up on the very idea of time. Or at least they give up on the convention of time as measured in hours. Wake, wash, work, repeat. Eat when hungry. Sleep when tired. Play when there are people to play with. The time these things happen is irrelevant. Really, what's the point of a clock built on the dichotomy of noon and midnight when the sun cycles in seasons, not days? In the town of Cambridge Bay, a popular stop for cruise ships plying the Northwest Passage, there is a huge sundial which, by dint of its position well above the Arctic Circle, has the unique feature of being able to tell time twenty-four hours per day during the summer. It's a favorite photo spot for the visitors, who contort themselves to construct selfies containing the dial, its shadow, their watch (with the *real* time) and their own self-satisfied and sleep-deprived mug. I've never once seen an Inuk there. I don't know what a traditional Inuit clock would have looked like if they had ever had the inclination to invent one. It probably would have been a little jar of ice, melting and freezing over the course of months. Maybe for a watch they could strap a vial of water to their wrist. Or they could do what they've always done and just look at the land. In the Arctic there are the two opposing forces of light and dark, warm and cold—but it is not day and night. It's now and then. Summer in the Arctic is all Yang, no Yin.

My first full day in Iviliiq began with my phone bleating out an alarm, insistent that it and the time it kept were still of some importance. It was 8:30 a.m. Normally I wouldn't need to set an alarm for a time that late. At my age, my body usually ensures that I wake with the sun, presumably in the hope that someday I will find something useful to do with the morning. In Iviliiq, however, my internal clock had become inoperable. Following my evening nap, I had gone out for a walk around town, tailed the entire way by three of the street hockey players. Despite their regular and repeated questions as to my name, where I was from, why I was there, and if I was cold, the trio turned out to be fairly good guides. Their tour included all of Simeonie's sights (confirming that his mother's house was the one with the dead caribou), but also took in a number of sites unique to the youthful underworld of small-town kids. I left them at the side of the school as they squirmed in through a broken window, and was back to the hotel by 3:30 a.m. I was in bed once again by four. Sleep, which seemed impossible at the time, set in a short while later.

After silencing my alarm I lay in bed for a moment attempting to sort through my sensations. I was awake, but not necessarily rested. I might have been hungry. I definitely needed to take a leak. The outside light pressed at the back side of the curtain with a little more intensity than it had during the night. Morning enough. I swung my feet out of bed and padded to the bathroom to begin the process of reassembling myself for a new day.

After I got dressed, I went back to the window. The scene outside was deserted. Where a few hours earlier there had been the noise and energy of an elementary school recess there was now nothing. No kids. No people. Nothing. It was a Tuesday morning in late spring. It was, presumably, rush hour. And there wasn't a living being in sight.

I wandered the streets and took in, for the third time in twelve hours, the same small collection of sights. In the absence of any activity the tiny town seemed even smaller. It was like an off-season theme park. The hotel itself was just a little off center, framing one edge of a cluster of buildings that looked to serve all of the community's commercial and administrative needs. The three other edges were bound by the Co-op, the school, and the RCMP. Between these sat a core consisting of a church (Catholic), the nursing station, the Hunters and Trappers Organization, and an administrative building that I took to be the Hamlet Office. Each had been assigned its own signature color: primary colors for the older, more important buildings, and a slightly wider and more garish palette for the secondary or newer buildings. Only the church was white, its squat steeple pressing up out of the snow like a schoolboy's erection.

I paused in front of the glowing orange building housing the town's administrative offices. Three flagpoles were aligned in front. In the center was the flag of Canada, shredded back to mid-maple leaf by the endless arctic wind. To its left was the almost cartoonish yellow and red Inuksuk flag of the territory. Intact against the elements, it must have been either a recent replacement or, being designed for Nunavut, been made out of a Kevlar weave. The rightmost pole carried a flag I had never seen before. With blue bars against a white background, its center featured a single walrus, standing improbably on its hind flippers. The beast was either playing a drum or humping a snow saucer, I couldn't quite tell which. I assumed it was the flag of Iviliiq.

I stood in front of the Hamlet Office and looked back over the empty town. The only sound I could hear was the flapping of flags on the masts behind me, the soft slap of slack sails on an abandoned ship. There were supposed to be nine hundred other people housed in the community but unless they had all left overnight, they were as effectively and efficiently hidden away as in a cemetery. It felt like I was playing a giant game of hide-and-seek and I was "it." I strained to hear anything that might betray the presence of other people but heard nothing. I started to walk and a bubble of my own noise rose up around me. My parka and wind pants rustled out the taffeta complaints of a prom dress, my lungs wheezed up a cloud of fog in front of me, and my boots squeaked with the slightly syncopated rhythm of my lopsided gait on the snow. I was a one-man band. A wheezy, wrinkly, jazzy ensemble hobbling across the snow. My limp is subtle but ever-present. Usually it is most noticeable on my entry from the wings onto one of the stages upon which I used to speak. To my fans it spoke of an untold adventure; to my detractors of affectation. The truth, always more prosaic, is that it is caused by a slight leg-length discrepancy, the result of an overzealous German nanny and a home-made high-chair that was significantly more resilient than my two-year-old femur.

I squeaked, wheezed, and rustled my way out of the core of buildings into the maze of surrounding little houses. Each house was accompanied by the detritus of a traditional economy—snowmobiles and sleds, upturned boats waiting for the return of water, clothing lines strung with the pelts of hares or foxes and, everywhere, scattered bits of caribou and the carcasses of seals. Animals and machines were all in various states of disassembly. It was the shop-yard of a factory that rendered wilderness into food, clothing, and the occasional jaunty hat. Any arctic animal that might accidentally wander into an Inuit town would probably recoil in horror like an Allied soldier entering Birkenau. I paused in front of one house to try to identify a particularly gruesome animal part and noticed the curtains flutter. A small child was standing sentinel by the edge of the window. I waved and the child disappeared into the darkness of the room behind. Aside from that child, the only other company I had on my walk were the dogs. One per house, each attached to its own little box by a long chain. They watched me with the same silent regard.

Then, without warning, the town was over. I walked between two houses and took twenty more steps into nothing. The snow sloped down to the ice and the ice carried across to the hills on the far side of the bay. A white, endless expanse unmarked by man.

CHAPTER 7

I heard a rearrangement of background noise from behind, the crescendo-decrescendo of a vehicle pulling to a stop on snow. It was punctuated with the percussive thump of a car door closing. Faint at first, then clearer, closer, a staccato squeak in the meter of a man. I read once that among the many Inuktitut words that deal with snow there is one—*qiqiqrijarpuq*—that means "to make the sound of squeaking while walking" and another—*qiqiqritaarivaa*—that means "to make a game of hearing one's footsteps." I can only imagine there are others that describe the effort it takes to stay silent. I suspect Inuit teenagers through the ages must have had a hell of a time sneaking back into the igloo after a late night out.

I continued to look out over the frozen bay while I listened to the person's approach. The squeak stepped up behind me. When it stopped, I turned. I was surprised to see that it was a cop.

"Having second thoughts?" he asked. He was looking into the emptiness past me.

"No," I said. My only concern with the trip at that point had to do with the fact everybody already seemed to know about it. "Should I?"

"You should be fine. You've got a good guide," he said, turning to me. I felt like I was under surveillance, as though he were gathering information to be used later at trial. "With a good enough guide any idiot can be a hero."

He was smiling, sort of, and had a relaxed posture. His hands were deep in his pockets, leaving the gun, Taser, and various other accoutrements of his police belt within as easy reach to me as they were to him. But his demeanor was as icy as the land around us. I got the distinct impression he did not like me. I wondered if this was police intimidation, Canadian style—the slipping of veiled insults into an otherwise pleasant conversation. Torture would be not offering to share a doughnut.

"Lance Brisebois," he said, offering a hand. His knuckle-crushing handshake was most definitely not Indigenous. "RCMP."

"I figured." The guy had a name tag with that very same information, a yellow stripe down the side of his pants, a gun, an imposing force-issued parka and the requisite Dudley Do-Right chin cleft. Idling behind him was a juiced-up pickup truck with the letters RCMP emblazoned across its side. He wasn't exactly undercover.

"I'm going to need you to fill out some paperwork before you head out," he said. "Contact information, travel plans, next of kin. That kind of thing."

This was obviously the "kind of thing" required in order to recover and properly dispose of a body. Brisebois was doing a little prophylactic police work to make things easier should his future services be required. It was a reasonable request, but I would have appreciated if he could have done it in a less grim manner.

"No problem," I said, trying to sound helpful. Cheery even. Delighted to fill out my own toe tag. "I can swing by the detachment later today if you'd like."

"I was thinking we could do it now," he said. "Do you mind coming with me."

Like authority figures everywhere, he used grammar to dress up an order as a question, without bothering to adorn it with genuine inflection. I wondered if this were a learned skill, something taught at Mountie School perhaps, or if Corporal Brisebois had innate talent. A natural asshole.

"Sure," I said.

I followed him to the truck. Brisebois held open the rear door to the pickup's cab. It opened into a caged-in space the size of a dog kennel.

"Sorry. I'd let you ride up front but, you know. Policy," he said. "Besides, I've got a lot of crap on the front seat."

He slammed the door. As he walked around the truck I looked through the wire mesh at the passenger seat in front. Under a bulky pair of gloves was a small and slightly disorderly stack of papers. Partially obscured under that was a book. Otherwise the space was clear. I suspected that the policy Brisebois was referencing when confining me to the rear was his own. I have had the occasion to ride in police vehicles a number of times in my life. Only once before had it been in the back.

The ride to the detachment was silent and short, a quick rewind of my previous tours of the town. I used the time to study the side of Brisebois' head. There was something about the man that reminded me of someone. Beyond the nondescript general coppishness of him—square jaw, small eyes, stupid moustache—he struck me as someone I had seen before, possibly somewhere outside the force. Yet, other than for his sideburn, a burly and ill-trimmed beast that hung in front of

44

his ear like a budding mutton chop, I could find nothing unique nor familiar about him.

We pulled up in front of the detachment. Brisebois grabbed his pile from the passenger seat and stepped outside. I reached for the door handle to follow after him. It wasn't there. I suppose it makes sense that they wouldn't put door handles inside the prisoner compartment of police cars. They probably don't have doorknobs on the inside of jail cells either. Like a dog, I waited to be released from my cage and was then led wordlessly up the steel steps to the RCMP office. Brisebois dropped his papers on a desk a few steps inside the door and gestured to the seat in front. He stepped around a corner and disappeared into the next room. I sat down and scanned the meager bureaucracy of the office. There were a few filing cabinets, a base station for a pair of radios, and a long, narrow table with a fax machine. A second desk, dusty and clear, occupied a space identical to the one I was at. The room looked to be set up as a two-member detachment, although there was no sign of Brisebois' partner. The walls were decorated with the usual collection of union posters, pinned-up memos, and an oversized portrait of Queen Elizabeth, looking appropriately unamused.

Two other photos caught my attention. They were small old black-and-white shots, simply framed, that hung beside a filing cabinet out of sight of the Queen. One was of a wooden fort sitting on empty prairie; the other of a small group of officers. From the uniforms I recognized the latter as being members of the Northwest Mounted Police, the great expeditionary force that helped settle the Canadian West, and the direct forerunner to the RCMP. Presumably the fort was one of theirs. I had spent a couple of years researching the NWMP as part of a book I wrote on Jerry Potts, the legendary Métis guide who almost single-handedly ensured the peaceful and well-policed settlement of the northern prairies. In the process of writing the book I retraced the entire route of their "great march west." If anyone could identify the fort, I figured it ought to be me. The building in the photo was of fairly rough construction, mostly of slim logs that stood straight up, as in a stockade. A Union Jack flew from inside. Outside, between the fort and a river, were a couple of tepees and a group of Indians sitting on the bald-ass prairie. I was fairly sure they were Blackfoot. I suspected it had to be an early photo of either Fort Macleod or Fort Calgary. My money was on Calgary. I got out of my chair to read the small caption lettered across the bottom of the photo.

— *Fort Brisebois, NWT 1876* —

Technically, I was correct. Fort Brisebois had been renamed Fort Calgary a year after its founding, when a near-mutiny ended the career of its egocentric commander and namesake. I did not, however, feel much joy with my ability to identify the place. Instead, I immediately checked the photo of the officers that hung below and confirmed two things. One: Inspector Éphrem A. Brisebois, the founder of the fort—a blowhard and buffoon whom I eviscerated with a chapter in my book on Potts—was central among them, looking every inch the prig I had made him out to be. Two: he looked a hell of a lot like Lance.

I looked back to the desk, to the book that was still partially covered by papers. I walked back and slipped it out from the pile. The front cover was facing down, but the identity of the book was without

46

doubt. Facing up—facing me—was the jacket photo of myself. Under that, this: "A relentless rebuke of one of the founding myths of the Canadian West, *Jerry Potts* strips the serge off the NWMP." I turned to the index (whatever my failings may be as an author, good indexing is not among them) and found several pages linked to "Brisebois, Éphrem A." I chose one at random and thumbed through to page 247. The book seemed to open naturally to the page.

Éphrem A. Brisebois. In my research I have never been able to determine what the A stood for. Pre-NWMP records show no sign of either an initial or a middle name. In Colonel James Macleod's terse exchanges both with and about Brisebois, the middle initial is never used, despite a variety of other colorful names and epithets he bestows upon his subordinate. But the 'A' became ever-present in Brisebois' own writing afterwards, a little flourish the man had permanently placed between his names, inked on his signature like a tattoo. Perhaps it stood for Affectation.

"Good book, eh?" Brisebois said, rounding the corner back into the room. He was carrying a manila folder and two mismatched mugs of coffee. "Well researched."

"The stuff about Potts, maybe." I snapped the book shut and placed it back on the desk, sliding it into the neutral space between the two mugs Brisebois had set down. I sat myself back in the seat opposite him. "He was a pretty remarkable guy."

"Macleod, too," he said. "*A lone light of competence on a force of misfits and remittance men.*"

"Did I write that?"

"You did." Brisebois took a sip of his coffee.

"Huh."

We watched each other in silence. Him holding his mug comfortably in the space between the table and his face. Me sitting back in a posture of false repose. I wondered what his relation to the Inspector might be, if he might be his great-grandson or more likely a bloodline or two removed. *Jerry Potts* had been published twelve years earlier, likely right around the time the man in front of me was finishing his training. The details of Éphrem's life were probably a lot fresher to Brisebois than they were to me. I realized there was no place I could take the conversation that would end in my favor. I had no move. He had me in checkmate in a chess game I had only just realized we were playing.

I sat forward and reached for my mug in a gesture of forfeit. The coffee was the color of a hush puppy, creamy and almost certainly excessively sweet. A double-double as Canadians like to call it, a candy coating concealing really crappy coffee. I took an unenthusiastic sip.

"So you've got some paperwork for me?" I asked of the folder Brisebois had in front of him.

I filled out a number of forms to document my identity. Home address and phone number were easy, as was next of kin. Under "emergency contact" I put my father, listing the number of the cell phone he hardly knew how to operate. Although he had long ago been divested of the powers that might be required in an actual emergency, he still occupied the position in a ceremonial role. Obviously I didn't expect that anyone was going to actually have to call him. If I had, I probably would have told the old man where I was going.

I had a bit more difficulty with the line that asked for an occupation. On customs forms I sometimes use *raconteur*, if for no

48

other reason than to solicit a guess of what it might mean. For a lark I have on occasion written *explorer*; in more sober moments, *historian*. I didn't feel comfortable using any of those titles with Brisebois watching. Instead, I entered *author* and moved on to the next form.

"What's this?" I asked.

"It's a map."

"Of what?" I recognize now that the question made me look like even more of an idiot. It was obviously a basic outline map, which I had assumed was of the Iviliiq area. I just didn't recognize the complicated pattern of bays, lakes, and islands in the unlabeled line map. It was as unique and indecipherable as a fingerprint.

"Of here," Brisebois said. "If you can just make a rough sketch of your intended route."

I couldn't. Beyond being unable to mark where we were going, I wouldn't have even been able to point out where I was.

"Just a vague idea of where you might be headed."

The pen was in my right hand. The paper was held down with my left. I had nothing to connect the two.

"We're going to the floe edge," I said. "I haven't worked out the details with Simeonie yet as to our exact route."

"Nothing?"

I put down the pen.

"Amazing," Brisebois said. He took the paper and pen from me and made a few quick marks, including an X and an arrow. It looked like a treasure map. He filed it under the other pages he had collected. "Do you know how long you're going to be out?"

"My flight home is in five days," I said. "Hopefully we'll be back by then."

Brisebois didn't respond. Instead he stood up and walked to a filing cabinet, which opened with an ill-lubricated creak. The papers, my file, disappeared inside. He stayed there, an elbow resting on the top of the cabinet. He had taken his coffee with him. The interview was over.

"Is that all you need?" I asked.

He took a sip of his coffee. "Yup."

I started to stand. Brisebois interrupted me when I was halfway off my chair.

"Before you go, would you mind signing the book." Again without the inflection. He held the pen out for me as one might offer an instrument of self-sacrifice.

"You can make it out to Éphrem."

CHAPTER 8

There was an anthropology student who spent a month in the field with me, using the job of research assistant to get closer to the material that was of interest to her. I was cataloguing the contents of a recently excavated latrine from an 18th-century exploration camp, a summer-long project that revealed nothing but the fishbones and fastidiousness characteristic of the Danes. Seriously, Scandinavians recycle too much. A thousand years from now no one will ever know they existed. Lindsay's thesis, the work she was doing on the side, involved interviewing local elders to trace the evolution of myth across the Arctic. I invited myself along on one of her interviews in the hope there might be some local knowledge about the place where I had been digging.

As we walked through the rain back to our camp, I reflected on the conversation we had just had with an elderly couple. I had been coming to the North for years and working alongside Inuit the entire time. Never had I heard any of them speak so candidly of spirituality. It felt like my first glimpse of a parallel world I had not known existed. Before the cold drizzle could completely wash away the warmth of their tea and bannock, I asked Lindsay about it.

"How widely do people believe that stuff?" I asked.

"That's what I'm trying to figure out. Some of those myths trace back in one form or another to Siberia. Assuming that's what you mean by *that stuff*."

"That's what I mean," I said. "But I was wondering more about how widely people believe it here. I've never heard anyone mention anything like that before."

"Have you asked?"

"No, but still you'd think it might have come up sometime in conversation."

"With you?"

"Yeah."

"Uh, no offence, but you're an outsider, and you're only here to look for traces of other outsiders. You're probably not someone anyone is going to be sharing their core beliefs with."

"But that couple talked freely to you," I said. "You're not exactly a local."

"No, but they invited me in specifically to talk about spirituality. They weren't just telling me stories. The only right I have to hear any of what they had to say is because I'm trying to help understand how those myths have evolved. If I'm not doing that I'm wasting everyone's time."

I mistook her cynicism for self-doubt. "Even when it seems most unproductive, Lindsay, data collection is never a waste of time. You can always make sense of it later."

She stopped walking.

"I completely disagree with everything you just said."

"Really?"

"Absolutely. Those myths aren't *data*. They're not artifacts I can stick in a drawer back at a museum. None of this means anything outside of how these people perceive it. It doesn't matter what field of science you're in—anthropology, archeology, whatever—context is everything. It's like your latrine. You can dig all you want but unless you know what you're looking at, all you're ever going to find is someone else's shit."

"Calling it shit might be a bit harsh, no?"

"Depends on whose project we're talking about. Look, it's a huge privilege to be able to talk to anyone about their beliefs. I've got incredible respect for this community. To honor that, I've got to make sure I'm doing my job. If all I want to do is drink tea and listen to old people talk, I should visit my grandmother."

"That sounds entertaining. Can I come watch that, too?"

"Do you want me to set the two of you up on a date?"

I laughed. Still, it stung.

I followed her to interviews for the remainder of our time in that camp, continuing well after I had given up hope there would be anything to learn from the locals about my Nordic shitter. I think some of our colleagues in the camp thought I was feigning an interest in Inuit spirituality in an attempt to get into Lindsay's pants. They were wrong. I wasn't so much interested in her or her thesis; I just thought it might be useful if I could learn how to get people to talk as freely as she did.

I owe Lindsay a lot. That summer's dig turned out to be a complete bust. As she put it, what we found really was just someone else's shit. Back at the university my department head—a young prima donna who seemed to publish a paper per week—began to put the screws into me to produce more, always managing to slip in a reference to my "upcoming" tenure review, after making clear his disappointment with my current performance. As managerial techniques go, it was simultaneously motivating and emasculating.

After the latrine fiasco, I decided to borrow a bit from Lindsay's methods and incorporated interviews of elders into the research design for the following summer's field trip. While my assistants mucked about in the rain, I sat sheltered in local homes sipping tea and talking to locals. Much of what I heard was utter nonsense. One possibly demented old coot spent an afternoon regaling me with an account of his Cold War encounter with a Soviet submarine, but some of it was gold. After my fifth day of interviews, I returned to camp with the giddy and impatient order that we pack up our work and move across the bay, a moment of inspired leadership completely out of character with what my team had come to expect. It was an unpopular decision met with murmurs of mutiny, particularly as my only contribution to the rushed disassembly of our dig was to grab a bag and scoop up all of the little numbered tags the team had diligently laid out over the site. My genius, however, was revealed two days later as the forecastle of a forgotten frigate arose out of the sand. It was a great find, and news of the discovery and of my use of local knowledge spread widely and rapidly. I was a hero, a modern-day John Rae, reassembling the last days of lost white men from echoes and artifacts. And at the same time, I learned how to tell a story.

You should trust that a culture that never bothered to figure out a way to write things down is going to develop a knack for conveying information through the spoken word. In every Indigenous community there are elders who are virtuosic storytellers, masters of cadence and tone who can stick a story into your mind as surely as had they pinned the notes to your forehead. When I found myself in one of those homes there would be no interview. There was nothing for me to say. You don't converse with that kind of storyteller. You just open your ears for them and hand over the keys to your brain. This is how the story of the frigate passed into my possession. Despite my reputation for embellishment and self-aggrandizement, the version of that tale I tell is true to the one I first heard. I know the story sounds too good to be true. It had to. If it didn't, people would have stopped talking about it ten years after the bloody thing sank.

Thus began my transformation from academic to entertainer. Like many who have made the same transition, I did it believing that this was where I would find the sweet spot as an educator. For a while, it was. I wove the tales I heard into the papers I wrote and the lectures I gave. I published widely. My classes were fully subscribed. Students were engaged. Awards were given. But over time I let my own telling of the stories I was supposed to be collecting take over. My writing migrated from journals and textbooks to magazines and bestseller shelves. My speaking platform moved from graduate seminars to guest lectures. I found success, if not tenure. You know your academic career is over when your alma mater offers you an honorary degree. The next thing I knew I was sitting at the captain's table. It sounds like a great metaphor until you find yourself eating a shrimp cocktail beside some prick in a white suit.

I thanked Lindsay once, indirectly. Many years after our summer together I wrote a nice acknowledgement to her in the preface of my book on the third voyage of Captain Cook, the research for which involved interviews with elders all through the Aleutian Islands. Since our summer together, Lindsay had gone on to achieve the academic success we all knew was coming, and at the time the book was published, she had just been appointed director of the prestigious International Circumpolar Institute. She never acknowledged my acknowledgement. She did, however, acknowledge my book. Lindsay personally penned a merciless review in the Institute's academic journal. *So many words,* she had written. *So little meaning.*

I thought of Lindsay as I walked back from the RCMP detachment. There was clearly a story left behind in that room, like a single gift left unopened under the tree. I wanted to know more about Lance, about his relationship to Éphrem A. Brisebois. I was curious whether the Corporal was the kind of person who was drawn to the North or the sort who was pushed from the South. I wanted to know what had happened to his missing partner. After my summer with Lindsay, I had become the sort of guy who could pull out all that information and more. Meaner, more reticent men than Lance have confided in me things they were only just admitting themselves. The fact that I know all the answers now (great-grandson, pushed, on stress leave) doesn't change the fact that when sitting across the desk from him in his office, I chose to leave it all untouched.

CHAPTER 9

I arrived back from the detachment to find Simeonie sitting on the steps of the hotel. He was smoking a cigarette. He took a long draw, then leaned back and released a cloud that briefly obscured the *No Smoking Within 5 Metres* sign that was nailed to the wall above his head. I caught a faint whiff of tobacco before the cloud was sucked away into the cold arctic breeze.

"What'd Woody want?" he asked. "You under arrest?"

"Ah, no," I said. I wondered whether the nickname was one Lance himself used or if it was something the community had bestowed upon him. "Not yet, at least. He had some paperwork for me to do."

"No doubt. Vital police work, I'm sure." Simeonie blew out another cloud. "Did he give you a beacon?"

I wasn't entirely sure what sort of beacon he was talking about, but I knew for certain the only thing I had left the detachment with was a vague sense of inadequacy. "Was he supposed to?"

"He shoulda. The government gave two to every community. Usually search and rescue keeps them. Woody here thinks the RCMP ought to have them. Wants to keep them secure."

"Why?"

"Probably so he doesn't have to go looking for anyone."

My feeling of inadequacy was morphing into insecurity. "Is that going to be a problem?"

"Not if we don't get lost." He took another drag on his cigarette, watched me as he held it in, then released a cloud to his side. "Besides, I've got a satellite phone."

I'd had a satellite phone once, bought on grant money for use during my summer research trips. It never found much use other than in the delivery of unactionable family news to a homesick crew. I had tried to take it when I emptied out my office at the university, but had made the mistake of placing it on top of a box-load of books. My department head plucked it out as I walked past him in the hall.

"Well, then. I guess we're set," I said. "When do we leave?"

"Gotta wait for the weather." Simeonie looked off into the indeterminate distance as one does when speaking of weather, God, or love. As is usually the case when people speak of such things, I saw nothing. The day might not have been exactly balmy but to my eyes it at least seemed reasonably non-malevolent.

"What kind of weather do we need?"

"We need wind we can trust," he said. "If it's blowing onshore it will bring in crap ice."

"And if it's blowing offshore?"

"It might take us with it."

"Huh," I said. "So which way is it going now?"

"Any way it wants."

As if to illustrate the point, Simeonie exhaled another cloud of smoke. It lingered in the space between us for a moment before an unseen force drew it past my left ear, around the back of my head and off towards the Hamlet Office to my right. As I watched the cloud disperse, I noticed the flags were extended stiffly in the opposite direction from earlier in the morning.

"But you still think we'll be able to get out before I have to leave?" I asked.

"Yep."

"Awesome."

"Should be able to get back, too." He pressed his cigarette into the snow beside his boot and stood up. "Store closes at seven. There's some stuff there you need to pick up today. If the weather's good we can leave tomorrow."

The conversation and the smell of his tobacco had me craving a cigarette. Although it had been years since I had smoked daily, I still found myself with a cigar or cigarette in my mouth often enough to maintain an almost constant craving. It seemed like a good time for a smoke.

"Before you go, do you mind if I bum a cigarette off you?"

"You didn't bring any up?"

"I don't smoke."

"You should have brought some up. They're expensive here."

"I'll buy you a pack when we stock up at the Co-op later."

"No need," Simeonie said, handing over the pack. He flashed a smile made up of a few irregularly spaced and yellow-stained teeth. "I don't smoke either."

I watched him walk away then popped open the pack to fish out a cigarette. It was one of those stupid Canadian packages, a flat, flip-topped square the size of a piece of toast. Two rows of cigarettes were lined up as politely as crayons. The smell of cut tobacco was beautiful and sweet, far more alluring than the sad-faced child whose photo took

59

up the majority of the package's front under an all-caps admonition that smoking causes orphans. I pulled a single cigarette along the underside of my nose before flipping it around to stick it to my bottom lip, then reached into my pants pocket for the lighter that hasn't been there for years.

The pack contained neither matches nor a lighter. I looked back up for Simeonie just as he stepped out of sight around the far side of a house. With the unlit cigarette still hanging from my lip, I headed inside to find a light. In the front room there was a single promising drawer. It held exactly the right sort of junk: a pack of cards, a cribbage board, batteries of uncertain charge, a Nicholas Sparks novel. I pawed through the loose sundries in disbelief that a lighter was not among them. A nearby cupboard contained a couple of jigsaw puzzles and a beat-up board game, none of which looked likely to contain all the requisite pieces. On the shelf above a filthy coffeemaker were three *Readers' Digests* and a dusty ball of yarn. The room reeked of boredom and the ineffective passage of unwanted time. I moved to the kitchen.

I rifled through every drawer in an increasing, nicotine-starved desperation. There were a dozen other ways I could harm myself (knives, obviously, a mallet, a distressing amount of lard), but not a single match with which to light a stupid cigarette. I was ready to give up altogether when I noticed the gas stove. I turned on a front burner, and behind the hiss of unlit gas loosing itself into the room, heard the faint tsk-tsking of an ignitor. Then, poof. The miracle of fire. With the cigarette between my lips I leaned over to suck in the flame.

"It'll be faster if you put your head in the oven."

I pulled back up. A large man brushed behind me. I guiltily hung onto my lungful of tobacco smoke for a second longer, delaying the inevitable greeting for a moment more of private pleasure. When I saw him lean into the fridge, I blew the smoke over my shoulder.

"I couldn't find a match."

The man turned around with a carton of milk in one hand, holding the refrigerator door open with his hip. He had the slightly disheveled look of someone who had either just gotten out of bed or was in the process of giving up on life. Rumpled but not yet lost. He looked like he could still pull himself together if he wanted to. Pants, for instance, would be a good start.

"That's because there aren't any." He took a swig straight from the carton, then wiped the milk from his stubble with the back of his hand. "Fire hazard. Manager's a bit of a stickler about these things."

"I suppose he wouldn't be very happy about this, then," I waggled the cigarette. "You're not going to tell on me, are you?"

"Don't have to." He placed the carton back on the shelf and released the door. "You just did. I'm Bob."

He offered me the same hand he had just used to wipe his face. I gave him the one that had been holding the cigarette.

"You're the manager of the hotel?"

"I'm the manager of the Co-op. We own the hotel." He crossed the kitchen and removed a bowl from a high cupboard. He held it out for me. "Seriously, though. Put that thing out. If you're going to smoke, you gotta do it outside."

I snuffed out my smoke against the bottom of the bowl, snapping the still-cold cigarette in half. Cut tobacco spilled out of it like blood.

Bob placed the bowl on the counter and busied himself with the process of making coffee. This involved a couple of trips to and from the front room and culminated with the dumping of a filter full of soggy grounds on top of the broken cigarette, which I had still been hoping to smoke once he departed.

"Are we the only ones staying here?" I asked.

"You're the only one," Bob said. "I'm just here to do my laundry."

"That explains the pants," I said. "I'm guessing that you don't get many guests."

"Not tourists, at least," Bob said. "If people are passing through here it's usually for work. Tradesmen and government folks mostly. We do get the occasional adventurer, though. Simeonie's clients, mostly."

"What sort of folks does he get?"

"Hunters, usually. Some scientists. Photographers. There's one guy that Simeonie has been guiding the last couple of years who comes up to film bears. French fella. Yves something. Maybe you've heard of him?"

I knew Yves. We worked for the same magazine, although as a visual artist the Frenchman was a lot higher on the totem pole than me. As with *Playboy*, we all knew that people didn't buy our rag to read the stories. And yes, I had heard of his bear project. Everybody knew about it. Although the project was as yet unfinished, and I knew of no one who could honestly claim to have seen an early cut, I had already heard rapturous descriptions of the film: epic, virtuosic, painfully beautiful, blah, blah, blah. It was to be a circumpolar opus on *Ursus Maritimus*. What I hadn't known until that moment was that he had done a lot of his filming in the Iviliiq area and that Simeonie had played a prominent role. It's due out next year, having been delayed due to Yves' need to go back north for additional footage and to capture a little human tragedy. It should be spectacular. You really ought to see it.

CHAPTER 10

There is an untold moment in the story of every great White discovery. It's the moment when our hero is gazing, gallantly no doubt, upon Xanadu. Through dogged determination, he has found his white whale. He has discovered El Dorado. And as he stands before a chimera that has been made manifest by him, and him alone, some local kid walks up and asks him what he is looking at.

Or more likely, "What's your name?"

Why it's Ernest, son. What's your name?

Edmund played soccer with the Sherpas. Amelia built paper airplanes with the schoolgirls of Fortaleza. Roald tobogganed with the kids of Gjoa Haven (although for what it's worth he was probably playing with some of his own children—the long, lonely winters Amundsen spent on King William Island have left a legacy of blue-eyed Inuit in that place). This petri dish of a planet was pretty thoroughly colonized long before anyone decided to tour it for fun. The real explorers, the first people to ever arrive any place, generally didn't document their discoveries. I would love to be able to read the journals of the captain of the first Polynesian canoe to land in Hawaii. *You're shitting me. Seriously? There isn't anybody here?* He must have felt like a genius. Or perhaps just awfully alone.

Every adventurer is first and foremost a tourist.

A few years ago a ship I was on made a port of call in Uummannaq, Greenland. To the dismay of our ornithologist, the majority of passengers signed up for a community feast, excited to partake in the once-in-a-lifetime opportunity to eat fermented auk. While the gray-haired adventurers tottered towards the high-school gymnasium, giddy and nervous as schoolchildren, I split off from the herd and headed up the hill for a bit of a break. We were at the tail end of a long voyage and I was getting tired of the crowd. Besides, I've had kiviak. There are very few foods that are improved by putrification. All I can say is that if those little birds are one of them, then they must taste god-awful fresh.

I found a rock providing a nice view of the town and sat down to consider a smoke. Dozens of steep-roofed little houses, most painted the same shade of red, were scattered atop pillows of granite. Behind me, the island's huge stone spire rose a few thousand feet straight into the sky. I watched a boy cycle absent-mindedly on a dirt road below. He noticed me and stopped. I waved. With that, the kid ditched his bike and started scrambling up the slope towards me, covering the distance in a fraction of the time I had taken. When he got to the base of my rock, he was panting. I held out a hand and hauled him up beside me.

"Why aren't you with your friends?" he asked.

"What makes you think they're my friends?" I replied. The kid looked confused. I decided I should give him an easier answer. "Kiviak," I said. I mimed barfing.

"You eat kiviak?"

"Once." I held up a single finger, then shook my head. "Never again."

"It's good. Makes you strong." My little auk-eating friend thumped his chest. "Are you strong?"

"No." I leaned towards him and tapped my temple. "But I'm smart."

For the next few minutes we went through the full menagerie of arctic animals—in Greenlandic, pidgin Inuktitut and English—as the boy interrogated me on all the creatures I had eaten. He had me beaten with walrus and seagull. I one-upped him with musk-ox and alligator.

"Do you eat bear?" he asked.

"I've eaten black bear." It was a small bite and I was coerced, but still.

"Not black bear. Nanoq."

I had not. I have read all of Gerrit de Veer's diaries. His record of the Barentsz expedition's overwintering on Novaya Zemlya in 1596 is a classic in my field. There is a particular passage in it in which de Veer documents the crew's vitamin A poisoning after having gorged themselves on a bit too much polar bear liver: *and we verily thought that we should have lost them, for all their skins came off from the foote to the head . . .*

"No. Not nanoq," I said.

"You should."

"Because it will make me strong?"

"Not strong," the boy said. He had known me for five minutes and had already, quite astutely, written off the possibility that I might ever achieve any semblance of Inuit fortitude. "Alive." His eyes widened as he said it. There was something a little spooky about the boy, but at the same time I figured he was probably just echoing some

66

bullshit his grandfather had told him.

"Alive, hey?"

The kid raised his eyebrows, remaining silent. An Inuit affirmative.

"Well then," I said. "I guess I'll have to eat a bear."

"Promise?"

"Promise."

The boy seemed to accept this. He jumped off the rock, his landing punctuating the end of our conversation. But instead of heading back down the hill towards his bike, he turned away from the town and towards the mountain. "Come with me," he said. "I want to show you something."

A local child who wants to show you something is almost invariably a more interesting guide than a hired professional. You'll miss some key sights—a kid in Agra might choose an abandoned caboose over the Taj Mahal—but you can be sure their itinerary won't be one covered by the guide books. With no idea where we were going but with a sure knowledge that I had nothing better to do, I lowered myself from my rock, brushed off my ass and followed the kid as he headed up the hill.

It was impossible to carry on a conversation due to the fact the boy was always surging ahead of me. Seriously, it was like chasing a balloon across a parking lot on a windy day. That was probably a blessing as I had neither the breath nor he the English to fill the time with words. We crested a small rise and went down a short slope. Where the obvious route headed left and back up towards the base of the cliffs, the boy took us right and down into a deepening draw. He had us jump down a couple of sketchy outcrops, then shimmy down a crevice in the rock. Just as I was about to call an end to the adventure we came to a broad ledge. On it were the ruins of a small stone house.

"Cool," I said, stepping under the lintel. I looked back out over the wall that framed the bottom half of what once was a window. "Whose place was this?"

The boy shrugged. "Come," he said.

Apparently the house was not what he wanted to show me. He led me around the corner to a secluded part of the same ledge. There, a stone slab bridged a wide crack. He hopped in beside it and gestured for me to help. Together we pivoted the slab to the side.

At first I thought we had opened a grave. I was both disturbed and intrigued, and drew in closer to inspect the contents. Although super creepy, the thing inside was most definitely not human, at least not in its entirety. It had a dome-shaped and flat-faced skull, which I assumed to be that of a person (monkey parts being a bit difficult to source in Greenland), but it was small. I figured it was either that of a child or, most unlikely, the remains of some teeny tiny pre-Inuit people. The lower jaw, however, was something else entirely. Oversized and out of place, it jutted out in an angry underbite. Its sharp triangular teeth rose up and over the upper teeth and nose hole. It looked like it might be the jaw of a small shark. While those two bits were attached together, the rest of the fella lay loose and a little scattered in the trough. Two antlers arched together to create a rib cage, the pelvis was of bone—quite possibly an actual pelvis of some other animal—and the limbs were arranged out of driftwood. Desiccated sinew and long-rotted leather and fur suggested that the creature had been tied together. I suspected it had been dressed.

"What is it?" I asked.

"Tupilak," he said.

"Tupilak?" I asked. "Seriously? Like the little carvings?"

The boy nodded. He seemed pleased with himself for bringing me to this treasure. I looked back at the thing in its crypt-like crack. The tupilak I had seen were all carvings, creepy-cute little figurines churned out for tourists like those on my boat. They were small, pocketable, and most definitely not made out of human remains. I knew the basic outlines of the story of these tchotchkes—they had evolved out of some sort of shamanic voodoo doll that Greenlanders used to use—but I had no idea that originals were still in existence. I also never imagined that one would ever look quite so sacrificial. I leaned in for a closer look. I wanted to see if there was anything inside the chest cavity. I reached in between the points of the antler and pulled out a fist-sized rock.

"What are you doing?" the boy asked.

"An autopsy," I said.

"We should leave."

"In a minute," I said. "Hang on."

I dropped the rock back into its place and leaned in further to get a better look at the jaw. I ran a finger over one of the jagged teeth and felt the serrated edge. It was definitely shark. The jaw looked to be wired to the skull, but together the two weren't affixed to anything else. I cradled the back of the skull in my right palm and, with my left hand on the chin, raised the head out of the hole.

"Alas, poor Yorick! A fellow of infinite jest." I turned towards the kid and waggled the jaw as I started into a Fozzie Bear imitation. *Waka, waka, waka.*

The look on the boy's face was one of sheer terror.

"Don't," he said. "Please." He took a couple of steps backwards. "Stop."

We walked in silence back to town. I think he was mad at me for my indiscretion with the skull. You'd figure his Danish teachers would have taught the kid Hamlet, but I guess ancient taboos are more memorable than Shakespeare. As we passed my earlier sitting rock and headed down the final pitch towards his bicycle I made one last attempt at idle conversation.

"So what does Uummannaq mean?"

"Uummannaq?"

"Yeah," I said. I considered repeating it but wasn't sure about my pronunciation. To my ears it sounded like we were saying the same thing. "What does it mean?"

"Uummannaq," he said. He pointed at the town.

"Right. But what does the name mean?"

He looked at me like he was trying to decide whether or not I would ever make sense to him. "Where are you from?" he asked.

I pointed at the boat.

The map of the North is drawn in the ink of failure. For centuries, southern men have reinforced the hulls of repurposed ships and punched their way into the ice of the Arctic. Some were looking for treasure. Most were just looking to get out the other side. Many more came to search for those who had disappeared before them. Everywhere these outsiders went, they labeled the land with the names of their dead and the hopelessness of their endeavors. On Baffin Island, for instance, there is a spot where the 16th-century privateer Martin Frobisher mined hundreds of tons of fool's gold and blew a fortune in an ill-conceived attempt to establish an English colony in the Arctic. They named the bay after him. The chutzpah is quite something; it's a little like someone naming my high school gymnasium after me in memorial to the singular humiliation of my senior prom. Nowadays, with modern navigation systems and conveniently thin ice, cruise ships like mine glide through the same waters on little more than a collective whim and the pensions of upper-middle-class urban professionals. Every fog-shrouded little beach they pass is the deserted stage of historic tragedy. My job on these trips was to tell those stories of shipwrecks and starvation—ghost stories, I suppose— as satellites guided our ship safely through a sea of despair. We were walking, as it were, on a path made of bones.

Repulse Bay; Turnabout Point; Starvation Cove. These are the English names. The Inuktitut names are much less melodramatic: Naujaat (nesting place of seagulls); Igloolik (place of many houses); Qaviqsiti (place where you do a funny dance to make someone laugh).

For what it's worth, it turns out that Uummannaq has something to do with heart.

CHAPTER 11

After leaving Bob to his laundry, I headed to my room to do a bit of work. A week before I left for Iviliiq, my editor had sent back her annotated review of a manuscript I had been working on for well over a year. Usually I admire her heavy hand. In this case, however, she had largely given up on the line-by-line word-smithing I've been so reliant on in the past (my lifelong incompetence with the hyphen may have finally been revealed in this book). Instead, the margins of the manuscript were filled with her commentary. I had sent it to her knowing it needed work. What she sent back made me wonder whether that work was going to be worth doing. The first sentence, for instance, had an annotation which began, "This is crap. Start again."

I sat in front of my laptop for a good half hour, my fingers idled by my inability to think of an alternate opening. The whole time I tried to ignore a strip of masking tape stuck to the base of the desk lamp, on which was written the Wi-Fi password for the hotel. Finally, I gave in and leaned over to read the faded ink. B0real!5. The password fit all the usual encryption criteria: at least seven characters, a capital letter, a number, a symbol, a local reference, and a near certainty that the whole thing would be forgotten before I finished typing it in. I opened a browser window and carefully entered the combination of characters when prompted for the key. On my third attempt it unlocked the internet.

The northern internet is a tease. Theoretically, the world is there for the browsing just as it is in the South. There is no censorship, no filters. There is, however, an exceedingly thin and long line through which the World Wide Web must pass. For a southern man accustomed to instant gratification that's bad enough. What's worse is that everybody else in the world operates as if we're all on the same bandwidth. Colleagues still send bloated PowerPoint files. Friends still share oversized photos of their ephemera. An occasional bonehead still thinks I want to watch a video of a dog riding a skateboard. All of that crap insists on trying to squeeze through with whatever it is that I truly need to access on the few occasions I lower my guard and connect.

As emails dropped like constipated turds into my in-box, I searched for Yves. Specifically, I searched for any teaser video I could find that might show him in the Iviliiq area. The guy, as you should expect, has an extensive online presence, all of which is beautifully laid out in high-resolution, bandwidth-busting glory. I waited an eternity for a picture of the pompous ass to assemble itself on his homepage before realizing I had to click on his face in order to access any actual content. With the help of the hotel's wimpy Wi-Fi, I labored my way to his *Upcoming Projects* page where I encountered a prominently displayed, beautiful shot of a massive white bear hauling itself out of the water and onto the ice. The beast's coat clung to its muscles like a wet T-shirt. It was almost erotic, and at the same time, absolutely terrifying.

Clicking on the image opened a video that would not play. I was, however, able to drag the time-bar through the promo and see a series of thumbnails that hinted at what I was missing. At the four-minute mark I found a short stretch with a human. I zoomed in on the small photo, pixelating it to the point of abstraction. Even so, the gap-toothed smile and sparse goatee were definitive. It was Simeonie.

I let the computer tread water on that spot in the hope the video might play. After a few minutes it fell asleep trying.

I arrived at the Co-op at six o'clock and did a quick cycle through the store's five aisles in search of Sim. Aisle one had a sad display of wilted vegetables and a cooler of outrageously priced dairy. Aisles two and three had a collection of marginally more affordable dried and tinned goods. Aisle four seemed to be entirely stocked with fishing lures and ammunition. Aisle five had a snowmobile, diapers, and what appeared to be a Big Wheel, circa 1978. It was the only store in Iviliiq, the only shop many people in the town would ever see. Somehow, from this one was supposed to cobble together a life. I was hungry and depressed after one lap through.

With Simeonie nowhere to be found, I headed to the single, bored, gum-chewing cashier. I was empty-handed and out of place. She saw me coming.

"He's not here," she said.

"Simeonie?" I asked.

She raised her eyebrows.

"I'm the guy going out with him. We might be leaving tomorrow."

"I know."

"He said there were some things I needed to pick up."

As I said it she reached beside her till and pulled out a slip. I thought it was Sim's shopping list until I saw the prices neatly totaled up down the right-hand side. It was in fact a receipt. I scanned the list. The biggest ticket items were gasoline ($140), a case of Coke ($42), and a bag of oranges ($28). Everything else—rope, sardines, tea, biscuits—rounded it out to a total of four hundred and seventy-three dollars. It seemed we were going glamping.

"So . . . Simeonie already picked this up?"

Eyebrows up. Bubble blown.

"And I need to pay?"

"Yep."

A small line had formed behind me, headed by a woman holding a frozen pizza and a box of bullets. Her toddler peered over her shoulder from his perch inside the back of her amauti. I made a face for him and fished out my American Express card. The cashier made no move to accept it.

"Visa or cash only."

"Right," I said. I thumbed through the Monopoly money that filled my wallet. I had no idea how much it added up to but was fairly sure it was nowhere near what was needed. I stowed the American Express card back into its usual spot and handed her my Visa.

"Is that everything?" she asked of the nothing I had before me.

"Guess so," I said. "Actually, have you got a lighter?"

She reached into a box below the case of tobacco behind her and handed over a little yellow Bic lighter.

"That'll be four hundred and seventy-five dollars," she said.

I pocketed the lighter with the receipt and headed for the door, then turned back. The cashier was already busy with the woman behind me. They bantered in Inuktitut while they completed the transaction. Her child stared at me the entire time. I got the clerk's attention before she started with the next customer.

"Did Simeonie say where he was going?" I asked.

"No," she said.

"Any idea where I might find him?"

"Try his mother's."

The walk from the Co-op to Simeonie's mother's house took two minutes, not including a stop to talk with a small child who may or may not have been one of my middle-of-the-night tour guides. Although she acted as though she knew me, she repeated most of the questions I had answered before. Inevitably, we got back to the topic of why I was in her town. When I reminded her that I was going on a trip with Simeonie, she pointed to a man who was bent over securing a load to a long, low sled. Then she ran away. Alone in an empty space between my two guides, I thought how lovely it would be to have a child's sense of conversational propriety. I can think of a number of cocktail parties where I would have liked to have employed the same exit.

I walked to the front of the house. The dead caribou was gone, leaving only a smear of blood and a scattering of hairs stuck to the snow in its place. I doubted I would have been able to identify the place without its signature carcass had Simeonie not been standing in front working on his sled. The design was typical of Inuit sleds—two runners, each about ten feet in length, connected by series of flat cross-pieces. It was vaguely reminiscent of a shipping pallet, or maybe a picket fence blown over on its side, except the whole thing was held together with nothing but rope. I circled it and confirmed that there was not a single nail or screw in the entire contraption. It is an ingenious design; the play in the ropes gives the runners an independent suspension, allowing them to heave over and around hummocks of ice with nothing more than the pulling power of a few dogs. If I were to try to build such a thing I would probably empty a five-pound bag of nails into it and still get permanently hung up on the first heaved hunk of ice less than a hundred meters from town.

Simeonie finished fiddling with whatever he had been doing to the right runner and stood up.

"That's a nice sled," I said.

"That's a sled," Simeonie said, pointing to the snowmobile. "This is a qamutik." He pointed at the sled.

"The sled?" I asked.

"Qamutik."

"And the snowmobile is a sled?"

"Sometimes. Or just machine."

I had heard that before. Machine. There were other machines the Inuit used—TVs, airplanes, and coffeemakers all seemed fairly vital in the times I had been north, but the snowmobile apparently deserved the word all to itself. The omnipresent ATVs I had seen on my summertime research trips must have arrived a little later than snowmobiles and had to find their own word. Those were called Hondas, regardless of the make. The qamutik, in contrast, had no replacement, either in language or on land.

"Are we taking just the one machine?" I asked.

"Do you know how to drive?"

"Of course," I said. I eyed his machine to categorize the controls. I tried to remember if a snowmobile's throttle was thumb-driven, like an ATV, or wrist-cocked, like a motorbike.

"Then we'll take two. Did you get to the store?"

"Yes," I said. "The bill's all settled."

"Good. Then there is only one more thing to do."

"Wait for the weather?"

"Meet my mother."

CHAPTER 12

Simeonie led me up the wooden steps leading to the shed-like structure tacked onto the side of the house. These plywood vestibules are ubiquitous in the North, handmade add-ons to make the government-issued "Indian housing" moderately more functional for the climate. They are a combination anteroom, air-lock, freezer, and storeroom. As we stepped into the dim space, I was hit by the smell of death. My eyes adjusted slowly, revealing in turn a few hides, a cache of bloodied tools, the ribcage of some unknown creature and, finally, the head of a musk-ox. It felt like Hannibal Lecter's workshop. Simeonie stopped with a hand on the inner door.

"Take off your boots before you go inside."

"Here?"

He didn't answer, instead opening the door and calling out to the inside of the house in Inuktitut. I searched for something inorganic to lean against and wrenched off my boots. When I was done, Simeonie stepped back and held open the door to the house. I noticed that his boots were still on.

"You're not coming in?"

"Nope."

"Is there anyone else here?"

"Just my mum."

My quizzical look was met by his mischievous grin. He motioned me inside. I stepped from the dirty plywood floor of the vestibule onto the clean white linoleum of his mother's kitchen. From darkness into light.

"Good luck," he said. He pulled the door shut behind me.

After the gloom of the antechamber, the interior of the house was as bright and clean as an operating room. The space was small and spare. The tidy kitchen opened directly into a comfortable living room. From there, a short hall disappeared into the private areas. The entire home was well under a thousand square feet. Somewhere unseen inside was Simeonie's mother.

I stood by the door in socked feet, neither fully inside—I was in the home but most clearly not at home—nor able to leave. I was hobbled by convention. Only the occasional soft sound that rippled through the space gave me reassurance that I wasn't entirely alone. After an awkward silence that couldn't have lasted more than a minute, an electric kettle on the kitchen counter began to steam, working itself up towards a full-blown whistle. I decided this was invitation enough and walked over just as the kettle snapped itself off.

A voice called out from behind a wall, "Would you mind making some tea? I'll be out in a minute."

I don't really like making other people's tea. Do they want it in a pot or a cup? What kind of tea do they prefer—real tea or some sort of chamomile sleepy-time bullshit? How strong? How do they take it? My mother was a tea-drinker and so mistrusted anyone else's hand in her brew that I never once made her a pot, not even as she lay demented and diminishing, drinking cold tea out of a nursing home's detestable plastic mugs. Fortunately, Simeonie's mother's tastes were

80

simple and reasonably easy to figure out. Beside the kettle was a teapot. Beside the teapot were two china mugs. Within reach of all that was a single box of Tetley's tea—one variety, individually bagged. I dropped two in the pot and filled it from the kettle. Then I turned around and waited with the hope she would appear before I had to decide whether it had steeped long enough.

A small woman possessing the general size and dimensions of a barrel arrived from around the corner.

"So," she said. "You must be Guy."

"And you must be Simeonie's mother," I said. I offered my hand. In absence of real names, the secret handshake would have to do.

"Come in," she said. "Let's have some tea. I want to know more about you."

She loaded the pot and the mugs onto a tray, then added a small plate with a sad-looking loaf of cake. Bypassing the kitchen table, she led me across the imaginary line that delineated the start of the living room. She set the tray on the floor at the exact spot where a coffee table ought to have been, then, ignoring the perfectly good couch behind her, sat on the floor. Despite her less-than-lithe shape she moved with fluidity into a position with straight legs in front of her. They were splayed at a forty-five degree angle. When she leaned forward to pour the tea she folded over at the waist like a clasp knife. The old lady must have had the hamstrings of an Olympic hurdler.

"Please," she said. "Sit."

To my dismay she gestured at the floor on the opposite side of the tray, not to the comfortable-looking recliner off to one side. With an involuntary and only marginally-muted groan I lowered myself to the floor. I arranged my legs beside me and leaned over on my left wrist. Everything began to ache.

Simeonie's mother handed me my tea. "So what do you do, Guy? Are you a photographer?"

"I'm a writer."

Presumably her question was more about why I was there than what I did for a living, because my answer didn't seem to satisfy her. Perhaps the occupation has little traction in a place with an entirely oral tradition. Nevertheless, there was no way I was going to tell this woman I was a storyteller.

"A writer of what?"

"Books, mostly. Some magazine articles," I said. Snarky emails. Anonymous internet postings. Unpublished journal articles. I don't have to take pride in every word I write.

"I've never met an author," she said. "Simeonie has had a lot of clients come up from the South. Photographers, filmmakers, hunters, adventurers. He even had some eco-terrorists pretending to be whale biologists. But I don't think he's ever had a writer. Why did you come? Can't you just imagine a place like this?"

"I tried," I said. "Maybe it's a failure of the imagination, but I feel like I need to actually see the floe edge."

"It's bad fishing at The Edge right now," she said. "You should go inland."

"I can imagine a fish," I said. "I need to see The Edge."

I intended the comment to be playful, but recognized it might have come across as prickish. Simeonie's mother ate a piece of cake and regarded me as if she were trying to decide which of the two it were.

I explained. "I read a lot of history. People always seem to have trouble with the floe edge—they run out of water or run out of solid ground, they get locked in the ice, their ships get crushed. There's a lot written about people just hanging around The Edge waiting to die."

"White people."

"Yes, of course. White people."

"And this makes you want to go?"

"That and the animals. I hear there are a lot of animals."

"There are." She motioned to the wall behind me. Three framed photos lined the wall below a crucifix. One was an epic shot of two walruses, fighting. The second a beautifully-lit portrait of Simeonie, laughing. The third was of a bear, hauling itself out of the water and onto the ice. The fucking Frenchman had been here too. "But I know what you mean," she said. "The floe edge can be a mystical place."

"What do you mean by mystical? Do you mean special?"

"I mean mystical." She smiled. "Which is also special."

My time with Lindsay came back to me. I could sense a story there for the telling. I took a sip of tea to create the silence for her to continue.

"There are two worlds here," she said. "There's the land,"—she knocked on the floor between her legs—"and there's the sea. The land is boring, and weak. It's a place of sickness and starvation. A place for scavengers and idiots. Ravens and caribou. People are from the land. But the power is in the sea."

She paused. I took another sip of tea.

"The problem for wise land animals such as ourselves is how to access that power. Boats let us visit, but they are vulnerable. If we are not welcome or if we have offended the sea it will push up a storm. It will blow us away and we'll be lost forever. It will crush us with a wave. Or, if it is feeling lazy and we are unlucky, it will simply tip us out and pull us under. The sea is powerful, but it is capricious."

"Capricious?"

"Fickle, temperamental. Prone to sudden, unpredictable outbursts."

"No, I know what it means. It's just… your English is very good."

"They taught me well in residential school. *That capricious girl*, the priest used to say. It's good. I will use it to lodge my complaint with his god."

I took a sip of my tea and looked again to the wall above Simeonie's portrait. It was definitely a cross.

"Sorry," I said. "I interrupted you. Please go on."

"The ice is what lets the Inuit be a people of the sea. With it we can walk on the roof of their world. We can drive our machines, build our igloos. We can travel between our communities. And where the ice comes to an end, and the water begins, we can have access to everything that the sea will provide."

"Safely."

"Safer," she said. "It's still the sea."

"Do you think the seals see it the same way? A place to be out of the ocean but not quite on land?"

"I think that depends if there is an Inuk waiting at their breathing hole."

I raised my mug to that wisdom.

"You know, most of the southern writers I've read talk about The Edge as if it were a wall, some sort of impassable barrier that stymies whatever it was that they set out to do. You describe it more as a membrane. Like a gate through which things can pass to both sides."

She shook her head. "There are only two things that pass freely between the worlds."

"Bears?"

"Yes."

"And?"

"Spirits."

I looked back to the wall, to Yves' aqua-erotic shot of the wet bear. "I get bears," I said. "Tell me about spirits."

She eyed me for a moment. I knew she was trying to decide whether I deserved the story she was considering telling. My left leg was asleep and my wrist throbbed under the weight it was awkwardly bearing. I tried my best to look relaxed and engaged.

She shifted forward and refilled my tea.

"Do you know Sedna?" she asked.

I had heard of Sedna. Her story is, after all, one of the pan-Arctic myths that Lindsay had been researching on that trip so many years before. Recently, I have been spending a fair bit of time reading what Lindsay and others have written about Sedna to try and make sense of what happened to me out on the ice. What follows, however, is as best I am able to recall, the exact version of Sedna's story that Simeonie's mother, Ava Angalaarjuk, told me that evening in Iviliiq.

❋ ❋ ❋

85

There was once a man whose wife had died years before, leaving him alone to raise their young daughter. The two lived in solitude along the coast, for the man was shy and sad and unwilling to remarry. There was little food, since there were few animals, but together the family was able to manage a meager existence. Despite her hunger, this daughter grew into a young woman, a beautiful woman, and the word went out across the region that there was a potential bride in that miserly camp. Young men from far away began to visit in the hope they might marry her. The daughter enjoyed this attention and was excited to meet each new suitor, and over time, the idea of marriage began to interest her.

Her father, however, became increasingly sullen and unwelcoming. He would withdraw to tend to his dogs while the men went about their courtship, but from a short distance he would watch and listen to the young people laugh and whisper. When a man left, the father would return to his daughter. He would speak of the departed suitor's shortcomings, both as a man and as a potential husband. He would convince her of some moral failing she had overlooked. He would commiserate with her. "Someday soon the right man will come," he would tell her. "Like I came for your mother." Spring came and the suitors were as thick as mosquitos on a still day. The daughter would braid her long hair and look across the ice at the comings and goings of potential mates. "Surely that man would be a good husband," she would say. "He was handsome and his team was strong." "Not him," said the father. "His teeth were horrid." Or his nose was crooked. Or his smile was suspect. The father began to run out of invented failings. His daughter looked at him like he was mad. And so he started to invent features instead. He created the optimal suitor, a handsome, humorous, kind man. One with great teeth and dozens of dogs. The one man worthy of marrying his daughter. An imaginary man. He would take her to him. Soon.

When the ice finally broke, his daughter's excitement became unbearable. She would spend the day looking out to sea and asking her father when she would meet this prospective husband. Soon he had no choice but to load her into his boat and set off to visit the imaginary man and his family. After two days at sea, when the land behind them was long out of sight, they came to an island. "Here, father?" his daughter asked. "But this island looks empty." Her father replied, "It is bigger than it looks. They must be camped on the other side." He pulled up to the rocks. "Start walking while I tie up the boat. I'll be with you in just a minute." And he watched as his only daughter with her two beautiful braids clambered over the rocks and out of sight.

Then he pushed off.

He could not look back at the island as he sailed away and so he did not see his daughter as she watched from the hill. He did not see her climb back down the rocks and enter the water. With the sound of his own sobbing he could not hear the soft splashing as his daughter swam slowly after the boat. For hours, the woman pursued the boat, pushed on by anger over her father's betrayal, her beauty transformed by wrath. She caught up to the boat when they were out of sight of all land and she reached up with both hands onto the gunwales. The boat heaved to its side as she pulled herself up. Only then did the father recognize his disheveled daughter emerging from the sea. A fight ensued. The boat rocked violently, casting up waves which in turn became a great storm. Whitecaps rolled in from all sides. The boat was whipped around like a sik-sik in a dog's mouth. The father, knowing they would both drown, tried to push his daughter from the boat. But he could not pry her fingers from their death-grip on the gunwale. He could not make the storm stop. So he raised his knife and with one hard thwack chopped off

87

all her fingers. Like ten little carrots. They fell into the water beside her and, with the daughter, sank to the bottom of the sea.

The storm subsided and the father travelled on, believing his daughter to have drowned. But she did not drown. The daughter, Sedna, lives in a stone house on a rock plain deep under the sea. She transformed—her legs and feet into a thick tail, like that of a whale, her finely featured face into a silver moon swollen with sea salt and scorn. Her fingerless hands are like paws and her fingers, floating free in the depths beside her, became all the animals of the sea: the seals—nattiq and udjuk; the whales—arviq, tuugaalik, and qilalugaq; the walrus—aiviq. They are like her children, except unlike children they will do her bidding. And she watches us. From her stone house at the bottom of the sea, she judges us.

When she is content, she is calm and the sea is still. She'll release the animals to the surface, to our boats and their breathing holes. If she is happy, there will be a good hunt. But if we anger her, and Sedna is quick to anger, she will thrash about, her long hair whipping the water and churning up waves. She will call the animals to her side and keep them there. If we upset her, we will be hungry. Sometimes we can appease her anger. If we know what we've done wrong—if we've been wasteful in the hunt or disrespectful to the animals—we can make amends. Other times, if the insult is large and the hunger prolonged, a shaman will need to visit her. They will find their way down the long path to her stone house where they will sit and soothe her. They will ask what we have done wrong and what we need to do to regain her favor. And as she speaks, they will run their fingers through her wild hair like a comb and will re-tie her two great, beautiful braids.

My father was an angakkuq, a shaman. He wasn't shy about telling me about his powers either, especially about the things he had done when he was younger. He would tell me about some of the people he had saved. One time an old woman was very ill. The qallunaaq doctor said there was nothing that could be done, kind of like the doctors who come here now—there is nothing that they ever do. But this woman wasn't ready to die, not quite yet. So my father decided to save her. She got out of her death bed at the nursing station, put on her qamiqs and walked home. The nurse, a nun who could work a rosary better than a stethoscope, said it was a miracle. The doctor, a man of science, told her this was nonsense—that it was his medicine that did it. Ha! Tylenol must be very powerful medicine. The woman's family knew it had to be an angakkuq, they just didn't know who. And my father wouldn't tell. Like all angakkuit my father would never tell me nor anyone else what he was doing at the time. Only once did he let me know what he was up to, and that was when he chased a teacher out of town for being cruel to Simeonie. I bet that woman is probably still having nightmares somewhere down south. As he got old, I think my father wanted everyone to believe he was as powerless as an angakkuq as he was as an old man. But after he died we had a long spell when the animals didn't come and we had nothing to eat but caribou and berries. So he must have been doing something. After my father died it took two full years to convince Sedna to let her animals come back.

89

CHAPTER 13

By the time I left his mother's house, Simeonie was gone. The snowmobile and sled, or machine and qamutik, were outside. A large green tarp had been tied over the heap of gear. The entire assembly looked ready, hopeful for whatever conditions we would need to be able to head out of town in the morning. I reached to my pocket to check the time, forgetting I had left my neutered phone on the nightstand in the hotel. The sun had moved—not up nor down, but across—in such a way that I couldn't remember where it had been before or begin to guess where it was going next. I had no idea how much time had passed inside the house. My shadow stretched across the snow in front of me as I followed it back to the hotel.

Once again, the place was empty. I went to pour myself a glass of milk, but remembering Bob's milky maw, opted for apple juice instead. I didn't want to retire to my room quite yet—the problem in small towns is that, with everything so close together, there isn't the time to process any one thing on your way to do the next—so I took my juice and poked around the main floor of the hotel. There wasn't much to see. The kitchen and dining room had been thoroughly patrolled on my earlier search for a light. The small bathroom had been entered once and was not to be entered again. All that was left was a short hallway to a back room, and that is where I headed.

The room was set up as a meeting space with a large conference table surrounded by a haphazard collection of swivel chairs. Along the far wall was a glass cabinet filled with soapstone carvings. I assumed they were the work of local artists, brokered by the Co-op for sale to the few outsiders who passed through the community. I'd seen such collections before. Usually, the well-known carvers have their stuff shipped directly south, leaving only the uncollectible pieces behind. They're like the older kids in an orphanage—kind of cute, sort of sad, but neither cute enough nor sad enough for anyone to take them home.

I searched for a light switch. In the Arctic, summer light seeps into buildings like water into an old boat, but the gray light now diffusing into the windowless meeting room was too weak for me to get a good look at the carvings. I found a fluorescent tube running along the top of the cabinet and flipped it on to an annoying flicker and buzz. As expected, most of the art was schlock—a couple of crude little inuksuit, a gangly bear—but scattered among those pieces were a few that actually looked quite good. A happy little narwhal carved out of bone distracted me from the bug-eyed caribou with hands for a rack. Behind them was a priapic drum dancer, his back arched to the curve of the antler from which he was cast, who had Einstein hair made from a tuft of fur. Despite the years I spent visiting the North, I had a very limited collection of Inuit art. I'm as indecisive as I am picky, but I thought that any of those pieces would be a reasonable addition. Then I saw *her*.

She was tucked behind an awkward loon, visible but not obvious, like a beautiful, shy girl standing at the side of a high school dance. The stone from which she was carved was green serpentine, completely unlike the dull slate soapstone of most every other piece in the display. She glowed under the harsh light of the cabinet. I reached in and, rudely pushing the loon and a seal aside, pulled her out for closer inspection.

It was a nude, and spectacularly so. Like Michelangelo's *Prisoners*, the figure emerges out of an almost unadulterated rock base. The difference, though, is that while I have always assumed the prisoners are in the process of being freed from the rock, this woman is being consumed by it. She is being subsumed from the bottom up. A more timid artist might have used this as an opportunity to avoid overt eroticism, to escape the depiction of the sexuality the rock itself seems intent on destroying. The carver of this piece was not quite so shy. The woman's two legs join to become a single great thigh, and it's that thigh that then turns to a base of stone. But far from having her predicament swallow her sex, the artist went to great effort to detail it. Seriously, the thing has a mons pubis that is almost pornographic. I blush when I look at it.

And from there on up, she's a beaut. The belly is slightly protuberant and somehow looks like it would be soft. The breasts I am loath to describe because they are so clearly those of a young woman. Hopeful, maybe? Virginal, surely. But before you declare me a creep, allow me to carry on. Her shoulders are broad, almost manly. The same goes for her muscular back, down which run two thick braids that intertwine and end at the crack of her smooth, strong buttocks— an ass of, if not steel, then stone. As for her face, I have no idea. She holds her fingerless hands in front of her as if in grief. Even so, I can feel her emotion. It's not grief. It's rage.

I turned the carving over to check for a price sticker but found none. I flipped over an inuksuk and a heroin-chic seagull—forty bucks apiece. The drum dancer was one hundred-twenty. This Sedna alone had no sticker. She also had no signature—no name, shapes, or squiggles to prove her provenance. Regardless, I had to have her. I lay her down on the conference table behind me and pulled out my wallet. In lieu of cash, I pulled out my business card as an IOU and slipped it into the vacated space. Then I flicked off the light and took my treasure to my room.

CHAPTER 14

I woke the next day at noon. It seemed late but, then again, I had no idea what time I had gone to bed. I put myself together in a hurry and headed out to find Sim. I almost tripped over him on the steps of the hotel.

"Morning, Guy." He moved over a titch. I took that as an invitation to sit down.

"Slept well?" he asked.

"Seemed to," I said.

"Any interesting dreams?" It was an odd question.

"Not that I can remember, no."

"Good."

We sat in silence for a while. I tried to remember exactly what it was that Rachel had said when she recommended this guy. I was starting to think we were going to have a few awkward days out on the ice.

"So are we leaving today?" I asked.

"Doubt it."

I looked at the flags, at the sky, at some passing kids—anything to second this man's opinion that today was not a fine day to travel.

"Why not?" I asked.

"It's not good."

"What's not good, the wind?"

"Maybe. It's just not a good time to be on the ice," he said. "You should come in winter."

I looked around at the snow and ice. I wondered what the appeal would be of casting the same scene in dimmer light and colder air.

"To go to the floe edge?"

"No, but I could take you caribou hunting," he explained.

"Yeah?"

"Yeah."

I waited for more. I wondered if Simeonie really wanted to take me caribou hunting or if he was simply musing about how to get something more useful for himself out of his time spent guiding me. He sure didn't seem particularly inclined to take me to The Edge.

"I could build us an igloo," he said. "I'm a champion igloo builder."

I knew this. I had heard about it from Rachel when she had given me his name. Simeonie had won a regional championship at some sort of Arctic games.

"That would be awesome, Sim."

"We wouldn't have to go far," he continued. "Maybe just over there."

He pointed to some low hills across the bay. They looked much like the low hills in every other direction. I was curious why that would be the best spot for an igloo, but didn't think it was my place to question a champion.

"We could take a Coleman stove," he said. "I could make tea."

"That sounds great."

He was still staring at the spot. He looked distracted.

95

"Maybe some caribou skins to keep warm."

"OK," I said. I was unsure where his plan was heading.

Then, after a disconcerting pause, "There's nothing like making love in an igloo."

He said it wistfully. I thought about how difficult it can be to tell the difference between a man lost in memory and one daydreaming about the future. In either case, I thought I should bring the conversation back to the present.

"Why can't we make an igloo at this time of year?" I asked.

Simeonie broke out of his reverie and cast me a look that suggested I was either an idiot or a pervert.

"Wrong kind of snow."

We arranged to meet again after dinner to consider our options. I tried to impress upon him my schedule. He might be able to exist on a time scale of seasons and animal migrations, but I had a plane ticket and a series of speaking engagements awaiting me. Besides, I wasn't used to traveling north on my own dime. For the amount of money the airfare had cost me and the time it had taken to get to Iviliiq, I could have been whiling away the week pretty well anywhere in the world. Bali, for instance, would have been lovely. If I couldn't get to The Edge there was really no reason for me to have come.

I left Sim on the steps and went for a walk. I felt like I needed to blow off some steam and burn some time before dinner. Having already exhausted the sights around town, I followed the only road leading out—a three-kilometer-long gravel service road to the lake from which the community draws its water. On the way, the road runs past the fuel depot, sewage lagoon, and gravel pit. As a result, each one of the town's three municipal vehicles (garbage truck, water tanker, and honey wagon) passed me multiple times through the course of my walk. Every time they did—whether face-on on their way into town or when sneaking up from behind on their way back out—the drivers of these trucks would honk, wave, and leave me choking in a cloud of dust.

The road dead-ended at a little pump house at the edge of a lake. Compared to the sea next to town, the lake looked a lot less solid. A sloping shelf of shore-fast ice dropped under the water, leaving a dark gap the width of a city street between it and the surface ice a little farther out. The colors between the two sheets of white were beautiful—an icy rainbow from aquamarine through turquoise, to azure and, finally, a blackish sort of blue. I had started to shuffle down the slope to check out the water when I heard the sound of a truck coming up the road behind me. I didn't want to have to have a conversation with the driver as he filled his truck, so after checking to see that he was still out of sight, I scooted along the shore and out of view.

The footing was solid at the edge of the lake, the ice neither too slick nor too soft, and I was able to make good progress. I wasn't going anywhere in particular, I just found it nice to be off the road. Although the town was only a couple of kilometers to my left, and the service road a few hundred meters behind, I finally felt I was on my own. It wasn't the kind of solitude your conscious mind engineers out of the desire to be left alone, shutting down the social apparatus of your brain to render yourself functionally invisible. It was true solitude. It was the kind of alone in which I could dance and strip and scream without anyone anywhere thinking that I had gone mad. It was lovely. Not that I did any of that, mind you. At most I might have sung.

I came to the end of a bay. A well-travelled snowmobile track led up from its apex to a pass between two low hills. I considered turning around, but was curious. I looked back in the direction from which I had come and made a mental mark of where the road ought to be, then walked up the hill to see what was on the other side.

Not surprisingly, it was another lake, almost indistinguishable from the one I had just left. The same sheet of white. The same blue rainbow of open water along its shore. From the high ground I could see another lake beyond, and a fourth off to the right. Under the late spring's threadbare blanket of snow, the land was revealing itself to be made more of water than of rock. If you ever find yourself flying over the Canadian Arctic on your way between America and Europe, pull yourself away from the tiny movie screen for a minute and look down. The place is a house of mirrors, pockmarked and pitted and as wet as a saturated sponge. Remember that. When the world gets thirsty we'll know where to go.

I heard a whistle and turned towards the sound. Off to my left on the other side of a bay, a small group of men sat with their snowmobiles. One of them was waving me down. I looked around to see if he might be signaling to someone else, but found no one. I waved back, then trudged down the hill to say hello.

There were four men and three snowmobiles. Two of the men were futzing with something under the engine cowling of one of the machines. A couple of parts lay on the snow beside it. The other two men were sitting sideways on their machines sharing a joint.

"Hey," I said. "Everything OK?"

"Yep." He took a hit and offered the joint to me. I waved it off. "They're just drying it out," he said.

I had no idea what that meant. I remembered one of my Inuit colleagues once having to remove the spark plugs from a snowmobile in order to off-gas the extra fuel I had flooded it with in a failed attempt to get it started.

"Is it flooded?" I asked.

"You could say that." He called out something in Inuktitut to the men under the machine. A curt "Fuck off" came the reply.

"So what are you guys doing?" I asked. I had assumed they were hunters, but only one of them had a gun and none of the machines was connected to a qamutik. They weren't equipped for a hunt. Nor did they seem inclined for a picnic. That said, it seemed like a long way to go for a toke.

"Skipping."

"Skipping?"

"Yep. You?"

"Walking."

"Huh." He offered me the joint again. I considered it for a moment longer this time, then waved it off once more.

We stood in silence. I wondered how many explorers had had such inane conversations. Certainly it seemed par for the course for me—random encounters with individuals who seem no more surprised to see me than they are interested in talking to me. Surely I never saw much of this documented in the Victorian journals I used to research. *Finally made it past the Cauldron of Hell. May have discovered trace of Livingstone. Short conversation with small woman too busy with her knitting to confirm.*

The man with the joint took one last drag then snuffed it out with his fingers. He placed the roach in a Ziploc baggie, which he pocketed, then swung a leg over his machine and fired it up. He nudged forward out of a cloud of exhaust and drove up the slope away from the lake. I thought he was leaving, but no one else made a move. Instead they watched. The two men working on the one snowmobile closed the cowling and stood. The third guy shifted in his seat. We all watched the first guy as he reached the top of the hill and looped around, coming to a stop pointed back down in our direction. Then, with a whoop, he floored the thing.

In my limited experience on snowmobiles I have never found them to be particularly nimble when it comes to either steering or stopping. They are, however, freakishly fast. This man was driving towards us at full throttle. Behind us was a stretch of open water fifty meters wide. He was closing the distance faster than I could process what was going on, but as best I could tell he was about to have to make a choice between killing himself and killing us all. I waited for him to make some miraculous last-second adjustment in course. Instead he flew past us—calm, straight and unflinchingly fast—and drove straight into the lake.

Or, rather, onto the lake.

The snowmobile slowed a little and sagged backwards like a broken couch. The track, still under full throttle, churned up a rooster tail as it thrust the machine forward. The snout and skis held high out of the water like the head of some proud and panicked horse. Amazingly, the snowmobile carried across the water. It reached the ice on the far side of the opening and rose out of the lake, turning the low-pitched throb of the engine in water into a high-pitched whine of complaint. The sound faded as the driver aired out the machine in a wide, ridiculously fast arc out on the ice.

"Jesus," I said. "I didn't know those things could float."

"They can't," said the guy on the second machine. "They skip."

"Seriously?" I looked around the lake for spots where the lake ice was contiguous with the shore. "Why wouldn't you just drive around?"

"Sometimes there's no way around. Sometimes on the sea ice the only way across a lead is to skip."

A change in tone and an increase in volume signaled the start of the snowmobile's return. Once again he was aiming directly at us, this time approaching the open water from the solid surface of the lake.

"Isn't that dangerous?" I asked.

"Beats swimming."

After his successful second crossing the driver pulled into his previous parking spot and killed the engine, returning the scene to relative silence. Steam hissed off the exhaust. The men bantered like young men do when they're screwing around. We started into a conversation of sorts, them asking the usual questions about where I was from and why I was here, me deflecting their enquiries with my own questions about what they were doing and what life was like in the community.

At most I could keep one or two of the men engaged in the conversation—it, or perhaps me, was not interesting enough for them all to make the effort in English. Every few minutes one of the men would start up a machine and take a shot at skipping the open water, each time under the watchful eye of his friends. I was never fully able to determine whether they were doing it for fun or for practice.

At one point one of them asked if I wanted to give it a try. I assumed they were joking. Regardless, I declined and took it as an opportunity to take my leave. I wished them well and started back along the lake.

"Where are you going?" the first skipper asked.

"I have to get back to town," I said. I had turned to face him as I answered but continued to walk backwards, in part to make a point of my leaving.

"To Iviliiq?"

"Yeah." Like, seriously. Where else would I be walking?

"It's that way." The guy motioned with his head in a completely different direction. One of his buddies sitting on the machine behind him pointed to a snowmobile trail leading to a low pass between two formless hills. I turned to look at the path I had chosen—a different snowmobile trail leading to a different pass between two equally formless hills. The shiftless sun shrugged behind a cloud.

"Want a ride?"

The men dropped me off at the Co-op. The late afternoon rush was in full swing: snowmobiles and ATV's idled in front of the store; a couple clumps of loiterers watched me and smoked; families and children came and went. I took a deep breath and walked into the cloud of exhaust and second-hand smoke that clung to the steps of the store. I drew a moderate amount of attention—nothing unusual, I suspect, for an unknown White man driven into town on the back of a hunter's machine—but I suspect in local lore that ride of convenience has by now probably become the first of my rescues. At the time, however, I was simply hungry and a little cold. I wandered the aisles and scrounged up some overpriced, unappetizing crap, then squirrelled it back to the hotel for dinner.

CHAPTER 15

I cannot fully justify what happened next. For what it's worth, I was, as previously mentioned, a little hungry. I was also a bit miffed at the cost of the bag of junk I carried with me from the store. I hadn't been sleeping particularly well. More than anything, though, I was getting antsy. The trip was folly enough as it was. If I didn't get to the floe edge it would be idiotic.

As I approached the hotel, the one thing I knew for certain was that Simeonie was not there waiting for me as he had promised. There was, however, a note stuck to the door.

Iffy about tomorrow. Call me: 4423.

I really should have eaten. Instead, I dumped the bag in the dining room and went straight to the phone. After a few rings someone picked up, initiating the conversation with something entirely unintelligible in Inuktitut.

"Simeonie?"

More Inuktitut. It could have been anything.

"I'm looking for Simeonie," I said. "I'm the guy who's supposed to be going out with him tomorrow."

"I know who you are."

"Is Sim there?"

"No."

I waited for more information. An offer of assistance, perhaps. I got silence.

"Any idea when he'll be back?" I asked.

"Maybe later?"

"Can you have him call me at the hotel? We've got to work out the details for our trip. I really have to get out on the ice tomorrow."

"Will do."

The phone went dead. I swore and tossed the handset at its base station. It slid over the counter and fell into the garbage can. When I went to retrieve it, I found it had landed in a cold pile of discarded spaghetti. I swore again.

I wanted to cloister myself in my room and stew, but realized I wouldn't be able to hear if Simeonie were to call or come back. Instead I went to retrieve my laptop with the intent of wasting time in the common room. I came down with both it and the bottle of whisky I had smuggled into town to share with Sim in celebration at the floe edge. If the trip wasn't going to happen then I sure as hell wasn't going to leave the bottle unopened—in the history of exploration, no man has ever carried alcohol out of the wilderness. I searched the kitchen for appropriate glassware (it was a good single malt) and found none. In the freezer I located a lone tray of desiccated cubes under a sketchy block of ground beef. Freezing my ass off in the Arctic and here I was wanting for a piece of ice. I retreated to the common room to drink scotch neat out of a coffee mug, the upper-middle class equivalent of imbibing out of a paper bag.

The computer opened to my marked-up manuscript. I wasn't in the mood to work so I minimized it. I opened a Web browser and set it to loading a news page, then went to my mail. The computer chewed on the task before the first of the messages began to squeeze through, landing like the first drops of rain at the start of a brief summer storm. When it was over, there were fifty-two messages. Thirty I could junk without opening. Fifteen I gave the courtesy of a read. I flagged six for a later response. That left one open on the screen in front of me.

It was from my boss at the magazine. Not the publisher or the editors—the actual bosses over whom most of the writers and photographers fawn—but instead the manager of the speaking tours, the woman who doled out the top gigs in big halls that had increasingly become my bread and butter. Her message was both chatty and clear; inarguable, in the style of better bosses everywhere. My part in the upcoming multi-speaker tour to Hawaii was cancelled, to be replaced by a solo road trip through Idaho and Utah. I was to shelve the talk on James Cook and George Vancouver and rehash some tired old shit on Brigham Young's Vanguard Company. A forced trade of Polynesians for pioneers, concert halls for church halls.

I refilled my mug.

The email offered no real explanation, unless "reorienting overarching themes in light of current geo-political considerations" was intended to mean something. I scanned the new itinerary, which consisted of a long rural ramble from Boise to Las Vegas, retracing the steps of many a fallen Mormon. Even the end of the tour offered no consolation given they had booked my final talk for St. George, Utah, the night before an early morning flight out of Sin City. The message was clear: not on the company dime. Not this time.

I went back to the Web browser. Setting aside the news story that had finally finished loading (more missing migrants in the

Mediterranean), I went straight to the Events page at the magazine. The Hawaii tour was prominently displayed, now with the catchy title *Islands Unto Themselves*. The teaser promised "a conversation about conservation and colonialism with the people of the Pacific." The speaker list was largely the same as I had seen it before: a marine biologist with expertise in traditional fisheries; a glaciologist who was their go-to guy on sea-level change; and a dreadlocked surfer dude who seemed to travel the world on a traditional longboard, smoking pot with local stoners wherever he went ashore. The only change in the line-up was me, redacted and replaced with a colleague from the University of Hawaii, a woman whose academic opus was largely comprised of imaginations on the idyllic world we would all be living in if every explorer had simply stayed home. Or better yet, drowned.

I searched the list of upcoming events for my own tour, finally finding it under "Regional Offerings." Clicking the link led to an unflattering photo of me beside the announcement that details were still to be determined. The itinerary was identical to the one Margaret had emailed, except that the website had labeled it as tentative.

I poured some more whiskey. You should recognize that it can be difficult to judge volume in a container with opaque sides. I started to write a reply to her email but found I couldn't corral my emotions well enough to arrange them into words. I deleted what I had written and walked to the window with my mug. I was feeling a sense of frustration similar to what I recalled from years earlier at the university. The one thing I gained when I lost that job was the certain knowledge that not all that can be said aloud ought to be committed to the page. Besides, it takes a lot less effort to talk than to write. I walked back to my laptop and called her.

"Hey," she said. "I'm guessing that you received my email."

"Yeah," I said. "I can't say I'm all that happy about it."

"I thought you were in the field."

"I am."

"With Wi-Fi?"

"I'm sort of stuck in town." Outside the window a child pulled a younger sibling by on a toboggan. "Anyway, Margaret, why are you taking me off Hawaii?"

"Have you been reading the news?"

I had been peripherally following the rising protests by Native Hawaiians against, as far as I could tell, everything. A camp had been set up at the Captain Cook monument at Kealakekua Bay.

"Seriously? You've pulled me because of that?"

"Yesterday the protesters pushed the monument into the bay," she said. "I really don't think this is the right time for a White guy to come in and start telling stories about how the British discovered them."

"Oh come on, Margaret. It's just history."

"It's not their history."

"That's bullshit," I said. "I can't believe you're letting yourself be intimidated by a bunch of fucking hooligans."

"And that's why we're not sending you to Hawaii."

I tried to dial it down a notch. I took a sip from my mug and was, in that moment, happy I didn't have ice. The clinking would have been conspicuous.

"Isn't there some way?" I asked. "I could focus my talk on Cook's death. Moana could tell it from their side. That would keep them happy, wouldn't it?"

107

"Moana? Seriously? You're unbelievable. But no, that wouldn't keep anybody happy. Besides, she refuses to work with you again."

"Oh for fuck's sake, Margaret. The warrior princess has had it in for me for years. We used to work together fine until she decided to make me her whipping boy. The last time we shared a stage I was booed off."

"I remember," she said. "I was there."

"And?"

"And you're not going to Hawaii."

We counted down the silence of a telephonic stare-down. When it was clear the argument was over and that she had won, Margaret resumed with an overview of the alternate tour. I grunted an occasional acknowledgement but otherwise stayed silent. I could haggle over the details closer to the date, when I had a bit more negotiating power. I stopped paying attention entirely somewhere around her mention of the Pocatello Book Festival. I was thinking that the sole benefit of a solo tour was the opportunity it would afford me to be completely alone.

"Hey," she said. "You still there?"

"Mmm." I coughed on a bit of misplaced whisky. "Yep. Sorry. You cut out there for a minute."

"No problem," she said. "I was just saying that the itinerary isn't finalized yet. There are a few sites that we still need to confirm. I'll send you a final schedule within a week or so."

"Swell," I said. "Is that it?"

"Pretty well. Except for one thing."

"You're sending me to Hawaii?"

"Yeah, no. I'm hiring an assistant to travel with you."

"You've got to be kidding," I said. "You're assigning me a handler?"

"An assistant. Someone to help you with the local arrangements and logistics, the driving, that kind of thing. It'll give you a chance to focus on your work."

"Have you considered that I might not want to focus on my work?"

"The thought has crossed my mind."

I signed off with a promise to check back upon my return south. Margaret left me with an oddly prescriptive *stay well*. I shut the top of my laptop with an entirely unsatisfying click. Honestly, I miss the therapeutic heft of an old rotary phone. I was very much in the mood to slam something but, as it was, all I had was my scotch.

I refilled my mug.

An aside. As a paid public speaker I am, first and foremost, a professional performer. And like any semi-serious actor or singer, I rehearse. I have to. It is as easy to pick out a speaker who has not practiced his talk as it is to identify a singer-songwriter who has never before sung in front of an audience. They read from their notes, they glance at their slides. They hem and they haw. They stutter. They suck.

I don't.

What this means, however, is that over time I have developed a tendency to talk to myself. If conditions are good, no one will know. I'll pace through a presentation alone in my office. I'll talk in hushed tones in a locked bathroom. Like a shy Roman Emperor, I'll address a city from behind a high hotel window. When walking in public, I'll hold a cell phone to my ear and hope to look and sound no different than any other asshole. On a train—well, on a train I look crazy.

Regardless, I've been doing the speaking circuit and rehearsing my talks in this way long enough that I think I may have short-circuited the part of the brain that serves to keep one's inner monologue securely contained. It's still largely functional when all is well, but when I'm stressed little bits leak out like air from an untied balloon. As my wife used to say (lovingly, once), I'm mentally incontinent.

I sat alone at the table with a closed computer and an open bottle of whisky and carried on in conversation with Margaret. I let her know, cordially, why she was wrong to reassign me, why my story of Cook and Vancouver would be a salve to the situation at Kealakekua Bay. I gave background to an imaginary news person. I welcomed my Hawaiian colleague to the conversation, then eviscerated her with a masterful refutation of her entire body of work. In my empty Arctic hall, the crowd cheered me. How much of this was muttered aloud is unclear to me. All I know is that at some point I had risen in my oration with mug in one hand, bottle in the other, and spun around to find a silent group of gape-mouthed children watching me through the window.

I froze. My right hand clenched into a fist around the handle of the mug. The little gang of thugs and I regarded each other with mutual trepidation. Theirs understandable, faced, as they were, with a madman. Mine perhaps a little less excusable. A girl on the right waved meekly, her white mitten a little knitted flag of surrender, and I began to settle.

Then the punk on the front left hammered on the window with the bare knuckles of both hands. RATATAT-TA-TAT-TA-TAT-TAT. I hurled the mug at his snot-nosed face. The window exploded into a crystalline web of shattered glass, but stayed in place. The mug's ceramic shrapnel skittered across the floor.

The kids, unharmed, squealed and stampeded away across the snow. I grabbed my laptop and fled up the stairs to my room.

CHAPTER 16

I have a recurring stress dream. I know I'm not alone in this. It's a variation on the classic exam stress dream (looming high-stakes final in a course you had forgotten you were taking), but tuned toward my own occupation. I've known professionals with their own versions of the dream. There was a drummer who would find himself backing a band whose music he did not know, a pilot who would realize mid-flight that he had no idea where he was headed, and a lawyer who would stand before a jury without a clue what her defendant had done. In mine I'm on stage, usually in a venue much bigger than those I actually play, standing in front of an audience hushed in anticipation of what I have to say. It's at that moment I realize I'm giving a medical lecture. I look at the podium monitor and see a title slide that says something along the lines of "Recent Advances in the Diagnosis and Treatment of Paediatric Pheochromocytoma." To make matters worse, I usually can't operate the clicker. On occasion I'm not wearing pants.

On the morning of my third day in Iviliiq I was awoken from one of these dreams. I was trying to understand a question that had been posed by one of the pajama-clad surgeons in the front row when a loud rap on the bedroom door delivered me from the lecture hall and back to my bed. Sunlight strained against the back side of the curtains of the hot, stale room. The strangled sheets were wrapped around my legs like a dhoti. I wavered between the two worlds, not entirely sure which was real until a second, louder, knock chased the dream completely. I rolled off the bed and sifted through the clothes on the floor for a pair of jeans. Then, presentable only in measure against the nothing I had on before, I answered the door. It was a kid, a girl. For a moment I saw an expression suggesting excitement or pride. She was no doubt pleased to have been asked to wake the qallunaaq. The expression didn't last.

"Are you Guy?"

"Sure," I said.

"It's time to go."

"Now?" I rubbed one of my eyes to get the sleep out of it as I attempted to bring the child into better focus.

"Ready?"

"Almost." I scratched my belly. "Give me fifteen minutes?"

"OK." The kid turned and started down the stairs.

"Wait," I said. "Where am I supposed to go?"

She leapt down the last couple of steps onto the landing. "Angalaarjuk's house," she said. She took one last look at me, then fled through the dining room and out of the hotel.

Despite the two days in which I had had nothing to do but wait and complain, I had done little to prepare for my trip onto the ice. My only true accomplishment had been pressuring Bob into letting me keep the room while I was gone. It seemed like it should have been an obvious request—I was going to need a place to stow some of my belongings and it was difficult to imagine there was going to be a run on the rooms of the otherwise empty hotel. Still, I'd had to suck up to the fat man like he was doing me some great favor.

113

I shut the door and stepped through my cast-off clothes to open the curtains. The sun illuminated the space like a flood-lit crime scene. I started filing my scattered belongings into two hastily constructed categories: 1) things I needed on the ice; 2) things I didn't. The task seemed fairly straightforward. Later, when I had more time, I would have the opportunity to question almost every decision I had made. Even so, many of the choices that I would come to regret were not entirely my fault. The packing of books, for instance, requires some foreknowledge of the duration of one's trip. The same can be said of underwear.

After a few minutes, I stood overdressed and underprepared in the middle of the room. The dresser was stuffed to overflowing with electronics and unwanted clothes. My deflated duffel sat zipped and resigned to adventure on the bed. I decanted the dregs of the bottle of scotch into the flask I intended to share with Sim at The Edge, spilling, as I always do, an equal volume over the lip onto my hand. I dumped the empty in the recycling pail and wiped the desk with a dirty sock, then stepped back to examine the room. The only thing left out was Sedna, sitting alone and exposed on the desk. I admired her for a moment, then heaved her up off the desk and buried her deep in the bottom drawer, safely stowed under some dirty underwear and a whisky-infused sock.

The scene in front of Angalaarjuk's house was unchanged from my previous visit—Simeonie's snowmobile attached to the qamutik, no sign of the driver. This time, however, his machine was running. Its idling engine thrummed a rhythm my heart stepped up to match. I set my bag on the snow and fiddled with the ropes in the hope I might find access without screwing up Sim's work. I stopped when I noticed his mother watching from the door.

"Good morning, Guy."

"Morning, Ava." I abandoned the sled and walked to the base of her steps. "Beautiful day for a Ski-Doo, isn't it."

"Ee," she said. "It would be a better day to go fishing."

"Maybe we'll get to fish, too. Really, I'm at Simeonie's mercy," I said. "Have you seen him?"

"He went to gas up your machine." She was leaning against the door frame, studying me. "Is that what you're wearing?"

I looked down at my outfit: a stupidly expensive mid-weight parka, bomb-proof pants that could be used to ski down Denali, top-of-the-line gloves, and the best boots I have ever owned. I was a Gore-Tex astronaut. When I first put the ensemble together, I had wondered if the pants and jacket might be a bit too matchy-matchy. I figured Ava was probably thinking the same thing.

"Too much?" I asked.

Ava shrugged. "Too much money, maybe."

"It wasn't too bad," I lied. "Besides, I need a lot of this stuff for work."

"You dress like that to write?"

"Not writing," I said. That uniform rarely included pants. "Research. I used to do a lot of fieldwork in the Arctic."

"You did?"

"Yep."

"In Nunavut?"

"Nunavut, NWT, Alaska, Greenland... all around the North actually."

She reviewed my outfit again. "Your feet are going to get cold."

My toes were already cold. I had assumed that was unavoidable. "They should be alright if they stay dry, no?"

"Have you been to the floe edge before?" She knew I hadn't. Still, she waited for me to confirm my ignorance. "Come inside. I'll lend you some qamiqs."

I stepped into Ava's antechamber of death as she was lifting the head of the musk-ox off the top of the chest freezer. "Hold this," she said. She opened the freezer's lid and leaned in. When she emerged she was holding what looked to be a gigantic pair of furry leg warmers.

"Take off your boots," she said.

"Are you sure?" I looked around for a place to put the head. "They're pretty good boots. They're waterproof."

"There is no such thing as a waterproof boot."

It was in complete contradiction to what the salesman at REI had told me, but it was certainly in keeping with my own experience of other boots. I put the head on the floor and wrenched off one boot. Ava handed me a qamiq. Whether it was the right or left, or even if there were a right or left, was lost on me. The qamiq was made of caribou from the ankle up and bearded seal for the foot. The liner was some type of felt that folded into a cuff near the top of the calf. The cuff itself was embroidered with beads. It was beautiful, but smelled like roadkill.

"Does it fit?" she asked.

"Sure." It felt like a small sleeping bag for my lower leg.

"Good. Put the other one on."

"I'll be OK," I said. "I don't want to trouble you." I trusted Ava, but was doubtful anything that had to be stored in a freezer was going

116

to be warmer than my hand-crafted Tyrolean boots. Besides, I had once accidentally traded a Canada Goose jacket for a Bolivian llama poncho in a very similar encounter and had vowed not to let it happen again. She held out the other qamiq and said nothing.

I was carrying my boots back down her steps when Simeonie pulled up on a second snowmobile. He killed the engine and dismounted. It sputtered back to life, rallied for a moment, coughed out a little death rattle and expired. Simeonie was several steps away when it finally died.

"Is this all your stuff?"

"That and these," I said, waggling my boots. I watched his expression for any sign of what he thought of my footwear, but got nothing. He bent down and unhooked a rope from the side of the qamutik. Without undoing a single knot, he folded back a section of the tarp and opened a perfectly-sized space for my bag. After he stowed my gear and resealed the sled, he rose up and brushed off his knees. I noticed he was wearing rubber boots.

"Ready?"

"As I'll ever be."

"Are you OK with this machine?" he asked. "It's a Bravo."

It looked leaner, older, and altogether less muscular than its partner. "Looks perfect," I said.

"Good. Fire it up," he said. "I'm going to say goodbye to my mum."

Sim trotted up the steps and disappeared into the vestibule. I walked over to familiarize myself with my machine. Every snowmobile I've ever been on has been basically the same. They are all very much the inbred descendants of the one that was first cobbled together in some Québec sugar shack. The Bravo, more than most, still had the look of something made out of castoff bits of motorbike and lawnmower. Its wispy handlebars held the two key controls, with the brake lever on the left, the thumb-throttle on the right, along with a couple of other switches that I thought best not to touch.

I twisted the key to the start position and braced myself for an attempt on the pull cord. From previous experience with starter cords I know that I'm more likely to tweak my back than ignite the engine. My first attempt accomplished absolutely nothing. The cord whiffed back as it recoiled from my feeble effort. On my second try, I pulled harder and nearly fell over. My third and fourth tries were done in rapid succession, the latter sounding like it almost turned the engine. The fifth through eighth attempts had the desperate intensity of a man trying to beat a small animal to death.

I paused to catch my breath. I pushed one of the superfluous buttons twice more thinking it might be a prime, and in the process flashed the headlights at a child who was already walking my way. I figured I had one last chance to save face. With all my might, I yanked on the cord so hard I thought it might break. Like the lawnmowers of my youth, the machine humored me with a half-assed hint at internal combustion and then returned to silence. Simeonie walked up as I leaned frustrated and sweating against the seat.

"It's a bit of a bitch to get started, hey?" I said, trying to conceal my shortness of breath.

"Can be." He leaned over the handlebars and pressed a small green button with his left hand. The machine fired up. He revved the throttle with his right thumb, then, confident that the engine was

118

reliably on, stepped back from the machine. "That's why I installed the starter." He smiled his gap-toothed grin.

Simeonie led me through the town at a processional pace. I think every kid I had seen over the preceding days came out to see us off. One of them ran along beside my snowmobile for a block with a variation on the same series of questions: *What's your name? Where are you from? Where are you going?* We were the world's smallest parade. Even Bob waved goodbye as he walked by on his way to the hotel with another bag of laundry. Then, just past the church and around the back side of the municipal garage, the snow-packed road we traveled narrowed to a trail and then dipped down the slope to the shore. The trail weaved through hummocks of ice heaved up at the beach by the tide, cut between two seracs that stood like sentinels at the entrance to town and emerged onto the smooth flat ice of the bay. Simeonie looked back over his shoulder to make sure I was still with him, then opened up the throttle and aimed for the horizon.

PART TWO

CHAPTER 17

After three days of uncertainty and inaction, we were finally moving. Fast and straight, away from land and onto the sea. I was too focused on piloting my machine to look back, but I could feel the town receding behind us. We had broken free of its gravity. I was released from frustration and ennui. There was nothing to stop us now but The Edge itself. I was soothed by the movement. Like a baby being bounced on a knee, I was content.

I suspect you've had the experience of being on a flight full of people who, after having been calm as cattle through ten hours of trans-Atlantic confinement, are riled into near-riot when the plane stops short of the gate. As animals, humans seem to have a compulsion to keep moving. It is odd, really, given how sedentary we tend to be. We are as fidgety as meerkats, but at the same time, we're as lazy as slugs.

I once made the mistake of booking a ride on one of Amtrak's morose vestiges of transcontinental travel. After trundling through the industrial rot of the Midwest—part tour, part exhibit in a museum of American decline—we gained the plains and began to pick up speed. It felt a little like the engineer was running through the gears in preparation for an attempt on the mountains farther west. It was, for a moment, almost exciting. Then a bang and shudder were followed by an unmistakable slowing. Throughout the car, passengers looked up from their word-find puzzles and put down their Yahtzee cups to take measure of the train's new cadence. A cautious re-acceleration a few minutes later somewhat settled the crowd, but didn't last. Power was cut and the train limped to a stop. The locomotive sighed and stood steaming like a spent racehorse. We were somewhere outside Minot, North Dakota and were going nowhere. Worse, we were within sight of the Interstate. As the color leached out of the prairie sunset and the sky dimmed to darkness, we were left with only two sources of light. One, the slack emergency illumination in our moribund carriage. The other, the headlights of cars on the Interstate. Bright and relentless; seventy-mile-per-hour meteorites streaking towards civilization.

Now, you would have to presume that nobody was in a hurry. I suspect it has been a very long time since there has been anyone on a train in North Dakota who was in a rush to get anywhere. Over the empty hours of travel that preceded our breakdown I had gotten to know a number of my fellow passengers and I knew for a fact that there was not an expectant grandparent or angsty businessman among them. No one was on their way to a meeting, a marriage, or a funeral. It didn't matter. As we sat, the passengers started to stew. Within an hour, all the lost energy of our impotent little train began to vent through their ears. The conductor, a small man who failed to fully inflate his uniform, made a couple of trips to our carriage to inform us of the nature of the problem (unknown) and the progress of its repair (none). Each visit ratcheted up the ire of the passengers. His final update, in which he informed us that a replacement locomotive *might* be on its way, was followed by a wildly hurled muffin passing within a foot of his head. I noticed that after closing the door in retreat the man looked back through the little window with a mixture of fear and contempt. Then he locked the door.

For the next two hours the inmates planned their rebellion. With a dramatic flourish, one man pulled the emergency brake, an act of defiance diminished by the fact we weren't moving. While one group formed around the highway-side emergency window to discuss the possibility of walking to the Interstate, another gathered at the head of the carriage around our own Fletcher Christian to plan a mutiny. I suspect that if he could have gotten the engine running, he would have taken command of the train and set the Engineer and Conductor adrift to stern in the caboose, *à la* Henry Hudson. They had started to break the lock when a bump and the weak squeal of wheels signaled the reanimation of our train. Within minutes the mutineers were back in their seats. An hour later most everyone was asleep.

Throughout the entire episode there was a single passenger whose demeanor remained unchanged. An older woman, traveling alone, who sat by a window on the dark side of the train, a paperback splayed open on her thigh. At the height of the rebellion she had been having a snooze, but later, as movement rocked the rest of the passengers to sleep, I noticed she was awake, once again staring into the nothingness of the North Dakota night.

At the time I admired her composure. As a middle-aged man I am well-positioned to both respect the tranquility of my elders and envy the energy of our youth. I can see the appeal in both parkour and the porch. It seems to me now, however, that age is just one of the many forms of defeat that beats out of us our innate imperative to move.

I thought about that train as we tracked across the bay. I thought about Henry Hudson and Captain Bligh, about how mutiny is so often born out of a sense of being trapped, unmoving, or worse, drifting in a direction opposite to the way you want to go. I thought about my work, my former boss, my wife, a former lover. I thought about the state of my feet (warm) and my hands (cold). I thought about the breakfast I had neglected to eat, about the lunch Simeonie might have packed. My mind skipped through thoughts like a stone across a pond, a collection of concepts as random and superficial as a cycle through the channels on a hotel TV.

How long we traveled like this was lost on me. The featureless horizon provided nothing against which I could measure either the movement of the sun or our own progress. I wore no watch. The Bravo's crude instrument panel consisted of only a speedometer and an odometer. For ages I watched the odometer's numbers turn over, ticking with the consistency of a clock. The sun swayed in the sky above Simeonie. When we started out the sun had been up and to his left, the muzzle of the rifle slung over his back marking it like the hand of a clock. A little later it was off and to his right. Either two hours had passed or we had turned slightly east. Before I could figure out which, a course correction put the sun back dead ahead. The odometer continued its count.

At some point the random tangents of my drifting mind came back into focus on the instrument cluster. The odometer caught on a short series of terminal nines and rolled over to a newer, more even number. I had that special kind of epiphany you get when, once finally seeing the obvious, you allow yourself to feel more genius than idiot. At Sim's unwavering speed, distance *was* time. Fifty kilometers per hour; six minutes for every five kilometers. The odometer a metronome. I had been staring at a clock the whole time.

I hadn't paid any attention to what the dial read when we started from town, and so had no way to know how long we had already been out. I could, however, easily keep track of time going forward. I held back a bit from Simeonie to create a buffer of space-time between our machines and focused on the speedometer to maintain a steady pace. The first few kilometers rolled by easily, odd little minute-miles of seventy-two seconds apiece. Despite the clunky math, I had reimposed time on the world. I started to mark the even steps—six minutes at five kilometers, twelve at ten. Twenty-five kilometers would be the half-hour. We were sailing across the boundless ice of the Canadian Arctic and I was staring at the clock like a shift worker.

A couple hundred meters before the thirty-minute mark I noticed the space between us had narrowed somewhat. I was probably following a bit too close to the back of his qamutik, but I didn't want to miss the clock hitting the bottom of the hour. With one hundred meters to go, I was almost riding up on his sled. I pulled a little off to the side of the track and maintained my speed, focusing on the instrument cluster so as to not miss seeing the odometer as it rolled over to twenty-five. When it did, I looked up to see myself flying past Sim close enough to give him a high-five. He didn't look happy.

For the first time since we left town I had nothing but ice in front of me. An endless field of white marked only by a wisp of low fog in the near distance. I was giddy with freedom and speed. I slid the machine back into the center of the track and glanced back to check on my guide. He had fallen farther back and looked to be standing on the footrests of his machine. He was flashing his light.

I turned forward. The bank of fog, indiscriminate and distant only a moment before, was now clear and close, and was underscored by a straight, dark line. I realized that there was a rift in the ice—a black slash of steaming water stretching across my path. It was about one hundred meters away; a hair over seven seconds by my current reckoning. Forgetting for a moment that I was about as well-secured to my seat as a milk jug placed on the roof of a car, I hit the brake. And by "hit" I mean to say I crushed the lever in my left fist with such force that I thought my knuckles were going to pop. The machine heaved forward, pitching me against the plastic windscreen. Freed of my weight and still seized by the brake, the track locked. The engine either stalled or, more likely, was shut off by the impact of my right thigh against the kill switch. With no other sound than the sickly skitter of the front runners along the ice, I felt like I was flying. Or perhaps falling. A couple of hours and thirty minutes into my grand Arctic adventure and I was about to be swallowed by the sea.

With the tiniest bit of friction and the grace of God, the snowmobile stayed on the dry side of the abyss. I came to an almost complete stop a comfortable ten meters from the water, right at the transition point where the old scarred white ice on which we had been riding turned to the smooth, turquoise surface of new and nearly frictionless ice. With the clatter silenced, the machine slipped on in silence for another five meters, a slow spin accentuating the now completely frictionless state. It came to rest pointing directly back at Simeonie. He was in the midst of a long arcing turn to bring his machine and qamutik alongside my spot parallel to the crack.

I took a moment to convince myself that I was truly stopped, then dismounted my snowmobile. Immediately I fell flat on my ass.

The sealskin soles of my borrowed qamiqs were tractionless on the fresh ice. I pulled myself to a standing position by hanging onto the side of the machine but, like a toddler, I was unable to stay standing without support. I was crawling to the old ice when Simeonie pulled up and shut off his engine.

"You should try to stay off the new ice."

"You think?"

"Yeah," he said. "It's slippery."

I reached the scarred snow beside his sled and stood. I brushed off my knees. I watched my guide to see if there was going to be any other information. A humorous story about playing on ice in his youth, perhaps. Maybe a bit of science or traditional knowledge that might explain the otherworldly physical properties of new sea ice. Nothing. I turned back towards the crack. The trail we had been following continued straight off the other side. It was like someone had split open the fifty-yard line on a football field and inserted ten yards of nothing.

"So how do we get across?" I asked.

"We don't," Simeonie said. "We go around."

I looked down the length of the fissure. It appeared infinite, like the horizon had been picked up and placed at our feet.

Simeonie was looking at the Bravo. It sat on the clean ice between us and the water. It looked conspicuous, possibly even self-conscious. Like a dog discovered in a forbidden room.

"So, Guy?" he said. "Why did you park there?"

"I didn't, really. That's just kind of where it ended up." I said. "It wasn't entirely a controlled stop."

"You didn't see the water?"

"Not right away, no. It was hidden by the fog."

"This fog?"

Simeonie gestured along the crack. Sea smoke rose off the open water and weaved into a cloud that hung like a gauzy curtain over the lead. There wasn't another cloud in the sky. The message was clear. I had seen the water. I just didn't know it.

"Maybe you should follow me, hey?" he said. "Like, from behind."

"Sounds good," I said.

Simeonie stood and stepped up beside me. He gave me a paternal pat on the shoulder.

"OK. Now, let's move your machine."

After dragging the Bravo by the nose to get it off the new ice and repositioned alongside his own snowmobile, Simeonie fired up both machines and led us along the crack. Now traveling perpendicular to the path we had previously been taking, we were, I had to assume, making zero forward progress in getting to The Edge. Our pace had slackened significantly and, with the work of picking a route though the puddles and side channels bordering the lead, our speed fluctuated widely. My odometer was a clock no more. I followed Sim's qamutik with the mindlessness of a Grand Canyon mule. Any sense of time and momentum wafted away like sea smoke and disappeared into the fog.

CHAPTER 18

The fissure we followed was longer and more complicated than I had anticipated. With the open water on our left, my measure of success was simple: a turn in that direction was good, a turn to the right was bad. Occasionally the crack would narrow and jag to the left, Sim's speed would increase slightly and with it my hopes would rise. But then, just as I thought we were about to be delivered back onto the unbroken ice upon which we started the day, the main lead would send off a branch angled acutely across our path. Simeonie would slow to a near stop and wrestle his snowmobile and sled into a sharp turn to detour around the side channel. It felt like we were trying to navigate an escape through the creases on a giant's outstretched palm. After a while I could tell that even Simeonie was getting frustrated. The fluctuations in speed increased, lurching away from the lead at each obstacle and then creeping back slowly towards it.

He pulled to a stop on clean ice alongside the lead at the narrowest spot we had yet found, an open patch of water not much wider than a Manhattan sidewalk. He shut off his machine and signaled for me to do the same. After the constant drone of the engine and my thoughts, the silence was centering. The spotlight was on Sim. He swung a leg over and sat sideways on his seat.

"How badly do you need to get to The Edge?"

"Pretty badly," I said.

I didn't know what else to tell him. Like a father driving a car with a kid in the backseat—*how badly do you need to pee?* Or Irvine to Mallory—*how badly do you need to summit this thing?* Or me to my wife—*how badly do you need out of this marriage?* Pretty badly, I guess. Still, it would seem some negotiations would be better off with a bit more shared information.

"You don't want to go fishing instead?" he asked.

I shook my head. I liked Sim, but my trust in him was as a guide, not as a therapist. I wasn't going to try and explain my need to go to the floe edge, but I sure as hell hadn't come this far to go fishing.

"How hard is it going to be to find a way around?"

He shrugged. "Might not be possible. It's a dumb time of year."

It wasn't the first time he had told me that. When I had been negotiating the trip with him, he had tried to get me to commit to coming a couple of weeks earlier. I had pushed for the latest time possible, partly because of a speaking gig I didn't want to miss and partly because I hate being cold.

"It would be nice to have a drone, eh?" I said. "Get a look from the air."

"You have one?"

"Uh, no." I had been joking. "I don't even have a camera."

"Yves has a drone," Sim said. "It's great for hunting. Want to see?"

He reached into the pocket of his parka and pulled out an iPhone. I stopped him before he was able to start trolling through photos.

"So what are our options, Sim? Do we just keep poking along looking for an end to the lead? Can we skip across?"

"I could." he smiled. "But I'm not the one who needs to get to The Edge."

"So we go around?"

"Maybe."

There was a pause. Simeonie looked to the sky. To my eyes it was empty.

"So you really need to get there, eh?" he said.

"Yes."

"Are you warm enough?"

"Sure."

"OK." He squared himself to his machine. "Follow me."

Simeonie started up his snowmobile and tugged the qamutik back into motion. He pulled away from the water and steadily accelerated with a confidence I had not seen since we first came across the crack. He led us on a long, looping course away from the lead. It was not quite back in the direction from whence we came but it was certainly well off the direction we had been trying to go. Regardless, it was clear we were going somewhere. Freed from nitpicky navigation through fractured ice we were once again moving with speed. On the horizon, waves of distorted light assembled and reassembled themselves into a slideshow of mirage. In time, I realized that the image was settling into a clear picture of cliffs.

We were heading towards land.

For what felt like a good hour we travelled towards my hallucinated horizon. I strained to make sense of the landforms. Every time I achieved some certainty about what I was seeing or how far away it might be it would pop back out of focus, like a letter line in an optometrist's eye machine as she flips through the lenses. For a short while I got excited when the cliffs grew into what looked to be mountains, even though I knew there were no mountain ranges in that part of the Arctic. The speed of our machines and my familiarity with the delusions of earlier explorers gave me a measure of patience. As a man of science I might not be an exemplar, but I do have more conviction in the refraction of light than in the trickery of fairies. Even so, it can be hard for the mind to override the eyes as the ultimate arbiter of truth.

Arctic air is particularly adept at creating visual illusions. *Fata Morgana*—the superior mirage that can make objects, both imaginary and real, loom above the horizon—is a common phenomenon in the far north. I look for accounts of the phenomenon in the journals of the explorers I study. It really can be quite deceptive. The clarity with which observers address what they're seeing is a good marker for the degree to which they've gone insane or, occasionally, the dimwittedness with which they first set sail. Gerrit de Veer documented several days of debate after he saw the sun's early return in Novaya Zemlya: *Wherewith we went speedily home againe to tell William Barents and the rest of our companions that joyfull newes. But William Barents, being a wise and well experienced pilot, would not beleeve it.* De Veer dedicated the next several pages to the astronomical discussions, diverse wagers laid, and crew's exploration of the possibility that they may have overslept the polar night. In the end, the sky cleared and the counterfeit sun rose for all to see. De Veer collected his wagers and calmly moved on to record more pressing matters, leaving it for skeptics and scientists to figure out the Novaya Zemlya effect centuries later. But then, de Veer was sane, smart, and bored. Sir John Ross, on the other hand, was something else. Sighting mountains blocking the end of Lancaster Sound, Ross turned his ship around at what would later prove to be the eastern entrance of the Northwest Passage. Ignoring the objections of his officers who wanted to explore further, Ross then doubled down on his conviction and named his mirage in honor of the Secretary of the Admiralty. The imaginary Croker Mountains. It was not the wisest career move.

I had the patience to let my own imaginary mountains sort themselves out. Contrary to my experience with real mountains, mine got smaller the closer we got. They drifted down out of the sky and became cliffs again. Then the cliffs themselves began to shorten. The waves of distortion filtered out and the optometrist's last lens popped the picture into a final focus. Simeonie cut back on his speed and aimed for a long, low beach between two low hills. It was the same barren landscape that we had left on the other side of that godforsaken bay.

CHAPTER 19

Our return to land was difficult. The tide-heaved ice along the shore had been untracked by any machine. Unlike the well-worn path out of Iviliiq, Simeonie had to find his own route to trail a sled and an idiot off the sea and back onto land. When we got to the dry side of the shoreline he stopped to readjust the lines on his qamutik. I took the opportunity to stretch my legs. The wind-packed snow had a consistency somewhere between Styrofoam and concrete. It squeaked underfoot as I walked over to Sim.

"So what's the plan from here?"

"We cross," he said. "We can get to the floe edge from the other side."

"Awesome," I said. "What's this place called?"

"Which place?"

"This. The spot we're crossing. Does it have a name?"

"Everything has a name, Guy. The place we're headed is called Qarmaqtalik—*the place of the stone houses.* But the thing we're crossing is called Kitiqluk."

"What does that mean?"

He pulled off his right glove and gave me the finger. He was stone faced for a second, then put it away.

"It means middle finger," he said. "It's a peninsula."

"Huh."

"Looks like this." He gave me the finger again.

I thought back to the map Lance Brisebois had challenged me with in the RCMP office. I had a vague memory of a long, finger-like projection towards the bottom corner of the page. As I recalled, it was a long way removed from the marks the corporal had made to note our likely route. The man is such an ass, I thought.

We took a path that connected a chain of lakes through a series of squat, saddle-like passes. It was easy sledding and an obvious route. Although there were few signs of recent traffic, almost every hill had a stone inuksuk standing sentinel, each communicating its own secret, possibly ancient, message. In the south of Canada, inuksuit have become as ubiquitous and as meaningless as graffiti—roadside rock piles that say nothing more than "Hey everybody! I was here." In the North, however, they're vital. They say in no uncertain terms *you are here*, whether or not here is anywhere you ever intended to be. They watched over us as we crossed over Simeonie's middle finger peninsula, whispering to one another under the wind.

At some point we crested the spine of the land and began to descend back down, the frozen lakes stepping down to the sea like a series of locks. On the last one, Simeonie cut left and followed a side arm of flat ice bounded on both sides by dark bands of rock. He stopped on a broad plateau at the lake's end and waited as I pulled up beside him. Beyond us, a semi-circle of land sloped down to the sea at a small bay backdropped by three overlapping islands. The place was an almost perfect amphitheater. Even with the whole scene frozen solid, it was remarkably beautiful; I imagined it must be idyllic in the summer.

"Qarmaqtalik," Simeonie said.

"Excuse me?"

"Qarmaqtalik. The place of the stone houses."

He pointed to the near distance, to the spot where our pillowy rise tipped over the cusp of the hill and took its first step down into the amphitheater. There, partially obscured by drifts of snow, were the clear outlines of the foundation walls of five stone houses. They were about three meters by two meters apiece, each with its long access oriented towards the bay.

"Jesus," I said. "Thule?"

"So they say," he said. "Or maybe Viking."

I was pretty sure he was kidding about the Vikings, although I know some academics who have made the same mistake. There was some overlap in the time both of the groups came through the western Arctic and both left little evidence behind. The Thule, however, stuck it out, spreading across the top of the continent and giving rise to the cultures that remain there to this day. The Vikings gave up and went home. It tells you something about the toughness of the Inuit that they are the only people who can rightly call the Vikings wimps.

The Thule are a ways outside my wheelhouse as a historian, but still I was able to admire their settlement. It was a thousand-year-old footprint of whalebone and stone, sitting atop a beautiful amphitheater by the sea. Although I knew little about their culture, I had to respect their style. Of all the places I have passed through in the Arctic, this would be one where I'd want to build myself a house.

Simeonie clearly liked the spot as well and suggested that we take a break for lunch. As he put together the Coleman stove I tramped over to the stone houses. I wondered if anyone had ever excavated the site. Any artifacts of interest would be buried in the muck and under several feet of snow, so I put aside my occupational impulse to dig and wandered around the foundations. I was trying to get a sense of what the place might have been like when the bone arches were intact, supporting walls and roofs of hide. I'd seen the remnants of such homes before, but only then did it cross my mind that they probably would have smelled as bad as my boots.

The third house had the most extant walls. I climbed over and settled myself inside. I looked over my feet, snug inside Ava's caribou and seal qamiqs, and out the stone gap that marked the ancient door. I imagined myself part of a Thule family—a wife by my side, a few kids playing with the dogs outside. Sheltered from the wind and with the sun shining in off the bay, I was almost warm.

I woke up as Sim stepped over the wall. He had a small rucksack over one shoulder and his rifle in his other hand.

"Nice place for a nap, eh Guy?"

I sat up, moving as much inside my snow pants as my pants did across the ground. "Sorry, I didn't mean to fall asleep."

"No problem," he said. "Never turn down a chance to sleep."

He leaned the gun against the rocks and began to empty the bag. A thermos, two enamel mugs, a huge hunk of meat wrapped in wax paper, and an enormous knife. Lunch. He poured us both a cup of tea, then unwrapped the meat. It was a raw slab of something, frozen solid.

"Hope you're OK with caribou," he said. He used the massive knife to sever a hunk the size of his thumb, then sliced that in half again. He picked up a piece in each hand, offered me one, then immediately popped the other piece into his mouth. His thumb followed it in like a ramrod into a musket. He removed his thumb with a slurp as I took the first nibble off the edge of my piece.

"What part of the caribou is it?" I asked.

"Rump." He patted himself on the bum. "Are you an ass man, Guy?"

"Can be," I said. I took another nibble. "Really, it depends on the ass."

He sliced off a smaller piece, this one the size of his pinkie. He ate that himself, placing the handle of the knife in my direction so that I could serve myself.

"Do you like it?" he asked.

"Mmm," I said. I took another nibble. "It's great."

If there is anything I could compare raw frozen caribou to, it would be carpaccio ice cream. Theoretically, I suppose, it ought to be great given that I like carpaccio and I like ice cream. Still, hungry as I was, it was bit hard to stomach. Simeonie must have recognized my lack of enthusiasm. He reached back into the rucksack and pulled out of a box of Ritz crackers. Then he cut himself a third hunk of meat. I began assembling homeopathic servings of caribou on crackers.

We ate in silence. As I was refilling my tea for the third time, Sim gestured to the hill behind me. About a hundred meters away, silhouetted against the sun, a large bull caribou with an impressive rack was scuffing its hoof in the snow. Every once in a while, it would lower its head and hoover up a bit of ice and lichen. I suspect its lunch was about as bland and unappetizing as our own. At one point after it had scrounged up enough to ruminate on, it straightened and looked directly at us as it chewed. We were sitting within rifle range and we were eating its kind. It showed no sign of fear.

Simeonie had tensed slightly but made no move for his gun. I thought he might like the opportunity to catch it and wondered if he was hesitant because of me.

"If you want to get it, feel free." I gestured to the gun.

"You don't shoot a lone caribou, Guy."

"Why not?"

"You just don't."

"OK," I said. The animal went back to scraping at the snow. I figured I should probably leave the conversation where it was. After a minute I decided I couldn't let it go. There was obviously more to the story.

"Honestly Sim, what's the reason not to kill it?" I asked. "Is it because it might be sick?"

He kept chewing, staring at the bull caribou. The creature turned away, then disappeared over the far side of its hill. Simeonie took a sip of his tea and watched the spot for a moment longer, then turned back to me.

"My father taught me that if you see a caribou all by itself that it's a shaman."

I tried to read his expression. I had been having a hard time figuring out when he was being serious. At that moment there was no humor to his voice.

"Do you believe it?" I asked.

"I try not to," he said. "Our elders have a lot of stories. My dad had more than most. Most of my generation tries to be a bit more modern in how they think. More white. But sometimes it's hard to keep believing what you want to believe when you know what you have seen."

He took a sip of tea.

"What did you see, Sim?" I remember almost whispering it. Simeonie sucked at his teeth, then tongued the gap that sat in the middle of what was usually a smile. After a minute, he spoke.

"When I was young, my brother and I went out hunting on our own. We were a long ways north of town, farther than we should have been, when we came across a bull caribou. It was alone and we knew we should leave it, but at the same time we were cold and hadn't caught anything all day. So my brother decided he was going to shoot it. I knew what my dad had told us. I knew he knew. But Terry was older and he had a clear shot, so I didn't say anything. With my dad's 308 I couldn't see how there would be a problem."

"And did he get it?"

"I was watching through the binoculars when he fired. Terry hit it square in the heart. It was a great shot. But instead of falling, the caribou reared up on its back legs." He looked at me as if judging how much I was willing to believe. "Then it did a back flip."

"You're shitting me."

"Nope," he said. "Full back flip and a perfect landing. It took a second to straighten up, then turned its head and stared straight at us. Like this." Sim did a spectacularly spooky demon caribou impression.

"Jesus. Then what happened?"

"Then it disappeared."

"It ran away?"

"It disappeared."

"Holy shit."

"Tell me about it," Sim said. "Scared me shitless."

"So what did you do?"

142

"I didn't know what to believe. Neither of us wanted to talk about what we had seen so we did what we would always do. We went to the spot where it had been standing when it was shot. We thought maybe it was wounded and we could track it, but there was nothing. No blood. No shit. No tracks. There was no sign that there had ever been a caribou anywhere near that place. So we went home and told no one. A year later my brother died. The only record of it ever happening is in here." He tapped his temple.

"So what do you think? Do you believe it was a shaman?"

"It wasn't a caribou."

Simeonie drained the last of his tea then shook out the mug onto the snow beside him. He wrapped up the leftover meat in the wax paper and stowed it and the crackers back in the rucksack.

"Ready?"

CHAPTER 20

We walked back from the stone house, Simeonie carrying the rucksack, me the rifle. Although I have never been much of a sportsman I have spent enough time in the Arctic and in the western US to be familiar with how to carry a long gun. Barrel down, finger nowhere near the trigger. I knew there were a lot of ways I could lose Sim's trust. Waving a loaded weapon around wasn't going to be one of them. He looked over at one point as we walked, but said nothing. I took that as a success.

While Simeonie packed up the Coleman stove, I took a closer look at the gun. It was an ancient bolt-action rifle. The wooden stock was weathered and worn, the barrel rough with rust. It looked like an ignored antique, like something you might find in an old cabin. As quaint and useless as a butter churn. Except that it was loaded and ready to kill. I held it up to my shoulder and took sight towards the middle island in the bay.

"Do you hunt, Guy?"

"I have hunted," I said. "Mostly I just go hunting with other people and let them do the shooting."

"You don't know how to shoot?"

"I can shoot," I lowered the gun. "It's just I choose not to. I'm a lover, not a fighter, Sim."

"Why can't you be both?"

Because I tried. Because I failed. Because I'm not sure I'll be either ever again. I don't know, Sim. You tell me why.

"What kind of gun is this?" I asked.

"It's a rifle." He smiled. "Lee-Enfield Number Four. It's my Ranger's gun."

"Really?" I said. "You're a Ranger?"

"That I am." He gave me a half-assed salute. "I'm all that stands between you people and the Russians."

I shouldn't have been surprised that my guide was a Canadian Ranger. Every Nunavut town I've ever been in has had a small patrol and Sim was exactly the type of guy who was in each of them. A volunteer militia in matching red sweatshirts tobogganing around the Arctic as Russian and American nuclear submarines slip silently underneath them. It is such a Canadian approach to national defense—understated, admirable, and quite possibly completely ineffective.

I held the gun out for Simeonie. He motioned for me to keep it.

"You want to give it a shot? Maybe try a little target practice?"

"Here?" I asked. "Now?"

"If we wait until later it might not be practice," he said. "There are bears at The Edge this time of year."

"Aren't you supposed to be protecting me?"

"I will," Sim said. "Unless the bear gets me first."

He pulled the knife and box of crackers out of the rucksack and paced fifty yards along the ridge. He stopped at the edge of a swale blown in with snow and began slicing slabs off the surface. He asked me to stack them on the bare rock beside the crackers. Once he had a

145

suitable supply he stepped out of the hollow and back onto the ridge. I assumed he was going to line up the slabs as simple targets.

Instead he started to assemble them into a form. The legs first, followed by a rotund torso, then a couple of outstretched arms. He shaped the last slab into a disc and placed that on top of the shoulders. Then he reached into the box and pulled out three crackers. He pushed two into the snow for eyes and popped the third into his own mouth.

"Taa daa," he said through a mouthful of crumbs. He stepped back from his creation, a gingerbread snowman, five-feet tall, wide-eyed, and ready to die.

"Nice, but shouldn't we be practicing on a bear?"

"I'm no good at making bears."

He led me back to the qamutik, then walked me through the motions with the gun. Out of one of the many pockets on his parka he pulled two new clips, showing me the ten bullets they contained before loading the magazine. Then he handed me back the gun. I advanced a round into the chamber with the bolt.

"Ready?" Sim asked.

"Yep." I raised the gun to my shoulder and squinted down the sight directly into the eyes of my unblinking target. "Prepare to die, snowman."

I squeezed off a shot. The stock kicked back into my shoulder with a force as hard and unexpected as a punch to the back of the head. The thunderclap crack of the gun deafened my right ear, leaving my left alone to hear the echo of the shot as it rolled back over us on its return from the islands. With it I heard Sim's laugh.

"Did I hit it?" In the commotion I had neglected to pay attention to the target.

"You might have scared it," Sim said.

The target was intact. Its feet, however, were covered in orange shrapnel. I had made a direct hit on the box of Ritz crackers.

"Huh," I said. "Mind if I try again?"

"Please. You ought to get it before it comes after us for what you did to its lunch."

I advanced the next round and raised the gun. Simeonie moved the butt off the edge of my shoulder and more towards the center of my chest. I took sight and waited a moment to steady my breathing, then on a long exhale to slow my heartbeat, I fired my second shot. The repositioned rifle kicked back significantly less. My already-deafened ear was unable to complain. Still, the snowman didn't flinch. I was already advancing the next round as the echo reverberated across us. My third shot was another whiff. The fourth may or may not have grazed the target's hip. Only the fifth was a definitive hit. It blew off the snowman's right arm just below the elbow.

I lowered the gun to admire my marksmanship. "Not bad, hey?" I said.

"Not bad at all." Sim held out his hand for the gun. "Do you mind if I try?"

I handed the rifle over and took a step back. With the confidence born of a lifetime on the land, Simeonie advanced a round, raised the gun and fired a shot. It blew out the snowman's left eye. I was leaning forward to confirm what I had just seen when his second shot blew out the right. The echoes of the two blasts rumbled over each other in confusion.

"That should take care of him, eh?" Simeonie smiled at me as he loaded his third bullet into the chamber.

His final shot was taken with less care. I saw a skiff of snow flare up by a cracker-encrusted foot. I was somewhat heartened by the fact that not all of his shots were bullseyes, and that his last was, in fact, not all that far off my first. Simeonie had turned from the target before taking stock of his miss.

"I guess you can't get them all, hey Sim?" I said.

As I said it, fifty yards behind my guide, the gingerbread snowman fell on its face and shattered.

CHAPTER 21

I have no idea how long we were at Qarmaqtalik. At the time, I had been thinking it was midday. The stone houses were set in the blue and white bicolor flag of springtime in the Arctic. The sun, bright but distant, stood back from the scene like the parent of an adventuring child. Present and watchful, attentive but uninvolved. Facing directly into it I could almost feel its warmth.

As Simeonie secured the load on the qamutik I tried to warm myself up for the ride. My hands had become frozen in the time I had been gloveless at our makeshift shooting range. Cold had set in at my fingertips and crept upwards from there into my palms, like how a lake ices over from its edges at the start of winter. I windmilled my arms to force the recalcitrant blood back to my fingers. I flapped my hands. I cupped my palms and blew heat from my core into the space between them with the instinctive but idiotic belief that I might be able to hold onto warm air. I was blowing and fanning my hands like I was coaxing a small fire to light. Yet every time I thought I was OK, my frozen gloves would smother my fingers and snuff out the flame.

"Cold?" Simeonie asked.

"Just my hands." I had the finger of a two-hundred-dollar glove clenched between my teeth.

"Did you try peeing on them?"

"No," I said. "Is that a thing?"

"Could be." He pulled a pack of cigarettes out of a pocket and fished out a cigarette. "Can I borrow your light?"

I couldn't remember which of my innumerable pockets I had put the lighter in and fumbled with the snaps and zippers on several before I was able to find it. I tried to spark a flame but my enfeebled thumb could barely roll the wheel. Sim took the lighter out of my useless hands. He lit one cigarette, stuck it between my lips, then lit a second for himself. He slipped the lighter back into my breast pocket. I realized his hands had been bare the whole time we had been stopped. His thick, scarred fingers were dark with dirt and grease.

"How do you keep your hands warm, Sim?"

"I dunno," he said. "I'm Inuit. I drink the blood of seals."

"That keeps you warm?"

"Sometimes."

"Huh," I said. "I'm White. I eat granola bars and spend way too much money on gloves."

Simeonie took a drag. The end of his cigarette sparked.

"Also, my machine has heated handlebars," he said.

"Seriously?"

"Yep. You wanna try it?"

The two snowmobiles sat side-by-side. Simeonie's was juiced up and muscular, like an over-priced basketball shoe. Beside it, my machine looked like one of my dad's old loafers.

"Are you sure?" I asked.

"Why should I have all the fun?" he said. "We can switch for a bit. It'll give you a chance to warm up. It should be pretty easy sledding from here."

He waited for me to mount his machine and then pointed out a couple of the controls, focusing primarily on the heater switch. He turned on the engine. Almost immediately I could feel my hands begin to warm.

"Let me unhook the qamutik and you can try a little spin on the lake. Keep an eye on your speed—it's a bit more powerful than the Bravo."

Simeonie released the sled and slapped my shoulder like a man shooing a horse. I eased into the throttle and pulled away from our parking spot, entering onto the lake like a new driver onto a freeway. Freed from the load it had been towing, the snowmobile stuttered under my thumb's light touch. I gave it a bit more gas to even the ride, and before I knew it, I was ripping down the center of the lake at an easy eighty kilometers per hour. The speedometer's markings maxed out at two hundred fifty. I got the sense this wasn't for show. I turned into a side arm of the lake and, after checking that Sim was out of sight, opened it up. A few seconds later, at one hundred forty kilometers per hour and still accelerating, I chickened out and slowed to a stop. The machine thrummed under me. Clearly it had more to offer than I was willing to take.

I came back down the lake to Simeonie at a pedestrian pace. When I pulled up he was sitting sideways on the Bravo. The qamutik was attached behind him.

"What happened?" he asked. "Did you get scared?"

I realized that while I might have been out of sight I obviously hadn't been out of earshot. Simeonie knew exactly what I had been doing.

"Nope," I said. "I'm just enjoying the ride. It's a nice machine."

"It's an expensive machine." He swung a leg over the Bravo and started it up. It coughed up a cloud of gassy smoke. "Just try to stay behind me."

We followed a route down the ridge line beside the amphitheater to the bay. Simeonie found an easy passage through the tide-heaved shore ice, which was fortunate given the limited towing power of the Bravo and my uncertain control over his snowmobile. As we threaded our way between the islands, the site of the stone houses swung briefly back into view. I took in one last look. It was only when I turned away from the scene that I realized what I had seen. On the hill above our rifle range, watching us, was the caribou.

I stopped.

I stood up, leaving my machine idling. The sound of Simeonie's sled faded into the distance, leaving only the patient tut-tutting of my motor and the rasp of my own breath. I took a couple of steps back along our path and scanned the ridge. In the saddle that blocked the end of the lake I could just make out the doughnut-shaped depressions of the stone houses. On the hill to their left there was nothing. On top of the hill to their right, an inuksuk. There was no sign of the caribou. In the entire treeless, snow-encrusted expanse there was not a single sign of life.

I knew that my brain—high on exhaust fumes and low on sugar—had probably created the caribou out of the inuksuk. Still, I couldn't shake the feeling I was being watched. I had stopped in the gap between the outermost of the three islands, a narrow channel bounded on both sides by heaved ice and rock. It was a perfect place for an ambush. I retreated to the machine and looked over the island on the left. Flat-topped and barren, it was, as far as I could determine, unoccupied. I turned to my idling snowmobile and the island behind it, which was higher and more rugged than its neighbor. With the sun sitting behind and above it, it presented a complicated silhouette of shadows. I shielded my eyes from the glare and traced the island's snaggle-toothed top. At its peak one shadow loomed larger than the rest. I squinted to squeeze the shape into better focus. As I did, it disappeared off the ridge.

I reached for the snowmobile. I considered bolting, but the formless fear I was feeling hadn't quite managed to overrun my executive capacity. I checked on Simeonie. Still within view and heading in a straight line across the ocean, I suspected that it would be a long time before I lost sight of him. I was confident that with the load behind the Bravo and me on the faster machine, I would be able to catch him quickly. I revved the engine to reassure myself that it was still good to go, then, leaving it running, stepped around the snowmobile and walked into the cold shadow of the island. As my eyes adjusted to the shade, the features of the land came into relief—bare granite, stepped up in wind-blown blocks like an inverted quarry. It too appeared lifeless. The ridge line where I had thought I had seen movement was empty except for another stupid inuksuk. Of all their myriad functions in the North, I swear that some of those little guys are put up just to fuck with outsiders.

Relieved, I decided to avail myself of the opportunity to empty my bladder. A narrow corridor between two vertical slabs of ice looked as good a place as any. I stepped out of the open and into silence. The insulating walls of snow made my pissoir as soundproof as a recording studio. I spent a moment filling the space with the various rustles and zips required to free my unit from its Gore-Tex hibernaculum, then paused before peeing to enjoy the silence. I realized that if I stood completely still and silenced my breath that the sole sound was my heartbeat. The entire world, minus my heart, had come to a stop. I remember thinking at the time about how that was the exact opposite of dying.

Then, when I turned to take a leak on the wall, a bomb went off. A block of snow the size and shape of a football exploded off the ground in front of me. The sound, sudden and terrifying, was akin to what might happen if you threw a turkey into a fan. A riot of white feathers rocketed directly at my face. I ducked. I'm pretty sure I screamed. I most definitely peed on my hand. For what it's worth, it wasn't an effective way to warm it.

And then it was over. Ten meters away a willow ptarmigan in its winter-white plumage had landed and was strutting around to show its irritation at my intrusion. Any other bird would have just flown away. Ptarmigans (all grouse for that matter) seem to possess wings for the sole purpose of scaring people. It has to be one of nature's most ridiculous self-defense strategies—lay low, try not to be seen and, when that looks to have failed, wait until the last possible second to see if you can induce a coronary. Seriously, there is not a predator in the world that doesn't shit itself when a ptarmigan explodes into flight.

I was thinking about how stupid that entire class of birds is as I exited the ice corridor. While looking down to decide which part of my water-repellent ensemble would be of best use to wipe off my hand, I had the sudden realization that I wasn't alone. I stopped and looked up. There, standing beside my snowmobile, was the caribou.

"Hello, Guy," it said. "Is everything alright?"

CHAPTER 22

I had heard it clearly. The caribou spoke in the unaccented, even voice of a newsreader. The question sounded sincere, although its expression was hard to read.

"Excuse me?" I said.

"You screamed," the caribou said. "At the ptarmigan. I thought maybe you were feeling a bit unsettled."

"No. Not really."

"Cold?"

"A little," I said. "You?"

"I'm OK."

It was probably a stupid question, but then I hadn't prepared a list of the twenty things I'd most like to ask a caribou if afforded the opportunity. We stood in silence for a moment. I found myself wondering if it might be offended by my footwear. In the end, I decided to restart the conversation by stating the obvious.

"You speak English," I said.

"Mmm," it said. "A little. Just enough to get by, really."

I recognize that I hobbled the statement with an unnecessary adjunct. Faced with a talking reindeer, I was left questioning: one, if English was its second language; and two, exactly how much English a caribou needed to get by. *You speak?* would have sufficed. Fortunately, the animal was feeling helpful.

"So, Guy," it said. "I suppose you're wondering why I'm here."

"Among other things, yes."

"I belong here. The real question is why you are here."

Awesome, I thought. *A therapy caribou.*

"I'm here to see The Edge," I said. It didn't look satisfied so I explained, "It just seems like the sort of place I should have been to before."

"But wouldn't the sort of person who should have been there before been there before?"

"Mmm," I muttered.

"So again, why are *you* here?"

I didn't have an answer. I doubt it needed one. I tried to hold its gaze but the fucking thing stared me down.

"You know, your English is very good," I said.

"Thank you."

I wanted to leave. The animal, however, was closer to my snowmobile than I was. I couldn't engineer a way onto the machine without passing through its space. I looked down the ice at the distant speck that was Simeonie. The creature seemed to recognize my restiveness.

"I should probably let you go if you're going to catch him," it said.

"That would be good."

"Be careful, Guy."

"I'll try," I said. "Are you following us?"

"No. I'm not good on the ice. Besides, it's not a good time of year at The Edge."

"So I've heard."

The caribou didn't move from beside the machine. I didn't feel comfortable taking a step towards it. They are unpredictable beasts at the best of times.

"Do you mind?" I asked.

"Oh, sorry." It stepped backwards, awkwardly, as ungulates do.

I had a colleague once who specialized in the posthumous psychiatric diagnosis of historical figures. Diagnostic pathography, he called it. Although the man could be a bit of a bore—his emails to me were rife with phrases like *the erroneous conflation of taxonomy and phenomenology* and *the ontological persistence of epistemic non-verification*—his work was quite fascinating. It is a difficult job, teasing apart the sort of insanity that might lead a man to seek out adventure from the mental illness acquired when on it. Did duress unmask preexisting pathology or cause it *de novo*? Did the adventure go off the rails because the adventurer himself was off his rocker? Was he accidentally poisoned with lead solder, dog liver, syphilis? When the symptoms recurred on a subsequent adventure was it a relapse of mental illness or a sign of PTSD? The whole field is, as my colleague might put it, a conundrum of apodeictic judgement in the absence of pathoanatomical proof.

This particular pathographer's background was in art history. He had made a name for himself in the debate over Michelangelo's purported autism (where he was, as always, on the side of the disease—seriously, the man takes no joy from magic). Into my world of dead adventurers he came as an expert in the analysis of illustrations; he had an eye for the details in a doodle that might mark insanity. He was, for instance, the only historian to note the peculiar presence of a parakeet

157

in one of Franklin's early journals, which he said was a clear sign of either frontal-temporal dementia or an unfortunately located brain tumor. Sir John, it seems, may have lost his marbles before he lost his men.

Our final collaboration was on Meriwether Lewis (despondent depressive, alcoholic, unrequited love). I was well into my transition out of academia and into infotainment at the time and I may have borrowed a little too heavily on his ideas to flesh out my book, *Terra Incognita: The Minds that Mapped America*, Chicago, HarperCollins Publishers. I last saw him after a public lecture on the tour to shill said book. Having forgotten that the man lived in that town and, as such, having neglected to invite him to the talk, I was surprised to find him before me at the book-signing table. Unlike those in the line ahead of him, he didn't hand over his copy. It landed on my table from a height.

"Hi Clarke," I said. "Do you want me to sign that for you?"

"Oh, please do."

I flipped it open to the prelims and set my pen to the half-title page. "Anything in particular you want it to say?"

"Sure," he said. "How about: *To Clarke. For all your fucking ideas.*"

Then he walked away.

Interestingly, of all my former colleagues he's the only one who has kept in touch.

I pushed the machine hard enough to be sure to catch Sim, but not so hard as to risk losing control. I was spooked and confused by my encounter with the caribou. Although there was much of which I was uncertain, there was one thing I knew beyond a doubt: I did not want to be alone. As the islands receded behind me and the dot I was pursuing developed into the details of a man, I eased off the throttle and attempted to settle my mind. Being a rational person, my first thought was that I might have imagined the whole thing. Regardless, imaginary or not, I had still been conversing with a caribou. I considered the possibility that I could be going insane, but then had to weigh whether having the insight to question my own sanity made insanity itself more or less likely. I ran through a list of the diagnoses that Clarke had pinned on our dead adventurers to see if any of them were the sort of illness that might present with a talking caribou. There was no good fit. I canvassed all the encounters of my recent past for any that was less than perfectly normal. Nothing was suspect. Even the psychologist who took me in for some solo sessions after our spectacularly unsuccessful marital counselling discharged me from her care by saying "I'm fairly sure you don't have any Axis I disorders." I am a unique and free-spirited man, but I am rock-solid sane.

The caribou was real.

Besides, I thought, it couldn't have been a product of my own mind. If it had, the beast would have used my real name.

CHAPTER 23

I caught up to Simeonie at the edge of a long spine that tracked across the flats like a crease across a shirt. Slabs of ice were thrust up on either side, offset and stacked into a wall. Along their base, marking the junction of the sail to the solid sea, were smooth turquoise pools of seeped water and freshly-formed ice. The ridge extended, as far as I could tell, forever.

Simeonie had found what looked to be the most likely passage, a less steeply-angled section where the ridge was more ramp than rampart. The Bravo was on the far side. The qamutik, tossed up like a small boat cresting a wave, was on mine. Sim was sitting on its stern, facing me.

"Glad you could make it," he said. "I could use your help here."

"I had to pee," I said. "What's this?"

"Speed bump."

"No doubt." I looked down the length of the thing. "It's a pressure ridge, no?"

"That too."

"Are we going to be able to get across?"

"If you give me a little push it shouldn't be a problem."

I wasn't quite sure how much my pushing would help given the weight of the loaded qamutik and the pulling power of the Bravo but I was willing to give it a shot. As I stepped onto the new ice my right foot flitted left, wrenching my balance and my back askew. I steadied myself, then took a couple of tentative steps towards Simeonie's perch. My sealskin soles started to slip at the slightest slope. I stuttered into a series of quicker, smaller steps, each less certain than the last, until I was basically running in place. A few feet from the qamutik my footing gave way entirely. I lunged at the rear crosspiece of the sled. Prostrate on thirty degrees of friction-free ice, I hung from the sled like a man dangling from a rain gutter.

Sim grabbed my parka between my shoulder blades and heaved me up beside him with one hand.

"Jesus," I said. "I'm not sure how I'm going to be able to push."

"I figured you would use your machine," he said.

"Oh."

"But I'd be happy to watch you try that again."

"Yeah, no thanks." I brushed off the fur on the upper part of my qamiqs. The sealskin soles were bare. "You know, I'm shocked at how slippery these things are. You'd think traction would be important."

"For a seal?"

"Well, no. For a boot."

"Hmm," he said. "Are your feet warm?"

"Yeah, I guess so."

"And are they dry?"

"Yes."

"That sounds pretty good to me." He reached into his pocket for his cigarettes and motioned for the lighter. "Slippery never killed no one."

"Tell that to Mallory," I said.

"Who's she?"

"He," I said. "George Mallory. The first man to fall off Everest."

"Did he die?"

"Oh yeah. He and his climbing partner, a kid named Andrew Irvine. They disappeared into a cloud just below the summit and never came down. It took seventy-five years before someone found Mallory's body. When they did, he was still recognizable, mummified from the ice and cold."

"That happens," he said. "Why were they climbing it?"

"Because it was there."

"Because what was there?"

"Mount Everest. *Because it's there* is what Mallory was said to have said when they asked him why he wanted to climb it."

"That's a dumb reason to die." He had lit two cigarettes and handed the first to me. He took a draw, then leaned back and released a lungful of smoke. "So is that what you do for work, Guy? You tell the stories of dead men?"

"More or less." I couldn't remember ever talking about my work with him. I wondered if he had spoken about me with Yves and, if so, what that little prick had said. "I'm a historian, of sorts."

"Why?"

"Why am I a historian?"

"Why do you tell those stories?"

Because they're there? I thought.

"Somebody has to, no?" I said. "Most of these guys led interesting lives. Some of them suffered spectacular deaths. People always want to hear that kind of stuff. Besides, I think there can be a lot to learn from other people's misadventures."

"I suppose." He paused to take another drag. "It's just it doesn't seem like they're your stories to tell."

I've been involved in innumerable academic debates about cultural appropriation. I've argued both sides. Sitting on Sim's qamutik I was well-prepared to take the contrary position to his supposition. Seriously, who would be better placed than me to tell the tales of middle-aged White poseurs?

"I don't know, Sim. Somebody has to speak for them. The dead don't talk."

"No?"

"Not to me."

"No," he said. "Not to you."

We smoked in silence. I waited for him to continue.

"The thing I don't get about your people, Guy, is whether you don't have souls or if you just can't see them."

"You're talking about the actual soul?" I asked. "Of a dead person?"

"Yeah," he said. "Where are all the White ones?"

I am not a religious person. People usually figure this out fairly quickly on their own. As such I'm not often engaged in a spiritual conversation. But it seemed like a reasonable question.

"I think the general belief is that they don't stick around," I said. "Once you're free to leave why would you hang back to chat? You know—*how long, I beg of thee, will thy spirit be chained down to earth?* Surely eternal life should offer something more than this."

"I see how that could make sense," he said.

"Yeah?"

"For a qallunaaq, sure. I've been to Winnipeg. A week was enough."

"I know, right? I've seen a lot of depictions of heaven. None of them looks anything like Manitoba."

"How many look like this?"

We were two men, sitting atop the sole decoration on an otherwise empty, infinite stage. With a little imagination and a bit of CGI it could be made to look like anything. God's soundstage, maybe. Heaven as a holodeck. Without a body it might not feel so cold.

"So, Sim. To my eyes, we're the only ones around. Am I missing something?"

"I think you might be missing everything, Guy," he said. "For us, *sila*—spirit—is everywhere. But hey, it's OK that you don't see it. This isn't your place."

I took a draw on my cigarette and held it at the top of my breath for a moment before exhaling a balloon of dry mist and cold smoke. I was tempted to tell him about my encounter with Mr. Ed back at the islands, but wasn't yet sure it was something I wanted to share.

"So what should I be looking for, Sim? Ghosts?"

"Not ghosts," he said. "Guidance."

"I thought that's why I hired you."

"I can show you around out here," he said, wafting his cigarette over the ice. "But sometimes people need a little guidance in there." He tapped my forehead with his free hand.

"That's not the kind of adventure I was looking for."

"Neither was I."

"Well then, I guess I'll just have to keep my shit together and get a therapist when I get back south."

"Ee," Sim nodded. "That would be good."

I had been joking. Although, for what it's worth, I did have a therapist.

"So Sim," I asked. "Whose spirit guides you?"

He looked at me with an expression that told me I was nearing the limits of what he was willing to talk about. "My grandfather. Mostly."

"Your mother's father?"

Eyebrows up. Nothing said.

"And your dad?" I asked.

"Not so helpful."

The gap-toothed grin appeared again. His eyes, however, added nothing. I figured it was a good time for a drink, a toast to our mutual mortality. I climbed up on the qamutik and rooted around under the tarp to locate my duffel bag. When I found it, I thrust my entire arm deep in the bag and felt my way to the flask, like a veterinarian trying to birth a stuck calf. I extracted it, sealing the spaces as I withdrew my arm, and checked for leaks. It was dry and, thankfully, still full.

When I turned back, Sim was looking into a cloud of mist that hung above him like a speech bubble. I assumed it had come out of him, but then, before I had a chance to speak, he flicked the butt of his cigarette off onto the ice, straightened himself and, with one long inhalation, drew the cloud out of the sky and into his lungs.

Simeonie turned and caught me in mid-swig. I wiped my face with my sleeve and waggled the flask. "Fancy a drink?"

"What's that?"

"Scotch," I said. "I thought this might be a good time for a wee nip."

He checked his watch. He looked unenthused. I wondered if maybe it was still too early for a drink. It felt like we had been out for hours.

"What time is it?" I asked.

"One."

"Well that's OK, ain't it? A little early afternoon drink before we hit the trail again."

"One a.m., Guy."

"What?"

"It's one in the morning."

I looked to the sky. The sun smirked behind a cloud. South became North. East, West. I was beyond lost.

"Maybe you should save it for The Edge, eh?" He zipped his parka and sat up. "You can have a little celebration once we've made it. I want to get going before this wind picks up."

I hadn't noticed a wind, but then I hadn't noticed a half day passing either. I exhaled a little weather balloon of breath and watched as the wind pulled it over the far side of the ridge. Without having a clue which direction it had been blowing, there was no way I could tell if it had shifted during the day. I wanted to take another, bigger blast of Scotch but Sim was still watching. I pocketed the flask and zipped up my parka.

"OK, Sim. How do we do this?"

"I'm going to lower the qamutik down a bit, then you can nudge it when I start to pull it back over, OK?"

"Nudge it?"

"Just a little positive gravity, Guy."

"OK."

"Got it?"

"Got it."

He pulled himself over the top of the qamutik and boot-skied down the far side. I waited for him to turn to his machine, then pushed myself off and bum slid back down the slope like a kid on a playground slide. On the level ice I tripoded to my feet, then shuffled back to my snowmobile. *Slippery never killed no one, my ass,* I thought.

I started the machine and warmed my hands on the bars while Simeonie maneuvered the Bravo and dropped the qamutik back down the slope towards me. When he got it into position he pulled forward just enough to take up the slack and then left the machine idling. He hauled himself up the tow rope to the top of the pressure ridge.

"Ready?"

I moved the machine forward. Operating the throttle with one numb thumb, I crept up on the qamutik. The snowmobile thrummed and lurched in protest of our pedestrian pace. It felt like I was riding a race horse across a rope bridge. From his rostrum of ice, Simeonie motioned me into position. *Accelerando. Doppio piu lento. Ritardando.* Then, with a circle of his left hand and a flourish with a closed fist, he signaled me to stop. The nose of my snowmobile was tucked under the tail of his sled.

"Perfect," he shouted. "When it starts to move, nudge it."

He slid down his side of the ridge and jogged to his machine. It had stalled by the time he reached it. I took the opportunity afforded by his having to restart the engine to sneak another sip of Scotch. I had just gotten it to my lips when the qamutik creaked and started to heave towards the crest. I fumbled to stow the flask and lunged at the throttle. With the added muscle of my machine, the sled tilted forward and popped off the top of the ridge. I followed it, at speed. Released from resistance and still under full throttle from my thumb, the snowmobile launched off the arête and into the air.

I've ridden a wide variety of conveyances in my day: horses, mules, and camels among the animals; scooters, jet-skis, and motorbikes among the machines. Like most men of my social stature, I have embarrassed myself in Lycra on a far-too-expensive bike. I once jockeyed an ill-tempered llama through the Andes on a poorly conceived re-creation of the journey of Hiram Bingham III. On most any vehicle, I am a competent and generally well-balanced pilot. But on that day, rocketing off the ridge on Simeonie's machine, I felt like I was riding a dragon.

I landed hard and was splayed across the bench by the force of the impact. The machine loaded its suspension and heaved back up, bucking me off the seat. I managed to keep my grip on the handlebars—my only point of contact—and careened across the ice like Superman. The snowmobile executed a single high-speed S-turn leaving it on edge and lined up directly at the back of the qamutik. With brute force, I wrested my way back onto the seat, floored it to level the machine, and steered onto the empty ice beside my guide.

Simeonie saw none of my expert sledmanship. Instead, what he witnessed was me flying by under maximum throttle and minimum control. Having averted disaster with the qamutik I tried to brake. I had every intention of dismounting Sim's snowmobile and humbly asking for the Bravo back. The machine, however, was inclined towards a less amicable separation. The back end slipped out and the track, now perpendicular to our line of travel, caught an edge on a small crack of ice. In a beautifully violent demonstration of Newton's law of the conservation of energy, our linear velocity was converted to angular momentum. I was flung to the ground—smote, you might say—as the machine flipped over me and bounced side-over-side down the ice.

CHAPTER 24

I will credit Sim with this. As his snowmobile—an expensive and beautiful machine vital to his life in the North—lay in steaming ruin twenty meters farther along on the ice, his attention was, at first, focused entirely on my well-being. Face down on the ice, I saw the Bravo pull into my limited range of vision. The sound of its engine cut off and the scene was delivered into silence. I watched Simeonie's boots as he walked towards me. I noticed with my ear to the ice that they sounded different. Less squeak, more crunch.

The boots stopped a short ways in front of my face. Sim squatted to compress himself into the frame.

"You OK?" he asked.

It was a complicated question. In the midst of the accident I had recognized in real-time all the things that could have gone wrong. I surveyed my at-risk bits—limbs, head, thorax—and realized I had survived without significant injury to anything but my ego. I was mortified, but alive. For what it's worth, I did suffer a partial tear of my rotator cuff, which still causes me a fair bit of grief, particularly at night. At the time, however, I believed myself to be physically intact.

"I'm OK," I said as I rolled onto my back. "I think."

"Are you sure?"

"Yeah." I sat up. "I'm alright."

"You didn't break a leg?"

I wiggled my toes. "Nope."

"So I can't shoot you?"

"I'd rather you didn't," I looked past Sim to the upside-down wreck of his snowmobile. "How's the machine?"

"Dunno yet." He stood and offered a hand for me to haul myself up. "Doesn't look good."

From a standing position, I could see that the snowmobile was in far worse shape than I had initially thought. A mirror lay among a few unidentifiable pieces of plastic between us and the main wreck. The engine cowling and windscreen were crushed and partially extruded onto the ice under the weight of the machine. On its skyward side, one of the front runners was bent badly, pigeon-toed against its partner. We approached it solemnly, as one would a dying animal. As we got closer, I noticed the track had derailed and one of the little wheels that support it was missing.

"I'm so sorry, Sim. I don't know what happened. It just kind of got away on me there."

"It happens," he said. I am pretty sure he was lying. He walked around to survey the other side. "You OK to help flip it over?"

I doubt I contributed much given my damaged shoulder, but even so it felt like the machine weighed a ton. We managed to heave it onto its side and then rolled it onto its gimped runner and dislodged track. There was worse damage to the topside. What remained of the windscreen and the engine cowling was pancaked flat and pushed askew.

"Yikes," I said. "Can it be fixed?"

"Everything can be fixed, Guy." He reached for the key and in doing so pulled the entire ignition assembly off of the steering

171

column. He slipped it into a pocket of his parka. "We just can't ride it."

"How are we going to get it back to town?"

"Gonna have to tow it," he said. "On the qamutik."

The already fully-loaded sled lurked behind the humble Bravo. It looked like an improbable job already. I couldn't imagine how it was going to be able to haul that plus another man and the ruined hulk of the bigger snowmobile.

"I guess I broke the wrong machine, hey Sim?"

I honestly expected that my trip to The Edge was over at that point. I know there are those who believe I bullied Simeonie onwards, but it's simply not true. I was aware of the grief I had caused that man and was shaken, both physically and psychically, by the events of that day. I was ready to give up. It was Sim who suggested we carry on. He told me we were within an hour or so of open water and that our trip back was going to be a slog. He suggested we head to The Edge, have a bite to eat and maybe a short rest, and steel ourselves for the work we'd be facing when we returned to the site of my crash. It was his idea.

We left the ruined snowmobile and carried on with the Bravo. Sim fashioned a seat out of caribou hides and some of the softer gear and ensconced me at the front of the qamutik. It was quite comfortable and almost fun, sliding along a few inches above the ice. I tuned my ears to the scraping of the runners and ignored the distant drone of the snowmobile, then pulled my hood forward like blinders on a bridle. With the man and his machine excised from my view, I could imagine I was being pulled by a team of dogs.

I thought about Knud Rasmussen's Fifth Thule Expedition. The Dane had passed not far from our spot on his epic three-year crossing from Greenland to eastern Siberia, travelling the entire way by dogsled. He covered thousands of miles by either running beside or riding atop a qamutik identical to the one I was now on. Not long before my own trip to Iviliiq, I had re-read his journals with the ill-formed thought that I might be able to write a book about the great man. I gave up partway through *Across Arctic America*, when I realized his own English translation was better than anything I could write. Rasmussen is a god among explorers and ethnographers. His route over the top of Canada wound around and beyond all of the northern places I have ever been, a suture sewing shut any claim I have ever had on adventure.

The only omission I could find in Rasmussen's writings is any suggestion of boredom. For three years, he slid across the Arctic at the speed of dog, sleeping in igloos through the long polar nights and camping in mosquito-infested muskeg during each summer's thaw. Yet all the while, he seems to have done it whistling some Viking showtune. If he was ever bored or frustrated he didn't let on. Few adventurers do. Shackleton says nothing of the hours spent playing cribbage on the poop deck of the Endurance. I've never come across a game of tic-tac-toe in the margins of a whaler's journal. No one ever says a peep about masturbation. The closest any *gallant gentlemen* has ever come to copping to a little time-numbing self-abuse is to pen an earnest letter to his dearest. But seriously, there is a fine line between adventure and ennui. Even Edmund Hillary (apiarist, alpinist) had to trek for a month behind a yak to find the base of Everest.

However comfortable Simeonie had made my seat on the qamutik, I couldn't help but feel I had been banished there. There was plenty of room for a passenger on the snowmobile's bench, but the option of a ride up front was not on offer. When I was a child, my father would, on those occasions when we were unlikely to be caught by either the local police or my mother, let me ride in the bed of his pickup truck. It was a secret honor I would always accept, even if whatever excitement I was likely to feel would be well worn off before we reached his destination. I remember spending a lot of time tucked up out of the wind against the back of the cab, listening to muffled music and watching through the window as my dad took me on one of his little adventures, drinking coffee and singing to himself as he drove.

I couldn't tell if Simeonie was singing to himself, but the ride on the qamutik turned out to be just about as cold and boring as those in the back of that truck. I was dressed better than my younger self—my long underwear alone probably cost more than my entire eighth-grade wardrobe—but the wind still worked its way into me, worming through layers of Gore-Tex and fleece until it peeled the Merino right off my skin. I was being delaminated by the cold. I tried to hunker down, but along the ice the wind was equally strong and came with a fine spray of snow that sand-blasted my face. Dermabrasion, Nunavut style. My very own Arctic spa. I put on my goggles. I tightened my hood. I zipped up my parka as high as it could go, catching my beard in the process. After a minute of futzing around with the zipper to free my face, I made a run-through of all the other fasteners and zips on my outfit to seal myself against the cold, like a solo sailor battening down the hatches on his sinking ship. I tried, briefly, to get Sim's attention, but got no response. So, with nothing left to do but suffer and wait, I wrapped myself in caribou hides and shivered myself to sleep.

CHAPTER 25

When I woke, the snowmobile's drone, the scrape of the sled on ice, the whistle of the cold, dry wind, were gone. In their place was the tropical, calm slap of lapping water. Buried under furs and lying flat on the qamutik, I realized I was no longer moving. Or rather, I was no longer moving *laterally*. I had the distinct sensation of being afloat. Bobbing, like a boat. At the time, it was quite novel.

I sat up out of the skins. One hundred feet in front of me was The Edge. Not just of the ice, but of the world.

The white, flat expanse of solid surface ended in a clean, crisp cleft. Beyond that—above and below the whitish-blue blur that I took to be the horizon—was an infinite sky. Clouds floated on either side. The reflection was so perfect I felt I could climb underneath and look at it from the other side.

I stood and walked towards the water. The effect was that of the world's most elaborate infinity pool. A seal popped its head out, sending ripples through the reflected clouds. *Hello*, I said. It said nothing and slipped back into the sky.

"Morning, Guy. Sleep well?"

I spun around to face Simeonie. He was elbow deep in the engine of the Bravo. I didn't know if the *morning* comment was facetious or if it was an accurate statement of time. I also found it difficult to judge the quality of my sleep without knowing if I had

176

been asleep for minutes or for hours. Certainly I felt well rested, if cold and stiff.

"Sure," I said. "Is everything alright with the machine?"

"Nothing is right with this machine." With a grunt he wrenched something unseen, then extracted a grease-covered hand. "If it was a dog I would shoot it."

"Ah," I said. "But you can't eat a machine."

"What?"

"That's what they say, no? The difference between a snowmobile and a dog is that when all else fails you can always eat your dog."

"What the fuck, Guy? Why would you eat a dog?"

"I thought that's what people say."

"Nobody says that." Simeonie turned to walk to the qamutik. "You're gross."

He peeled back the tarp and revealed a corner of the load. He tossed my duffel to the side and rooted around underneath. I was feeling a little peckish and hoped he might be starting to assemble brunch. Instead, he pulled out a jerry can and a toolbox and walked back to the Bravo. I didn't want to get in his way, so walked over to the qamutik to see if I could find where he had stowed the food.

"What are you doing?"

"I thought maybe I could put something together for us to eat," I said. "Are you hungry?"

He stopped and put down the jerry can. "Why don't you go for a walk or something? I'll make lunch after I'm done with this."

"Are you sure?" I asked.

"Please," he said. "Go."

I looked along the edge. "Is it safe?"

"If you stay on the white side, you ought to be OK."

"Which way should I walk?"

Sim glanced both ways along the ice and muttered something I didn't catch. "I dunno," he said. "Try that way." He pointed past me. "Just give me fifteen minutes alone to get this done, then we can eat something and get out of here."

I watched him for a minute as he resumed working on the machine. The rifle was leaning against the seat. I was inclined to ask for it—I've taken flack in the past from Inuit when I've gone for a walk unarmed in polar bear country—but decided to leave it. It wasn't like I was planning on going far.

Like a zoo animal pacing out the perimeter of its enclosure I padded along the ice, keeping a constant six-foot buffer between myself and the edge. My earlier problems with traction, combined with a new unsteadiness underfoot, made me cautious. The water appeared almost still, the ice more so. Even so, I swayed as I walked, like a drunk.

I trudged along with an eye to sea, hoping to spot some sign of the legion of animals I had expected. Sea smoke wafted in and out of view, a magician's hands first revealing then disappearing some uncertain shape. There was something out there—whales maybe, ice—but I couldn't lock onto anything long enough to focus before the fog would wash it away. I remembered Alexander Mackenzie's claim of having seen whales in the mouth of the river that now bears his name. Fog and ice may have been playing tricks on him as well, in addition to thwarting his attempt at a pursuit: *It was, indeed, a very wild and unreflecting enterprise, and it was a very fortunate circumstance that we failed in our attempt to overtake them, as a stroke from the tail of one of these enormous fish would have dashed the canoe to pieces.* Sure thing, Alex. For what it's worth, we know you were looking for the Pacific.

I heard a sigh and stopped. Behind me was the seal. Although it was stationary and staring at me, I could clearly make out the vestiges of a wake spreading behind it. I was being followed.

I turned and walked for a minute more, then stopped and knelt down as if to tie a shoe. It's a transparent gambit at the best of times, more so when wearing qamiqs. I peeked under my right armpit and saw the seal hanging back, watching me. I stood and walked a ways, affecting an air of insouciance. After a while, I began whistling a marching tune. Then, just as I entered into its rousing finale, I aborted the song and spun on a heel. The seal skidded to a stop. For such nimble creatures, they have lousy brakes.

"Ha!" I said. "Caught you, you little bugger."

The seal looked past me as if it had found something of interest on the empty ice.

"Why don't you come up here?" I said. "We could walk together. Maybe get to know each other a bit."

It turned its gaze to me with a stare that shut me up. Until that moment, I had always found the animals cute. Cuddly even. We watched each other in silence for a while longer until I cocked an imaginary rifle, took sight, and popped a shot at it.

"Bang," I said. I got him right between the eyes.

The seal stared at me for a moment more, then turned its nose to the sky and disappeared.

I watched the sea return to stillness and then resumed my walk. The whole while I had been out I had been careful to keep the edge of the ice a steady distance to my right. Now, however, there was another edge an equal distance to my left. My route petered out at a point about twenty paces ahead. Sea smoke steamed off the water on all sides, obscuring any landmarks. I looked back to the seal for advice, but it was gone.

Everything I knew about the floe edge suggested it should be a single, mostly straight line. This was not the case here. The new edge led back roughly in the direction I had walked, so I decided to explore it further. I figured as long as I kept the water on my right I couldn't get lost. After a few minutes, I lost sight of the original edge— presumably more due to fog than distance—and with it lost any sense of having changed direction at all. The only clue was the semi-obscured sun, now hanging in a different part of an otherwise identical scene. I was either walking back towards the qamutik or I had travelled through time.

The wind stiffened and chased the steam off the water. The cold cloud wisped around me and over the ice to my left. Offshore, the mirrored surface of the sea shattered into ripples. The ripples gathered into waves. In a breath, the ocean had turned malevolent. A father's rage. With the fog cleared, I was better able to see what I had been following. To my right, across a break of open water, was the endless expanse of ice I thought I had been on. To my left, a little ways across the ice on which I was walking, was the ocean. The rolling water at my side narrowed to a crack less than a hundred yards ahead, where the two sheets became one.

I quickened my pace.

The freezing wind bit at my face and thrust itself down my shirt. I pulled my hood up and tucked my chin into my shoulder for protection. I couldn't look ahead without my eyes watering in the wind, so stared at my feet instead. I counted steps. I figured fifty should get me halfway there. At forty, I snuck a peek.

I was still a hundred yards away. I shifted into a run. I have always been more of a middle-distance runner than a sprinter and conditions that day (wind, footwear, twenty pounds of outerwear) were far from ideal. Still, it seemed to take forever to close that hundred yards. I got to the point where the lead on my right was only a stone's throw across. I could see the spot where the two floes connected but couldn't reach it. It was like running in water, as in a dream. I bore down into my highest gear and like the miler I've always imagined myself to be, I sprinted to the finish. I passed the crack and slowed to a trot, then stopped to catch my breath.

From behind me there was the sickening sound of bones breaking. I watched as the crack carried past me on my right. It sliced into the solid ice ahead of me and cleaved the world in two. As the water widened beside me, I felt like I was being pulled backwards along the route I had just traversed.

There was a gunshot, a single crack. Echoes came from every direction—the original from somewhere in front of me. I ran towards it. I tried to follow a straight path but the sun, faint through the fog, kept falling to my left. The wind shouldered me to the side. I stumbled to the ground.

I heard a shout and looked up. Through a parting in the fog I saw Sim standing by the qamutik, gun at his side.

There was water on both sides of him.

"Where the fuck were you?"

"You told me to go for a walk."

181

"I said to be back in fifteen minutes!"

Sim dropped his gun against my duffel bag and started to untie the tow rope from the qamutik. I bent over to catch my breath and nearly fell over. The gentle bob of the ice had increased, like a canoe when cast off from a dock. There was a loud sick creak followed by the sound of water sloshing.

"Fuck." Simeonie looked back over his shoulder then continued with the rope. When he had unlashed everything from the qamutik, he tied a couple of the loose ends together, made a few quick coils and dropped them in a pile on the ice. "Don't let that go."

The coiled rope was attached to a long straight stretch. Sim ran along it to the Bravo. The other end was hooked onto the back of the machine.

I ran after him. "You're leaving me here?"

"If I don't get to the other side we're both going to be stuck here." He turned the ignition and pressed the starter button. The machine wheezed a refusal.

"But what am I supposed to do, waterski across?"

"Do you want to drive it, Guy?" he asked. The engine's reluctant wheeze diminished to a raspy whimper. "You think you got this? Because so far you're not doing so good."

Simeonie gave up on the electric starter and moved around to the pull start. With a single yank, he ripped the cord off the Bravo. The machine came to life like a whipped pony. He leaned into the cloud of smoke and detached the tow rope's heavy hook, then reached behind his back and latched it onto his belt.

"Trust me," he said. "But whatever you do, don't let go of the rope."

He jumped on the machine and steered it towards the sea-side of the floe. I could feel the ice tilting under its weight. He maneuvered into a position aimed directly at the gap, a spot that a minute before had been five meters across. It was now thirty meters wide and growing. Sim revved the engine twice. The little Bravo responded with tinny rattle, then the two of them charged into the abyss. The rope, snaking along behind them, snuck up behind my ankles and yanked my feet from under me.

I hit the ice just as they entered the water. The high-pitched whine of the Bravo muted into a rheumy chortle. The machine sagged and slowed. Lying on my side on the ice, I watched as Simeonie leaned back and with great skill and full power wrestled it into position. The Bravo picked up its pace and changed its tune. One-third of the way across the lead, it took the posture of its stronger cousins, the ones I had watched crossing the channel outside of Iviliiq just a couple of days before. It rose high out of the water and struck a note of victory.

Then it went silent.

The Bravo had stalled. A cloud of steam rose in the silence around Simeonie. The machine bobbed briefly, then disappeared. I lost sight of Sim in the tempest the sinking snowmobile stirred up. I struggled to my feet and stared at the spot where I had last seen him, terrified that he had been pulled below. As the mist and bubbles subsided, Simeonie appeared, alive and afloat.

He waved with both hands like scuba divers do when they want to signal that all is OK.

I waved back. I meant it as encouragement. *You're going to be alright. Just swim over here.*

He waved once more, this time with one hand.

I knew that when he got to back onto the floe he was going to be dangerously cold. I worried that I would lose him to hypothermia. I glanced towards the qamutik; I wondered what I could use to warm him up. I had my eyes off Sim for only a moment. But when I looked back at the water he was gone.

I stepped forward, uncertain. Behind each wave was a shadow, a shape. In a flash of spray I was sure I saw his face, but then saw it again in a different place. I thought I spotted his hat. Then his hand. For a moment I was convinced I saw the silhouette of a man just off the edge. I yelled Sim's name at it as it dissolved into nothing. The wind and sea rearranged every shape I saw into water. Then, on the surface of the ice, I saw the one thing I could be sure of.

The rope was sliding off the edge.

It had a more direct line to the water than I did and was moving fast. I raced to intercept it and managed to catch the end just before it went over the side. I slipped onto my ass, dug my heels into the ice and ground to a stop at the water's edge. Arm-over-arm, I heaved the ice-encrusted and soaking wet rope out of the water. It was heavy, but the more I got in the easier it became, a little like reeling in a fish.

And like most of my experiences when landing a fish, when I got to the end of the line, the hook was bare.

CHAPTER 26

I kneeled at the edge, numb with a combination of cold and incredulity. I stared at the spot I had last seen Sim. I was ready to jump in, to swim to his rescue. All I needed was a sign he was there. Something to break the surface, anything to release the tension. But there was nothing. The only trace of the disaster was a small slick, a glint of oil left behind by the Bravo. The slick gathered together, swirled into a tight vortex, and was swallowed by the sea. A wave wiped the surface clean.

The wind that had cleaved the ice carried over the gap and lashed at my face. Waves rose on the water's surface. The void widened into a nascent sea. On its far side I could still make out a line of white, the edge of the sheet of solid ice we had traveled on from Iviliiq, receding into fog. I held onto the hope that the sky would clear and I would find Sim standing sentinel on that floe, like the caribou on its ridge. I imagined him hauling out onto the edge like a seal. But I saw nothing. Whitecaps rolled out of the fog and spilled onto the ice. I called Simeonie's name into the cloud but there was no response. I screamed. There was no echo.

I watched and I waited, my despair tempered by disbelief. Mist settled on my beard. Around me, the loops of rope I had cast aside froze into the ground like roots. It seemed impossible that Sim could be gone. This was supposed to be a minor job for him, a short side trip

185

to help earn the income to fuel his machines and stock munitions for the real work of being an Inuit hunter. It was to be more inconvenience than adversity. I knew I had pushed him a little with regards to the timing and had insisted we make it to The Edge. Still, compared to the adventures he had done on his own and with other clients, this was surely more a nuisance than a risk. I had heard the concern in Ava's voice. At the time I believed it was more about me than him. If anyone were going to get hurt it should have been me. Not Sim.

My eyes watered in the wet wind, letting loose tears that froze to my lashes. I turned away from the water to clear the ice from my eyes. When I looked back, the far edge had disappeared entirely.

In time, the wind diminished and the sky brightened above me. Under a blanket of fog, the ocean started to settle. The squall passed. A tiny clearing in the cloud opened to my right and flitted across the stage to the left. A peepshow, revealing nothing but naked ocean. A flash of what would be my ruin.

I wondered how long it would be before someone started looking for us. Surely, there were people in Iviliiq who would worry if Simeonie were not back home in due course. I thought about the vague trip plan I had filed with Brisebois and his attempt at sketching our route. With that man in charge it would be close to a week before anyone set out, and even then they'd probably start off searching somewhere else. I recalled the conversation I'd had with Sim when I returned from meeting the Mountie, particularly the comment about a beacon that "Woody" hadn't bothered to loan out. Then I remembered the phone. Sim had said something about a satellite phone.

I tried to stand but the sides of my qamiqs were stuck to the ice. I peeled myself off like a Band-Aid and walked to the qamutik, leaving behind two patches of fur and a fossilized rope. I wanted to run, but my pant legs had frozen into stovepipes.

I pulled back the tarp and dismantled the contents of the qamutik. I started methodically, with items I thought I should try to keep dry on the tarp, impermeable miscellany on the snow, but grew impatient the deeper I dug. When the sled was stripped, I turned to the various containers I had cast aside and took them apart in my search. In the end, I eviscerated the load, leaving the bare skeleton of the qamutik surrounded by entrails of its former cargo.

It looked like a yard sale at survivalist camp. The phone was nowhere to be found.

I paced the periphery of the debris field, lurching like Frankenstein's monster in my frozen pants. I've been accused in the past of not looking hard enough for things I've declared irretrievably lost. *Man eyes*, my wife called it. I think it came in handy for her during our divorce. I tried to remember what Simeonie had been wearing, whether he might have had the phone on him when he skipped across the lead. I took an inventory of all the belongings I had seen him transfer in and out his pockets. The only item I was certain he had on him when he went under was the pack of cigarettes. It was too bad as I could have used one right about then.

"What the fuck, Sim," I said. "Did you bring a satellite phone or not? Because if you didn't, I've got better things to do than waste my time looking."

I looked over my mess and into the fog. *Such as what, exactly?* I thought.

I sat on the qamutik and considered my next steps. In the fog and flat light I could see no sign that the ice was moving. Still, I could sense it. The roll of the floe I had felt when we first arrived at The Edge had become untethered, freed like a fluttering kite.

I left behind my mess and walked back to the water. I could feel the heave of the ice increase the closer I got. When I arrived at the two patches of fur and the fossilized rope, I turned left and started along the edge. Keeping the water to my right, I counted steps. Through the mist to my left, the qamutik flickered in and out of sight like a lighthouse. I reeled along the edge, my step-count clicking forward like an odometer. I slowed up at step number four hundred and seventy-four. Five steps in front of me was the rope.

The math was easy, if imprecise. Circumference is equal to diameter times pi. Four hundred and seventy-odd steps around a somewhat circular shape should equal roughly one hundred fifty steps across. My pace is about a yard. The piece of ice I was on was one hundred fifty yards wide. I was afloat on a ballfield.

I looked back over my floe. It was obvious we had broken off the shore-fast ice; the crack I had followed after Sim set me off on my walk—the one that left me winded as it looped past him like a ligature—had cleaved us off from the world and set me adrift. I was sailing to sea on an offshore wind. I had read of similar events, both in the historical record of polar exploration and in the rare news item out of the North. On occasion, an Inuit colleague would share their own story. Invariably, it involved a patient wait, usually for rescue but on at least one occasion for a change in the wind or current and deliverance to a distant land. I realized, however, that there is a survival bias in those stories. Nobody knows what happened to those who just drifted away and died.

In some ways I was as well-prepared for the situation as anyone could be. I had read hundreds of accounts of men who had found themselves in similar despair. A broken mast halfway around the Horn. A broken leg on the summit of K2. A lot of broken spirit, the occasional broken heart. Some died, some did not. There is only so much you can learn from the swan song of a single narcissist. I, however, had assembled a choir. An entire ensemble of survival and despair. What I lacked in experience I could more than make up for in erudition.

There is one account of the death of Henry Hudson that has him take up the oars of the little lifeboat in which he was put adrift and set off in pursuit of the *Discovery*. It is said he kept up for the better part of a day, until his mutineers got tired of being chased and raised another sail. Even if the man never was seen again you have to admire his gumption. But Hudson at least had oars. I didn't even have a boat. I was adrift on an ice floe at the start of the Arctic summer. I had no guide—I had just watched the man drown—and no snowmobile. I had a bit of caribou jerky, but no crackers. Most important, I had no way to contact anyone anywhere in the world and, quite possibly, nobody who would give a shit I was gone.

I once partnered with an epidemiologist to calculate the mortality rate among Victorian adventurers—forty percent if you count direct death, she had said, sixty percent if you include alcohol and venereal disease. I figured I was safe from the latter, putting my odds of survival in the same ballpark as leukemia. A coin toss, then. *Pollice verso.* The key to survival, the epidemiologist had claimed, was in the attitude. It's the same sort of bullshit that some people say about cancer.

The epidemiologist and I had produced a catchy little monograph titled *Observations on the Causes of Mortality among Explorers*, with her doing the majority of the work and me mostly just opening my treasure trove of journals and regaling her with stories. We did get into some spirited debates about what actually killed my men. Laurence Oates, for instance. I said chivalry. She settled on gangrene. The project was our only collaboration as the manuscript never did get published. I was, however, able to find a home for much of the data in a subsequent book. The epidemiologist, as far as I can recall, quit academia to work in a county health department.

Regardless, what was of interest to me now was our top-five list of non-infectious causes of death. I could remember it clearly, as I had helped with the layout of the sidebar in which we presented the data. They were:

1. Exposure
2. Starvation
3. Trauma (this she sub-categorized)
   i.   Drowning
   ii. Fall from heights
   iii. Animal attack / envenomation
4. Nutritional disorders
5. Suicide

I felt fairly confident *vis à vis* a fall from heights. I also figured that in my predicament, starvation would trump any nutritional disorder. I didn't want to contemplate the possibility of animal attack or suicide, but noted that in either case Simeonie had left me his gun.

That left drowning, exposure, and starvation.

I had my to-do list: stay dry, stay warm, have a bite to eat.

CHAPTER 27

Step One. I needed a change of pants.

In my rush to get out of the hotel I had taken a somewhat crude approach to layering. Namely, I had put on almost everything I owned. On my lower, wet half, I had the outer layer of Gore-Tex, some pile pants, high-tech long johns, and orthopedic underpants. The latter, purchased from a distractingly attractive physical therapist at the time of a long-since-healed groin injury, are my go-to gonch for any semi-athletic activity. My top, largely dry half, was covered with more Gore-Tex, an outrageously expensive soft-shell jacket, a fleecy sort of hoodie, a microfiber yoga shirt, and another couple hundred dollars' worth of long johns. On my feet, I was wearing at least four socks. The ensemble wasn't everything I had packed, but it was close. I knew I had stuffed some remaining clothing in a drawer back in my room, swaddling Sedna.

I reached for my duffel bag to see if I had brought anything onto the ice that I could cobble together into a new outfit. I found several more pairs of socks (take that, gangrene), a cable knit sweater, a couple of extra T-shirts, a pair of jeans, and a baseball cap. My wardrobe options were binary—Polar adventure or weekend at the Cape. The sweater in particular was quite nice, if a bit twee. I placed it, and everything but the jeans, back in the duffel bag.

For those of you whose experience with winter is limited, you should know that denim ranks just below chiffon among the most useless materials from which to fashion a snowsuit. I learned this at the same time I learned to ski, as a marginally-continent six-year-old, decked out in matching jean jacket and pants. Other than for the cut—bell-bottoms and ski boots work quite well together—the outfit was dangerously non-functional. It would be okay only if the temperature remained within a few degrees of freezing and I didn't fall down, in which event I would end up wet from the inside and out. If denim had not been one of our common causes of death among explorers, it was only because few explorers had ever been dumb enough to wear it.

Regardless, the jeans were all I had. I was starting to feel a burning in my thighs, directly under an area of frost that had formed on the shell. Moisture is the cancer of the cold; it creeps through your clothes and roots into your vital bits. I didn't know how deep the water had penetrated but I knew I had to isolate the dampness before it spread. I tugged off the qamiqs, noting that my socks were still warm and dry (thank you, Ava), then shimmied backwards out of my pants. The first under-layer felt a little damp so I peeled it off as well, then put on the jeans. They were snug (I was wearing long johns) and had a button fly—a bad combination in cold weather. I lay on the ice, on my back, and fumbled with unfeeling thumbs to get myself put back together, then pulled on the qamiqs and stood up. I ran on the spot for a minute to warm up the pants, much like one does when revving a cold engine. I had intended the jeans to be a temporary measure while I set my better pants out to dry. How that was going to happen, however, was unclear. I was on a foggy, flat expanse of ice under an anemic polar sun. The highest point on my island—at a hair over six feet above sea level—was the top of my head. In absence of any better idea, I set the pants down atop the tarp, weighed them down with my boots, and turned to the job of itemizing the contents of the sled.

I retrieved the pen and notebook from my duffel, along with a bag of licorice that I had found packed among the socks. I popped a piece in my mouth and wandered around the site with my notebook like a judge at a junior-high science fair. I had already worked my way through everything in search of the missing phone. On this pass, however, I intended to pay closer attention to the stuff I *did* have.

I was impressed with how comprehensive Simeonie had been. The qamutik was better stocked than my condo. There was a box that looked to contain enough tools and spare parts to repair most any malfunction of a snowmobile, short of total loss (in my case, of both machine and mechanic). There was an axe, the use of which so far above treeline escaped me. In Sim's rucksack was some leftover caribou and his enormous straight-bladed knife. Panna, I think they call it. The man's knife. It looked like the sort you see Japanese showman chefs fling about when they want to distract you from the fact that you're about to be served a most uninspired stir-fry. In a large Tupperware container I found the makings of a complete kitchen: a frying pan and pot, oil, salt, cheese grater, and French press. The excitement I felt when I saw the press led to frustration later on when I failed to find any coffee. I wasn't quite as excited by the grater, so the subsequent lack of cheese was less disappointing.

In the bottom of that kitchen bin I also discovered a complete two-person dinnerware set. I stopped my industry for a moment—long enough for a little cry—then packed it back up with the press and grater. I moved the box of cookware to the rear of the qamutik and set it beside the stove and kettle. I took the two jerrycans of gasoline and another container of kerosene and put them next to my makeshift kitchen. I had the beginnings of a camp.

I gathered up the skins from my unmade bed at the front of the qamutik. I had assumed they were all caribou, although as I stacked them I noted some variation in their color and plushness. Two seemed a reasonable match with the leggings on my qamiqs. The other ones, darker, smaller and a bit more mangy, appeared to be a closer cousin of my beard. Behind them was a large roll of cream-colored canvas. I unfurled it onto the ice and scattered from its center a set of wooden poles. A tent. Or, if conditions were to deteriorate, a sail. I dragged it over to the spot recently vacated by the Bravo. I know it is generally suggested that when camping in bear country one should take care to separate eating and sleeping areas, but my options for homesites were limited. I spread the gear on the ice and scanned through the parts to get some idea of how to assemble it. I've always found tents to function in part as puzzles, like enrichment for gorillas or OT for the enfeebled. It's not a challenge I'm usually very receptive to (typically I set up tents when beset by some combination of failing light, fatigue, biting insects, and rain). I left it for later and turned back to the qamutik.

The only thing left for me to inventory was a large plastic bin of food. I had rifled through it earlier in my search for the phone, but at that point I had purposely avoided thinking about what it contained. I steeled myself with a piece of licorice and boxed off the corner of a page in my notebook to document my provisions, then peeled off the lid and dove in.

My maternal grandmother lived through the Blitz. While she made it through the London bombings physically unscathed, she, like many of her generation, ended up crushed by privation. The kind of malignant frugality learned by surviving a war is both incurable and contagious; it spreads through a family as easily as tuberculosis. My mother, scarred by the scourge of her own mother's miserliness, first crossed an ocean and later married a glutton. It didn't matter. By the time I came along she had embraced her austerity with pride. Our pantry was as overflowing as any in America. My mother had no need to police our portions. Still, the woman could tolerate no waste. My father, like most Americans, was a man driven more by appetite than economy. He would polish off every bone like a dog. Together my parents would watch me as I ate, guarding the only path I had from the table to the sink. It was impossible to smuggle a crumb past them.

I've been conditioned from that childhood to always clean my plate. I've been known at times to lick it. The Inuit, who go so far as to suck the goo out of the inside of eyeballs, no doubt can relate. A hunter once told me that to waste food is to ensure future want (he said it while handing me a choice piece of omentum, which I later had to spit into a stream). My mother's family, being British, just took it as a sign of strong moral fiber and civic responsibility. Whatever the rationale, the compulsion to clean a plate is as useless in a land of plenty as it is dangerous in a time of need. It is a challenge to stretch out a finite supply of food when you've been habituated to hoover up everything in sight. I had two tasks before me as I examined my stores. First, itemize all that I had. Second, try not to eat it.

I set out my food on the bare slats of the qamutik. Sim appeared to have had a particular affinity for canned fish. I had six tins in total:

three of sardines, one each of oysters, mackerel, and brisling. The brisling were imported from Norway and looked particularly good, even if the Couche-Tard price sticker told me unequivocally that Yves had picked them up on his way through Montréal. I decided to set that last tin aside for a special occasion.

My journal, otherwise generally unreliable, documents clearly the food I had available at the start of my adventure:

Tinned fish

Sardines (3)

Oysters (1)

Mackerel (1)

Brisling! (1)

Bread, white (20 slices)

Onion (1)

Flour (2 kg)

Oranges (12)

Coke (9 cans)

Tea, decaffeinated (27 bags)

Caribou, rump (~200 g)

~~Licorice (bag)~~

I was curious about the three missing cans from the case of Coke. Besides the gasoline, it had been the single most expensive line item on the receipt at the Iviliiq Co-op. I knew I hadn't drunk any. I wondered if Sim might have snuck some while I had been asleep. I cracked a can and sat down on the skins to contemplate.

The tea was obviously useless. I hadn't known it was decaffeinated when Sim had served me earlier, although now I had a better understanding of the origin of my headache. The caribou was likely nutrient-rich and, although the allotment was small, its consistency would help temper the speed with which I ate through the rest of my larder. The onion was, as most onions are, as familiar as it was inaccessible. I decided to ignore it until either inspiration or desperation suggested a use.

The menu plan was straightforward. I would build it around the fish and bread, alternating sardines / mackerel / sardines / oysters / sardines, and space out those "meals" with oranges. The Coke (now eight cans) I could dispense on a tapering schedule as I weaned myself off caffeine. After that, there was enough fresh water in the puddles of snow melt that pocked the surface of the floe to keep me hydrated. With a half tin of fish and an orange a day, I'd have enough food for a week and a half. Surely, Brisebois would be able to find me by then. If not, I would break out the stove and flour and start to make bannock.

While there may be an art to rationing, it is for the most part an exercise in mathematics. I reckon the word comes from ratio. You have your numerator, a limited supply of something essential. Fuel, maybe. Water, often. In my case, food. And then you have your denominator. Technically speaking, the denominator is the number of person-days your finite supply needs to last. When William Bligh set off for East Timor in his open boat, he had an ounce of bread and a quarter-pint of water for each man, each day. A death would result in slightly more water for everyone, and perhaps a little something for each of them to put on their bread.

But William Bligh had a rough idea of how long he might be at sea. More important, he had a measure of time. Once per day, the sun would rise astern and set ahead. As it passed the zenith on its way towards night, Bligh would dispense order with an ounce of bread. My bounty was laid out in front of me, orderly and divisible, but how was I to know when I should eat? I was already lost in time at the time of the crash. I had no idea how long I had been asleep on the qamutik, or had been walking on the ice after I woke. How long I had sat after Sim had sunk was lost on me. I looked to the sky. The mutinous sun, adrift in the fog, mocked me.

I thought about my internal clock, the various chronometers that mark the hours with regularity. Caffeine withdrawal. Morning wood. That never-ending piss that starts each day. The daily dump, as dependable and conspicuous as a one o'clock gun. My body is a little Swiss village, with church bells that chime on the hour. Usually. As it turns out the body's clock is wound by the night. Even before setting out on the ice, the three days of continuous light had desynchronized my works.

I grabbed an orange and a caribou skin and paced off the eighty-one steps from the front of the qamutik to the water's edge.

CHAPTER 28

The squall had settled. The waves had dispersed, leaving nothing behind but a wobble on the water's otherwise smooth surface. It was a warped mirror; a sea made of mercury. I sat on the skin and watched my cast-off pieces of orange peel drift away. They moved of their own accord: reluctantly, randomly—like bystanders wandering away from a crowd. It was strange to not see them taken away, pushed in by a wave or carried out by a current. It didn't occur to me then that there was a current, a strong one at that, and that we were all traveling on it together.

The motion and soft sounds were hypnotic. Sitting on a skin, I started to loll in and out of consciousness. Momentary paralysis from the neck up, then a jerk back to life as my head fell over its fulcrum. Each sleep could have lasted only seconds, but in every one was a dream—a series of unresolved, vivid vignettes playing across my mind like previews before a film. Each dream was set on the same ice on which I sat. Their intensity contrasted with the dozy fugue into which I kept waking. As I passed in and out of sleep, reality and reverie dissolved into each other like blood into water.

In a waking moment between dreams, I saw that the seal had reappeared. It watched me, as pinnipeds do, its body-less head bobbing beyond the peels. I tried to focus on it, to let it know that I could see it too, but fell back into sleep. When I woke it was gone. I met it next in a dream. After that it seemed to travel freely between my conscious and unconscious worlds. In time it was joined by a few friends. Seals mostly. A walrus. A couple of narwhal for a bit. I assume that those animals were dreamt, but can't be sure. Honestly, arctic fauna has a mystic appearance even at the most lucid of times.

The seal was in a small group of its kin when it spoke. A dozen dark eyes watched me impartially, like a jury.

"Are you going to eat those?" it asked.

"The peels?"

"Yes," it said. "The peels. Are you planning on doing anything with them?"

"Um… no. You can have them if you want."

I heard a watery snort of derision from the right.

"I don't want them," the seal said.

"We don't want them," some other seal shouted.

The leader broke its gaze from me and shot a look at the interjector. When it was silenced, the lead seal turned back to me.

"We're here to ask you to keep to your side of the ice."

There was a murmur of consensus among the animals.

"OK," I said. It seemed a little unfair given the size of my floe compared to their ocean. "If it helps, I promise to stay out of the water."

"Good luck with that, asshole," some seal said. The voice had the same nasal quality, though a slightly different timbre. A bit more New Jersey to the lead seal's New York. I looked to my left, to where it had come from, but saw nothing but a ring of ripples. The group didn't look inclined to offer any assistance. Even so, I realized I should at least ask them for help.

"So hey, while you're here…" I said.

"Mmmm?"

"You haven't seen any other people, have you? A boat, maybe?"

"We haven't seen any boats," the leader said. "We avoid boats this time of year."

"Really? Because I could use some help. Somebody might be looking for me."

"Can't help you."

"Are you sure? Can you maybe keep an eye out for other people when you're swimming about?"

"People eat seals, asshole!" It was another heckler.

"Look, just stay up there," the leader said. "Leave us alone and we'll leave you alone."

It was clear some of the other seals weren't feeling as conciliatory. I thought I ought to address them. "Just so you know, *my* people don't eat seals," I said over the leader. "It's the Inuit who eat seals. I'm not Inuit."

"No shit," the leader sighed.

The heckler persisted. "So you're saying you've never eaten seal?"

A vague memory inserted itself between my mind and my mouth. The pause betrayed me. A chorus of barking rose up out of the water.

"It was just the flipper," I said. I had to shout over the noise. "It was in a pie. I was in Newfoundland."

One hooligan made a move towards the ice. Sensing a confrontation, I struggled to my feet. I was strangely sore and stiff for a dream. I suspected that sea mammals might be intimidated by limbs so I stretched out my arms, like an albatross. My challenger pulled up a few meters short of the edge. Another round of barking rose out of the water behind it.

"Just ignore him," a different seal called out. "He means no harm."

I looked to see where my support had come from. The voice sounded familiar. I refolded my arms. "It's true," I said to the gang. "I'm just going to mind my own business up here. I'll keep to my side."

I stood in a wordless standoff for a minute. One by one, the seals sank below the surface. Most in silence; one after mouthing *fuck off*. The leader gave me a watery raspberry, tilted its nose to the sky and disappeared. Behind and to its right, I saw one seal left. My defender. It was Simeonie, at least from the chin up. The ends of his Fu-Manchu moustache spread across the surface of the water. Whatever was below was obscured.

"Be careful, Guy." He turned his nose up and went under, again, trailing an ellipsis of bubbles.

I woke. The water was still. The wind was calm. The only sounds came from within my own body. The heart's baseline beat—steady, apace. My lungs' harsh gasp, entering late. I was still upright on the skin, but in the time I had been asleep the fog had cleared. I scanned the ocean for any signs of life, then turned and surveyed the ice. I felt, ironically perhaps, reassured to see that I was still alone. Blue sky and sun had washed the ambiguity out of my surroundings, leaving the cold clarity of sharp shadows on snow. The nap, and dream, had the undiluted intensity that often signals a need for real sleep. I had no idea how long I had been on the ice, or how much of that time had been awake or asleep. My accounts were, as usual, a mess. I suspected it had been at least two-and-a-half days since we had set out from Iviliiq, and in that time I had taken nothing more than a series of indeterminate and incomplete catnaps. It was time for a real sleep.

I stooped to roll up my little caribou skin yoga mat. I thought about how with the right attitude and a guaranteed outcome, my experience could be marketed as a high-end retreat. Certainly it was a bit more peaceful than some of the desert boot camps the senior staff at the magazine had become fond of taking. They had invited me once, to some scrabby shithole outside of Tuba City, Arizona. I declined, of course. Why anyone would ever entrust me with a firearm in the pretext of "team-building" is beyond me. But I was still able to draw offence from the short series of emails that followed my departure, before the group was wise enough to drop me from the cc: list.

I was thinking about that slight as I walked over to the edge to pee. I was trying to remember who it was in that chain of messages that had referred to me as Lady Franklin. When I looked down to finesse my buttons back into place I saw the orange peels. A little pile, at the edge of the edge. All of them very much on the dry side.

I sorted through my memories to try to place when it was that I had seen the peels in the water. I had no recollection of having tossed them there, but was just as certain I had watched them floating while awake as I was of having talked to the seals while asleep. Seeing them on the shore was as disconcerting as seeing someone else's face in the mirror.

I gazed past the froth of my urine and into the expanse of unmarked ocean. There was nothing there. I had to be alone. I scraped the peels over the edge with the instep of my boot and turned to walk back to the qamutik.

CHAPTER 29

It was no use just sitting around The Edge waiting for rescue. It wasn't like I could paddle the floe and with the qamutik squarely centered on it, it would be obvious to anybody who got near that they had found the right piece of ice. If I pitched the tent it would be even more clear that the camp was occupied. Then maybe I could get a real sleep.

All the tents I have ever used on research trips and treks have been ultralight erections of nylon and aluminum. Once, I paid an idiotic amount of money for a tent with titanium poles, convinced by the granola-munching salesman that the weight difference (about equivalent to a single flax-infused bowel movement) would afford me a bit of breath with which I could talk up my research assistant. It did not. Sim's shelter made no such promise of portability. Laying before me on the ice was a puzzle of heavy canvas, tangled rope, and lumber. From it, I was supposed to construct a shelter. If but for a bag of nails, I probably could have built a boat.

I had a vague recollection of Inuit colleagues assembling a similar sort of tent for use as a camp kitchen. It had looked straightforward enough. The key, if I remembered correctly, was the internal frame. I sorted through the pile of lumber and pulled out the center beam, along with a couple of cross pieces, four posts, and a few plywood joints. Two other poles, both crafted out of the shafts of old hockey sticks, didn't look to be part of the tent. One had a detachable tip—barbed and made of brass—connected to its spear-like shaft by a wound strip of sinew. It looked to be a homemade harpoon. The other—shorter, meaner, and with a fixed rusty hook—a gaff. Both read SHER-WOOD on the side, all-caps confessions of their earlier incarnations on the rink. The blood, fresh smears over old stains, could have been from either tour of duty.

I tossed the harpoon and gaff towards the qamutik, adding them to my one-gun arsenal, then set about erecting the tent. It was a struggle keeping the ends aloft while I secured the frame and stretched the canvas. I temporized by tying one end of the frame to the qamutik and another to the stove. I weighed down the loose sides of the canvas with jerry cans of fuel. I had booby trapped my own camp. If the wind had blown while I was fiddling with the ropes and futzing with the pegs my adventure may have ended there. But the wind stayed calm as I hammered every anchor I could find into the ice with the blunt end of the axe. I stepped back. The tent slouched but stayed up, the canvas sagging like the skin on an old man's once-strong chest. I tugged lightly on the flaps of the door and tested a couple of the key ropes. It seemed solid enough. I tossed the skins onto the floor and retreated inside for my first real sleep.

I fell immediately into a deep, dreamless state that cut off any connection I had left to either clock or calendar. When I woke, I had no idea whether I had arisen from a fifteen-minute power-nap or a ten-hour sleep. Sun diffused through the canvas and filled the tent with the same gauzy light as before. It was a room of clotted cream. My beard was slick with drool, my left arm asleep. I lay between caribou skins and fumbled through my thoughts. The clearest clue that time had moved on was the return of the wind. The tent puffed and rattled, more a billowing than a flapping, as air alternately filled then fled the half-inflated space. I was laying between the slack cheeks of a snoring giant.

I had left home on a Sunday. Of that I was certain. I had spent that night in the soul-crushing solitude of a Winnipeg airport hotel. That was the last time it was dark. On Monday, I had risen at dawn to catch the first of the small planes that brought me north. From that point on the sun had been my chaperone. I tried to calculate how long I had spent in Iviliiq before Sim and I set out. I could remember the various things I had done—the wandering, the conversations with Ava, finding Sedna—but couldn't recall which days they belonged to, or what time of day they had occurred. I was at Ava's in the afternoon, I thought. But if so, when did Brisebois drive me to the station? Did I walk to the water intake on the same day? I decided that all together it must have been three days in Iviliiq, another two, maybe three, since. It could be no earlier than Saturday. My flight out was on Sunday. Someone would be coming for me soon. I just needed to wait.

In the chronicles of castaways and other lost men, two patterns stand out. There are those whose industry and effort delivered them through time or space to their eventual rescue—Ernest Shackleton's crossing of South Georgia, for example. And then there are the others who lay back in the sand and cried (or whored, or drank, depending on their circumstance). Alexander Selkirk, the 17th-century Scottish privateer who in a moment of suicidal stubbornness let a perfectly good ship sail away, did a bit of both. His three-year sojourn in the South Pacific started with a few weeks pacing the beach in despair, before he headed inland and settled into the domestic industry that would later inspire *Robinson Crusoe*. You can almost hear him saying to his rescuers, "Right then, just give me a minute to feed the goats." I am no Shackleton or Selkirk. I was whoring and drinking and laying in the sand long before I ever became lost. But I knew that if I wanted the opportunity to ever enjoy any of that again I was first going to have to survive the ice. Regardless of how long I had been asleep, it was time to get up.

The wind grabbed the door flap out of my hand and whipped it between my face and the front of the tent. I ducked my head and scuttered to the qamutik. Since I had last been outside, the air had all been exchanged. The temperature had dropped, the sky had cleared. The sun, so aloof on the trip thus far, had stepped forward and scoured the scene with light. I squinted and shielded my brow, turning away from the sun and into my own shadow while I waited for my eyes to adjust. When they did, I cupped my hands—a mime's binoculars— and scanned the ice. All trace of cloud and fog was gone. The horizon, a smear of washed-out blues, was equidistant in every direction. A step below that was another line, the bright white cutoff of my own island's edge. The ocean, a moat, between me and the end of the world.

Blowing snow slid over the ice and around and through my thighs, leaving a cold that lingered in my long johns. I had discarded my jeans under the skins sometime in my sleep so turned instead to the pile of clothes I had left out to dry earlier. The fleece under-layer, a sort of sweatpants for the adventure-minded, was there, pinned under the guard of my unworn boots. The Gore-Tex shell, however, was not. I stared at the spot, trying to reconcile what wasn't there with what I thought ought to be. I ran through a rollcall of alternate possibilities. Did I repack them? Maybe I wore them into the tent?

With each imagined option eliminated, I became more certain of what I already knew—I had left two pairs of pants out to dry together, and now one was gone. The wind picked up and rattled the tent a little louder. A little nudge. A winked admission. *I did it*, it said.

I cursed my own carelessness for not having protected them better. I was at sea in the Arctic and had left my most important article of clothing secured by nothing but the empty weight of a pair of boots. I canvassed the immediate area in the hope they had gotten caught up on a piece of equipment or wrapped around part of the tent's rigging but they had not. I turned my back to the wind and scanned the leeward side of the ice. At first, I saw nothing. Then, through the sun's glare and my pinpoint pupils, I saw something drop off the edge. I jogged towards the spot and then, a few steps from camp, stopped. If my pants were in the water I was going to need something to retrieve them. I turned back to the qamutik and got the gaff.

I approached the edge not entirely certain where the shadow had been. The water was dark and calm. In the lee of the floe, little swirls and eddies distorted the surface before organizing themselves into rows of ripples a few meters out. The waves strengthened and merged before heading towards the distant froth of open sea. I paced the shore with my gaff in search of any sign of the pants. I couldn't see far under the surface—it was clear, but with a turbulence that distorted focus like Vaseline on a lens. I scanned the ocean nearby. Nothing. In the waves and whitecaps farther out, shapes and shadows thrown up by one wave were erased by the next. Optical illusions and imaginations for the most part, I suspected. Even if one of those shadows were my pants, they would be too far out. They were gone.

For the second time, I had lost something essential over the edge. The third time, I suppose, if you count my guide and his machine separately. I stared at that malignant sea. My memory augmented its empty stage with the image of Simeonie going down. I felt like I might vomit and took to a knee. In that moment, I saw a shadow slip under the ice.

I tensed as the inky water wavered. I waited, fist tight around the handle of the gaff. After a moment, I saw the shape again. This time, a peep—a hint of black edging out into the blue. I dove at it, plunging my arm into ice water. With the edge in my armpit, I swept the gaff under the ice. The first pass moved freely, with no more drag than that of my own freezing arm. I leaned in deeper and swept back. At the start of the second pass, I felt the gaff hook into something. It was heavy and the shaft trembled, as it would when trailing a length of wet cloth. I yipped with triumph and rose to my knees, then landed a yard of kelp.

I walked the seventy-two paces back to camp, half-dressed in defeat with long john bottoms and a soaking wet arm. My top two priorities—stay dry, stay warm—were not going well. If I kept losing things over the edge then my adventure was not going to last long. When I arrived back at the qamutik, I took inventory of all the gear I had left out in the open. Everything but the missing pants was in its place in my diorama of Arctic misadventure. My fleece pants were unmoved on the qamutik, weighted down and watched over by the boots. I tugged them free, knocking the boots off the qamutik and onto the ice. I had removed my qamiqs and had one leg inserted into the pants to mid-thigh when I stopped.

I had disturbed a crime scene.

It was not possible that my Gore-Tex shell—the most expensive pair of pants I have ever owned—had simply blown away. I had secured them under the boots along with the fleece pants. Until a minute ago, those boots were sitting lined up and at attention in the very position I had left them. How could the wind tease out one pair of pants while leaving everything else untouched? Even my gentle tugging on the fleece had toppled the boots like bowling pins. The wind would have had to at least done that. Hell, the wind would have taken both pairs of pants.

It must have been those fucking seals.

CHAPTER 30

I don't do all that well when I'm hungry. I get emotional. I say things I regret. I fixate on stuff that later seems trivial. I eat, then I move on. I rarely apologize. Time has tempered the emotion I felt at the moment I realized the seals had stolen my pants, but what I remember is a simmering rage. I didn't rail or scream. I stewed.

I moped about the camp and assembled an outfit from the cast-off clothing. It was like dressing a scarecrow. I pulled the fleece pants over my layers of underwear, then stuffed myself back into my jeans. It was a poor approximation of the pants I had lost. I fumbled with the fly and, failing, I cried. It was then that I decided I should eat.

I didn't want to mourn the pants more than necessary, nor did I want hunger to cloud my judgement. I wanted to properly examine what had happened and come up with a rational plan for my next steps. I wasn't entirely sure I was hungry (I find hunger clouds self-awareness as effectively as lust), but figured after my big sleep I would call it a new day. There might be little joy in rationing food, but what there is happens in a brief flash when breaking a fast.

As per my menu plan, my first meal was to be a sardine sandwich. I pulled out two slices of the most boring bread, volunteers from a loaf baked a thousand miles away without any expectation of ever going anywhere. Welcome to The Edge, white bread. I peeled off the top of the sardine tin, sampled one, then fingered the rest onto the open sandwich. Afloat on the open ocean and I was scraping fish out of a can. I used to fancy myself a bit of a gourmet. I would slow-cook eggs for hours at a temperature barely above that of a hen. I owned a truffle grater. But this was before the recalibrations brought on first by divorce and then by starvation. I no longer have any interest in the pretensions of food.

I tore the sandwich apart with my teeth, lingering over it only long enough to let each oily bolus squeeze down my gullet. When the last bit of bread finally cleared my throat, I opened a can of Coke and cleansed my palate with fizz. I amended the food list (Sardines 3, 2, Coke 9, 8, 7) and stowed my journal. Sipping at the bottom half of the Coke, I sat back and reconsidered the theft. The tent flapped idly beside me.

In those early stages of ice-bound exile, the contrast between paranoia and isolation was profound. In the fog or at the edge, I felt as though I were under surveillance. In the sun at the center of my floe, it seemed I was utterly alone. The only comfort I got from either state was the absence of its opposite. Whether or not the world of talking caribou and belligerent seals was of my own creation was immaterial. Either way, I was in trouble. I had no choice but to wait for outside help for my ultimate salvation—there would be no point in building huts or striking oars on my ship of ice. My job was to survive long enough to be rescued.

The first step, I decided, should be a survey. I would take my journal and pace out the dimensions of the floe. I might try my hand at a map. All successful defenses, mental or martial, are grounded in cartography. I would banish my demons with industry.

I walked into the wind with the sun at my back, opposite to the direction I had taken earlier in search of my pants. With the harpoon to steady my gait, I tapped out seventy-seven steps from the sled to the water. On that axis, at least, the qamutik was nearly centered on the floe. I made a note in my journal. I scraped an "x" in the ice and turned left.

My second circumnavigation was easier than the first. Both the sea and my mind were calmer than they had been in the aftermath of the tempest that took Sim. Although the ice still rose and fell with each swell of the sea, the floe felt more tightly tethered. I wobbled as I walked, but my course stayed true. I figured it was a sign I was finally getting my sea legs. I did note a touch of nausea, but at the time I was unsure whether this was due to motion or to lunch. It cleared with a few briny belches. I walked on.

At the quarter mark, pace one-hundred-twenty, the tent was aligned directly in front of the qamutik. The shore at this point was a bit irregular, a wart-like protuberance on my island's otherwise smooth edge. The surface was mismatched, the ice of the extension more ragged than the rest. I took a few steps onto it and heard it groan—felt it actually, through my feet. I hopped back to the main ice. I made another note.

The walk continued in this manner. Counting steps, making notes. Another hundred or so paces to the place of the missing pants, a quarter turn beyond that to the transit of the sled over the tent. The frozen ropes, now obscured under a carapace of ice, were ten paces short of the mark I made at the starting point. The floe's geometry was not particularly complicated—think Sri Lanka, but smaller. Still, I made sightings, jotted notes, and charted the space like I was

Magellan's apprentice. When I look at the journal now, almost none of it makes sense. No matter. I was mapping Atlantis. The continent I was exploring is gone.

At no point on that peregrination did I see any sign of an animal. I didn't spend a significant amount of time staring out to sea—were they to be watching, I wanted them to see me working my terrestrial claim—but if the seals or any of their spies were out there, they were keeping themselves hidden in distant waves. I kept a closer eye out for tracks on the ice. I recognized that tracking a seal was likely going to be different than tracking a deer (floppier feet, looser stool), but figured at the very least they would make a mess of the edge on their way in and out of the water. Anytime I came across a wetter-than-average spot I'd stop, pace about, squat to investigate. Nowhere could I convince myself that it was the work of anything more rogue than a wave. It struck me that even if the seals were to have breached the edge and gained access to my ice, they would be hard pressed to get to my camp. I hadn't paced out the interior in every direction, but in my early estimation the qamutik appeared to be almost centered on the island. At its closest, it was at least fifty yards from sea to sled. An excellent punt. A better return. I'm no marine biologist, but it seemed like a long way for a seal to shimmy.

I decided I was safe, from seals at least. I just had to gain control of my imagination. I sat for a bit at the edge and flipped through my journal, annotating my notes with a few doodles. I stopped after a while and simply stared into the sea. There were no shadows or shapes, no suspicion of company. I didn't conjure a ship or a shore out of the distorted horizon. I just listened to the waves and watched the dance of light on water. I let it be empty. I needed to focus. As long as I had food and stayed warm I would be OK. I had the ice. My only enemy was time.

I stood and brushed off my ass. After one last look over the placid sea, I turned away from the edge. The sun flashed across the snow and screwed itself into the back of my eye. The qamutik and tent were in sight for a moment, then were consumed in a fiery glare. Light—benign ether, passive as paint—became pure, malicious energy. I pulled my toque lower, squinted and took my bearings, then closed my eyes and walked blindly towards my target. Every ten steps I'd squeak one eye open and readjust my trajectory. Like a misaligned car, I kept pulling to the left. Each time I opened my eyes the pain was more intense and my vision more impaired. By fifty paces, I was walking blind. Seven steps into the sixth set of ten, I broke through the ice.

I didn't hear, or at first feel, water. Instead, it just felt like my foot had punched through the ceiling of the underworld. I fell forward with my left leg splayed behind me, knocking the air out of my chest as my belly made contact with solid ice. I wheezed out a string of curses and scrabbled at the surface. Pulling myself forward, I extruded my right leg from the hole, rolled twice, then scampered on four limbs a few feet away until confident I was on solid ground. Water flowed out of the fur and pooled around the sealskin sole of my left foot. A wet trail ran in a ragged line back to the spot I had broken through, a circular disc of slushy gray water about the size of a hubcap. It was in the middle of a white plain of otherwise unbroken ice.

I shuffled towards it, dropping to my knees to crawl the last couple of feet. There was no crack, no other fault or flaw in the ice. The edges of the hole were solid and polished smooth, the ice thick.

Below the surface was a deep, dark tunnel leading to the ocean below. It looked *maintained*.

It was a seal's breathing hole. And it was less than ten meters from my camp.

CHAPTER 31

After hours spent in the bright glare of sun splintering off ice, the inside of the tent was a relief. The canvas walls cast a linen light that was a balm to my eyes. With the exception of a residual twitch in my left eyelid, the muscles of my face relaxed, freed from their grimaced squint. Still, they hurt. It was the tear-inducing feeling of sand in my eyes. I stripped off my outerwear, lay back between the caribou skins and draped the cold, wet leg of my pants across my face.

In the opus of disappointment that is Arctic adventure, some of the saddest stories I've studied involve snow blindness. The death of Morty Macguire, Australia's sole representative in the league of Arctic explorers, may be among the worst. Morty survived Douglas Mawson's fatal foray into Antarctica only to sign up for the even more ill-fated First Polish Expedition to the North Pole. Left alone in Franz Joseph Land to tend ship while his expedition partners set off for glory, Morty made the mistake of loaning his glacier goggles to a Pole-bound colleague. He then went blind keeping watch for their return. Despite a progressive loss of vision and constant pain, the Australian diligently, if somewhat illegibly, recorded his daily observations. He developed an ingenious technique involving a long length of rope and a series of cairns to navigate among the islands on extended walkabouts, intent on marking and mapping the territory in case his team got lost on their return. It was on one of these multi-day journeys that the Poles did return, finding their ship, minus Morty, right where they parked it. I can't be sure from his logs (the journals, found under one of his many cairns several years later, are difficult to decipher), but it seems likely the ship sailed within sight, had only he been able to see. We don't know what the Poles were thinking when they set off without him. A navigational error led them to sail under flag directly into Murmansk harbor, where they were sunk. At the time, Morty was probably still feeling his way around the archipelago in an effort to find the ship.

I didn't have Morty's excuse—the noble gesture of lending a colleague a vital piece of equipment—nor did I have his perseverance. I did have a great pair of sunglasses tucked above the visor of my car, parked back home in an airport garage. The ski goggles I had brought north were fitted with clear lenses that, while serving beautifully as a windshield, were useless as sun protection. Sim's pair, worn almost exclusively around his neck, looked to have been much better suited for these conditions. He had taken them with him. I had no choice but to lie in my manufactured dark and try to sleep off the injury. If I were lucky the clouds would move in while I slept and I could continue to recuperate while getting on with my life outside. I pulled the pant leg along to a colder, wetter spot and willed myself to sleep, with the harpoon at my side.

When I woke, the pants were in place but no longer wet. I'd both been asleep long enough for them to dry and short enough to not have moved. I had no idea how long that might have been. Under cover and still closed, my eyes felt OK. I pulled off the pant leg and sat up. The tic returned. My left eye flickered like a fluorescent light.

I crawled to the door and pulled back the flap. A shiv of light lit up the tent. The pain in my eyes returned, more shards of glass than grains of sand. I squinted and sat back. The door fell shut. The light ebbed out like a tide. Soothed like a startled baby, my eyes began to settle.

Although I was better in the softer light of the tent, there was no way I was going to be able to spend significant time outside without some form of eye protection. Besides the pain, I knew that if I incurred any more damage I might, like Morty, lose my vision altogether. But my food was outside, as was any chance of rescue. Plus, I had to take a dump. I didn't care much for dignity, but I was neither going to die nor defecate inside my tent. I peeked out again. The sun poked me in the eye.

I considered my options. I had no glasses and my goggles were useless. By itself, the baseball cap would be ineffective, given that the majority of radiation was being reflected back up off the snow. It occurred to me that the Inuit had had similar problems prior to our flooding the market with knock-off Aviators. Their traditional approach was to carve snow goggles out of bone or driftwood with thin horizontal slits as their only aperture. You might have seen pictures of them—they're one of the coolest-looking emblems of the North, an icon of Inuit innovation. I actually had a pair, at home. They were one of the many artifacts of adventure on display in my study.

I didn't have any driftwood or bone, but thought I might have just the thing to mock up my own version of Inuit snow goggles. I pulled my toque down over my eyes, threw open the door flap and ran out into the light to the qamutik. I grabbed the case of Coke and Sim's knife and retreated back inside the tent. I emptied the box, lining up the cans—two empties and seven intact—along a wall, then checked the dimensions of the cardboard against my face. The narrow end was an almost perfect fit. I creased the box and tore it in two, then, with the knife, sliced off its top. I fashioned matching arms off opposite sides in such a way that they had pre-formed hinges at the corners. From there, I carved the short end into the face piece. It was nothing fancy, just a horizontal strip with a notch for the nose, but with a few revisions, I got them to fit snugly. I had perfected the cardboard-box blindfold. I removed them; then, with the tip of the knife, punched horizontal slits an inch long and a millimeter thick into each of the eye pieces.

Voila. Soda pop snow goggles. Inuit ingenuity had nothing on me.

I pulled my toque over my ears to lock them in place, then fumbled around in the dark to find the harpoon. I had some business outside to attend to.

I pulled the snow goggles down to the tip of my nose and leaned in to inspect the ice. A thin dome of frost had formed over the hole, covering the clear water like an inverted crystal bowl. I poked it with the tip of the harpoon. Three light taps. I stood up, looked over the distant water, then flipped the harpoon over and bashed the ice in. I used the blunt end to stir the shards into the water. The opening in the ice was almost the exact size and shape of a toilet, although it was slush-filled and level with the ground. An almost perfect squatter. I pulled three layers of pants together to my knees and lowered my ass over the hole. After a minute of silence my right thigh started to shake. My bowel took no notice. I shifted my feet to transfer more of the load to my left and pushed a little harder.

I heard a bark from the distance and almost fell in the hole. I braced my right hand on the ice and readied my left by my belt, as I scanned the sea. The water was empty but for a single seal. The creature approached the edge, stopped, then strained its neck high out of the water to see what I was doing.

"Seriously?" it shouted. "Are you shitting in a breathing hole?"

I settled back into my squat and bore down.

"C'mon, man. I've got to breathe through that thing."

"You seem to be doing fine out there," I said, catching my breath. "I'm not sure why you need a breathing hole at this time of year."

"It's just the idea of it," the seal said. "Honestly, who does that?"

"Yeah? Well who steals pants?" I strained again, punctuating my point with a fart.

"What the hell are you talking about?"

"YOU GUYS STOLE MY FUCKING PANTS!" I gave up trying to defecate. I dipped my hand in the hole and splashed my ass with ice water.

"Why would we do that?" The seal looked around to see if there was anyone else who had heard the accusation. "Do we look like we need pants? I'm not sure if this is news to you, buddy, but seals ain't got no legs."

"I don't know why you would steal my pants." I reached deep into my many layers and adjusted my junk. "All I know is that when I went to sleep they were here and when I woke up they were gone."

"Did you consider the wind might possibly have taken them?"

"It wasn't the wind," I said.

"A bird, maybe? Ravens like to steal things."

"Do you see any birds?" I opened my arms to the sky.

"Because I don't. As far as I can tell it's just you and me out here, my friend, and I don't have my pants."

"You're crazy, man."

You think? I thought. Sleep-deprived, sun-blind, constipated, and alone, I was awaiting rescue on the last cube of ice in a leftover drink. Dissolution or absolution, whichever came first. All the while, I was in an unwanted battle with a band of pirate pinnipeds. The stress was definitely getting to me.

"I can't hear you," the seal said. "Are you saying something?"

"Wait there a minute," I said. "We need to talk."

I took a knee and gathered my gear from the ice. I put on my gloves and picked up the harpoon. When I stood back up, I planted it beside me like a walking stick and started towards the edge.

The seal, alarmed, surged backward. A bow wave wrapped the back of its neck like a ruff.

"Whoa, whoa, whoa… what the hell is that?"

I swung it up into both hands like a drum major might. "This?" I gave it a twirl. "It's a harpoon, I think."

The seal zigged farther away. Its eyes were a bit buggier than usual. "Jesus Christ, man. Is that *blood*?"

I slowed and lowered the harpoon to my waist. "Um, might be."

The seal looked over its shoulder and barked.

"Look," I said. "It's Sim's harpoon. It's just something I found in his stuff. I'm not planning on using it."

"Like the gaff? Are you also not planning on using that? Don't think that we haven't been watching you. You seem pretty well set up for someone who's not planning on doing anything."

It ducked its head underwater. Bubbles broke onto the surface, releasing unintelligible sounds into the air. I shuffled closer. The seal caught me as it came up.

"I can see you, you idiot. Stop right where you are."

I stopped and put the harpoon on the ice by my feet. "Better?"

"No."

In the distance I saw another seal surface. My flippered friend had called for reinforcements.

"Look, I've got no interest in a battle. I've got enough going on up here without having to fight you. If anything I could use your help."

"Oh yeah? What for? You gotta resole your boots?"

The second seal emerged behind the first. After a short exchange, the new one strained out of the water to get a look along the ice. It saw the harpoon, then shot me a foul glance and settled back into the water. The seals started into a muted conversation, turning away from me to conceal what they were saying. Within a minute they were arguing. I reached out with my toe and started to roll the harpoon towards me.

"Don't even think about it," the second seal said.

"I wasn't thinking about anything," I protested. "I was just stretching."

"As if. Keep your hands where I can see them, asshole, and step away from the weapon."

I was being threatened by bowling balls bobbing a few meters offshore. There was nothing stopping me from just picking up the harpoon and walking back to camp, but with the sea full of seals I figured I ought to humor these two. I stepped back a few paces.

"Now kick it to the water."

"Excuse me?"

"Give us the goddamn harpoon." The second seal, angry to begin with, was going all bad-cop on me.

The first one leaned in. "He can't," it said. "You made him back away."

"Why can't he kick it? He's got legs."

"Yeah, that's not how they work. He has to walk over to it first."

The first seal looked back to me, sized up my limbs. "That's bullshit," it said. "C'mon. Kick it into the water already."

"He's right," I called out. "I can't reach it from here. Besides, I don't think I can kick it that far. If you want, I could carry it to you."

"Fat chance, Stretch. You keep your hands off the harpoon. Do you think we're stupid?"

Honestly, I had never put much thought into the intelligence of seals. Dolphins, certainly. These guys weren't dolphin smart.

The seals had started conferring again. The first one seemed to be arguing for detente, the second was holding its line. I waited for them to come to an agreement. I was getting cold.

"Look," I said. "Why don't I just back off a bit more and one of you can come up here and get it for yourself."

They stopped talking. I walked a short ways back towards my camp. When I thought I had put enough distance between us I turned back and faced the seals.

"How's that?" I shouted. They remained silent, watching me. "You're welcome to hop up and get it. I'll stay back here."

They sank slightly in a small swell, but otherwise stayed motionless.

"No?" I called out.

Nothing. I was talking to a couple of coconuts.

"Fuck it," I said. I walked back to the harpoon. With my approach the seals began to bark and bob. When I bent over to pick it up they dove backwards and disappeared under the surface.

CHAPTER 32

The qamutik wouldn't budge. It was too low to the ground for me to get the leverage I needed to either push or pull. I could squat and bend, contort my body and load myself like a spring, but all the energy I put into it came back out of my feet as they let go of the ice. I heaved, yanked, and assaulted the thing, but the runners were stuck. Sweaty with the effort of wrestling with it, I set up my duffel as a bean bag chair, cracked open a can of Coke and sat back.

My plan had been to barricade the breathing hole with the qamutik. I was certain that the seals had used the hole to gain access to my camp. I figured if I could reposition the sled I could use it like a trap door (or toilet lid, as need be) and keep the creatures out. From the seals' side, the slats of the sled would be like the bars of a prison window. It was a great plan. But the qamutik was unmovable, and my defenses remained breached. I needed to find some other way to fortify my floe.

The two most obvious alternatives—to keep watch or to move camp—were non-starters. No matter how much the perpetual light kept me up, there was no way I could go entirely without sleep. Unless I used my body to cover the hole while I napped, there were going to be times when it was unguarded. As for moving, the camp was already at the center of the floe. There was no place I could put it that wouldn't be even closer to water. Besides, it had been a feat to get the tent up in the first place. It slouched in its spot like an old, hobbled mule. Trying to relocate would risk losing it altogether. The camp would have to stay where it was.

My greatest fear with the open hole was that the seals would come back and ransack my food. Their prank with the pants was a nuisance, a bit of delinquency that I assumed had been intended to intimidate. But if they stepped up their vandalism and went after my food, it would be murderous. I was tempted to move the entire cache into the tent with me, but knew that would be breaking the first commandment of backcountry camping: you do not eat where you sleep. My battle at that moment may have been with seals, but I was still in bear country. I remembered my conversation with Ava about the floe edge. *There are only two things that pass freely between the worlds,* she had said. *Spirits, and bears.*

In my summer research camps in the Arctic we had always enforced an absolute prohibition on food in sleeping areas. Never mind the fact that when it comes to polar bears we too are food, the hope had been that the smell of the kitchen might be more enticing than that of the tents (the latter a fug of dirty wool and sexual frustration that fermented in the twenty-four-hour sun). In more bear-dense areas we took the extra precaution of erecting an electric fence, a knee-high tripwire that encircled the camp. It was a fairly anemic defense as there is only so much current you can generate from a solar-charged car battery that far north, but if we were lucky it would slow a bear long enough for someone to grab a gun.

I had asked Sim about electric fences before we left town. Specifically, I wondered if the hunters of Iviliiq ever used them. It seemed like a reasonable question. I mentioned it in part to show that I had at least a little bit of wilderness experience. He laughed.

Inuit don't build fences, Guy.

Ah, right. I suppose no wood.

No boundaries.

It was true. In my time in the North I have never seen an actual fence. There are no barriers, there are no gates. The only trespass is that defined by respect and taboo. I think this goes for animals and people alike.

I shook out the last bit of Coke and was about to crumple the can when I had an idea. Even if I couldn't electrify a barrier, I could still make a trip wire. And while technically you can't trip a legless creature, neither are they able to step over a line. I walked to the breathing hole and paced out two perimeters. The smaller one, a circle centered on the hole itself, was fifteen yards; the larger one, surrounding the qamutik and tent, was fifty.

I've never been a knitter, but surely there had to be more yarn than that in a cable-knit sweater.

The hours of effort that went into the construction of the tripwire may have been the high point of my time on the ice. I was focused and efficient. I was hopeful. For what felt like the good part of a day, I didn't think about food or death. I had purpose. Never mind that I was building defenses against a gang of seals, I felt like I was in control.

I started by taking the axe to the qamutik. Sorry, Sim. I left the runners and most of the sled intact, but hacked off a few crosspieces for use as fence posts. I conserved wood by splitting them, like kindling. I was more or less trying to make survey stakes. Four slats gave me twenty stakes. If I needed more, I could come back.

I pulled my sweater out of the duffel bag and retreated to the tent so I could work without goggles. I hesitated longer to disassemble my sweater than I had with the qamutik. In the cream-colored light, it looked more blue than I usually pictured it. I couldn't recall buying the sweater and couldn't imagine replacing it. Still, I had gotten a lot of good use from it, particularly on northern trips and in the woods. I held it to my nose and inhaled a mix of wood smoke and sweat. To a dog, the sweater's smells would tell stories and betray secrets. To me, they triggered nothing more specific than nostalgia. Memory attenuated into emotion.

I started by picking at the pre-existing hole in the right cuff— an imperfection acquired early in my ownership (beer, bike) that had surprisingly never progressed. By the time I got to the elbow, I had a good-sized pile of yarn. I probably should have stopped to measure at that point but I was on a roll. Besides, I didn't see the point of a one-armed sweater. When I finished there was enough yarn to fence off the entire floe had I wanted to, as it turns out there are a couple thousand yards of yarn in a sweater. I also had a very nice, and quite stylish, cable-knit vest. It was navy blue and smelled of the sea.

I built both tripwires that day. The long one was an ellipse surrounding the camp. Its primary purpose was visual definition and reassurance. Inside that line I felt safe. I recognized early on that it served no real defensive function. I tripped over it regularly, and each time I did it put up about as much resistance as a spider web. Over the course of my stay on the ice I modified that barrier with a number of openings, gaps like the undefended gates of an old walled city. It was the smaller tripwire surrounding the breathing hole that was the real fortification. That one was a circle of two lines—the first a few inches off the ice, the other at knee height. It wouldn't be strong enough to stop a seal, but they would have to knock it down if they were going to try to get by. That's where my genius came in. I cut off the tops and bottoms of the empty Coke cans and strung them from the wire. To that, I added modified bits of sardine tin. It took some effort with the spacing of the cans—I wanted an alarm system, not wind chimes—but in time I had it done. After every meal, I could hang some trash and improve on my invention.

I stood back and admired my camp. A single line of yarn encircled a space scattered with gear. In the middle stood a semi-tumescent tent and shattered qamutik. Outside the perimeter, in a circle of yarn tinseled with trash, was my shitter.

I was wearing a cable-knit sweater vest and Coke-box sun goggles. And I was king.

PART THREE

CHAPTER 33

I gave up trying to calculate the passage of time in increments of hours or days. Instead, I used a metric constructed out of accomplishments and fatigue. I farted around the camp, tinkered with my lines, and patrolled the edge. I spent a good deal of time staring at my food. When I felt myself growing tired, I entered the tent, employed an abbreviated bedtime routine and fell fast asleep. Then I woke, reversed the process and left the tent. All the while, nothing would change. The same light breeze. The same harsh light. Scattered items in the foreground, fuzzed out horizon in the distance.

When southerners first experience the Arctic summer they're usually most disoriented by what happens when they're awake. Golfing at midnight. Fishing at three. *OMG, I'm going to be awake forever.* Being awake in the midnight sun is neat, at first. But crazy comes after you when you sleep. In the South, time goes on when you're in bed. Things shift in your sleep. By the time you get up, even from a nap, the light will have changed. The hue and intensity, the direction of shadows, are your first cues. Then you'll notice that someone had their fingers on the thermostat, fiddling with both temperature and humidity. You'll probably walk past the clothes you cast off and find something more appropriate to wear. Birds will have started to sing. Or, if they had been singing, they will have stopped. Every sense will say to you, *I've been gone for a while. It's good to be back.*

There is no such shift in the Arctic. Waking up in the northern sun is like stepping out of a closet into a well-lit room. The only change will be inside yourself.

I woke with no idea how long I had been asleep, but wasn't inclined to lie around. Sim tended to visit me in my idle moments inside that tent. I wormed my way out of the skins and got dressed and stepped outside. My eye twitched in protest. The sun glared off the surface of the ice, casting a light as bright and sterile as that of a surgical suite. I put on my Coke-box goggles, picked up the harpoon, and stepped over the boundary. It was time to go on patrol.

I started to the right edge. Unless I needed to use the hole (straight ahead, past the qamutik), my route to the water was perpendicular to the camp's axis and directly to the right. It may have been the natural preference of a right-handed person. It could have also had something to do with avoidance. Sim's spot was on the other side. It was a place I didn't like to linger. I would pick up my pace as I passed it.

I stepped over the line and started my step count. This was another habit. I was becoming lazier with my journaling so the numbers didn't matter as much. I was also tending to get more distracted in my thoughts and occasionally would lose count. Even so, the counting had become compulsive. At times, I would pace from the edge to camp and back again in order to get a number I liked. That morning, I got to the water in seventy-two steps, give or take.

I stood in the sun at the edge of the ice. The wind and the water were calm. I turned into the breeze and walked. Offshore, a bank of fog drifted past, partially obscuring a choppier sea. To my right was the white, sunlit surface of solid ice. To my left, doubt. The ocean was up to something. I used my step-counting as a tactic to avoid constantly checking over my shoulder and out to sea. Once every twenty steps I'd stop and peer into the fog. There was, at one point, something there. A grayish-white shape in the darker gray mist. I could never hold it in view long enough to know for certain that it was real, but the regularity of its appearances—always showing up a little to the left of where it had last been—suggested that it was moving. Hallucination, I would think, ought to be more random.

I ignored the apparition and continued my walk. Straight, it seemed to me. All the while the camp to my right rotated on its axis. As I walked, the tent revolved around and in front of the qamutik and the qamutik in front of the hole, then the hole came back out from behind both. It was the slow, celestial dance of planetary alignments put in motion by my pace. I passed syzygy (tent - sled - hole) and was well along the other side when I realized the ratty ice previously at the point was gone. I walked back and lined up my markers. In place of the piece that had groaned under my weight was a clean, solid edge, indistinguishable from any other. I looked offshore to see if I could find it adrift, but found only water and fog. I know I noted something in my journal at that point, possibly annotated a map. Whatever I wrote, I can't find it now.

I continued my patrol. I was stepping over the ice tomb that contained Sim's rope when the seals showed up. First one, dogging me from a distance, then two more. When they had quorum they approached the edge.

"Whatcha up to today, colonizer?"

I ignored them and kept walking.

237

They barked occasional insults at my back, none of which I understood. Between their taunts, however, I could hear them talking among themselves.

"How far do you think he can throw that harpoon?"

"Him? I doubt he could even throw it out of his tent if he were sitting inside. We're safe."

"I dunno, he looks pretty big."

"They all look big, you idiot. It's perspective. Keep up."

There was another round of barking. I picked up my pace.

"He's limping. Do you think he's injured? Jesus, if he's injured already this ain't going to last long."

I stopped and turned to face them. The lead seal was almost rear-ended by the next.

"I can hear you," I said.

They bobbed in silence.

"I'm not injured. My limp is because of a leg length discrepancy. I've had it since I was a kid."

Nothing but stares.

"Whatever," I said. "You should be so lucky."

I turned to walk on. I heard the slosh of seals starting back up.

"What's he got on his eyes?"

"Oh, for fuck's sake." I peeled off the Coke-box goggles and held them out for the seals to see. "They're sunglasses, all right? Maybe you don't realize this but it's kind of bright up here."

I was squinting into the light. The pain was intense. My left eye began to twitch.

"You made your own sunglasses?"

"Yes."

I couldn't tell through the tears which seal was talking. "Any other questions?"

"Do they work?"

"Kind of." I wiped my eyes and put the glasses back on, tucking the cardboard arms under my hat. "They take the edge off at least."

Through the slits I got a better look at the seals. There were five, all staring at me in silence. I couldn't believe I had been goaded into having another conversation with them. Their usual leader was in front. I waved it closer.

"Listen, buddy," I said. "What would it take to get you guys to just leave me alone?"

The seal sidled up. "Are you offering me a bribe?"

"Might be."

"Well then," it said. "I guess that depends on what you got."

I had no idea how to bribe a seal. Particularly when the sum of my possessions was scattered within sight.

"How about some sardines?" I said. "I can give you a tin of sardines."

"A can?"

"Yes."

"Of fish?"

"Mmm hmm."

The seal stared at me. I got the sense I might have lowballed it.

"Hey team," the seal shouted. "Bigfoot here wants to give us one whole tin of sardines. Whatcha say? Should we let him go?"

More barking. This round sounded more like laughter.

"Yeah, that's not going to do. We got lots of fish. Besides, we got orders."

"Orders?" I scanned the water behind them. "So what, you're going to take me in for questioning?"

"Not yet. We were just told to keep an eye on you. Make sure you're not up to no mischief."

"We're a patrol!" a back-up seal sang.

The leader looked down and shook its head. It signaled me to lean in, then continued in a wet whisper.

"Seriously, Stretch, the boss ain't happy. And between you and me, things around here get a bit ugly when the old lady is in a snit. You may be OK if you stay away from the water, but nobody's going to guarantee your safety if you get too close to the edge."

"Is that a warning or a threat?"

"Both."

More seals had arrived. I counted eight, maybe nine. It was hard to be sure as the ones in the back kept popping in and out of the sea. The fog farther out could have concealed an army.

"Well then," I said. "I'll try to keep to the dry side."

"I hope you do," the seal said. "But maybe pay a bit more attention when you're counting steps. The ice ain't what it used to be."

"What's that supposed to mean?"

"I'm just saying that judging by what happened to your friend, I'm guessing you don't swim too good."

The fish-breathed beast was so close I could have speared it in the face. Its posse rose a bit higher in the water and shifted forward. I stiffened. I looked back at the camp. Tent; qamutik; hole, reading from left to right. I was back to where I had started; my circumnavigation was complete. It was time to get away from the edge.

"Listen, Bob." I tried to match the seal's tone. My voice wavered. "I appreciate your concern. But tell your boss that if she's going to threaten me then she can come up and do it herself."

I clenched the harpoon in my fist to conceal my shaking hand.

I turned my back on the seals and started on a straight line to my camp.

I didn't look back. My stride was a little longer, my posture more erect.

I got to the qamutik in sixty-eight steps.

CHAPTER 34

Oranges ~~12, 11~~, 10.

I didn't know for sure if I was due an orange. It could have been stress eating. Regardless, I needed to figure some things out. And with the smell of the seal's breath still fresh in my memory, I wasn't feeling up for another fish sandwich.

I flipped through my journal to look for any notes I had made on the dimensions of the floe. The accounting was poor, but what evidence I had seemed to suggest the ice might be shrinking. I climbed on top of the qamutik and scanned the full panorama. My domain, a wet white disc, was more ragged than I had thought. I had spent so much time patrolling the border that I hadn't noticed the fissures filling the interior. The ice was etched like elephant skin. Pools had formed at a few fissures' forks, bleeding into each other through a latticework of shallow channels. I knew the floe was thick from looking down the breathing hole, but it was clearly rotting. And beyond the ice, along the shore on its every side, little waves were eating at the edge, as industrious as ants.

My world was a clock, counting down.

I could feel myself afloat. The ice, at times, had felt like land, surrounded by water. Now I couldn't purge the sense of the water *beneath* me. A dark, wet world, as infinite as the sky. Seals swimming free. Whales and walruses passing below. All the animals, conspiring.

And deep down, unseen on her stony plain, Sedna. Waiting. An alien realm on the flip side of my floe. I held onto the sides of the qamutik as though it were a raft.

I had been resigned to a longer stay, a slow burn of food and sanity while I awaited rescue. I realized now that time itself was rationed; I could linger only as long as my ice stayed solid. There can be valor in a waning demise—a withering hunger, a languorous freeze—that appeals to the Romanticist in me. Death in a dunk tank does not have the same grace. The image of Simeonie in the water came to me again. His surfacing in the mist. His wave before disappearing. The gesture looked different in my mind this time. He was beckoning.

It was then I wrote the two letters that are inked into my journal like a regrettable tattoo. I stowed the notebook and considered the possible ends to this adventure. None, aside from rescue, was particularly palatable. I decided to review my alternatives. That is to say, I began to think of how I might kill myself, if it came to that. Drowning was the most obvious option. It would be easy enough to step off the edge. But the image of Sim haunted me. Plus, the whole point of suicide was to avoid dying in the water.

My options on the ice were more limited. I figured hanging would be impossible given the rope was frozen into the floe and there was nothing from which I could dangle. I doubted I would be able to garrote myself with yarn. That left the knife and the gun. I'm squeamish around blood. It would have to be the gun.

The rifle was leaning against the front of the qamutik, indifferent to my thoughts. *They have to be looking by now*, I decided. *It can wait.*

In the annals of adventure, a pattern emerges. Impatience sparks action, action invites disaster. For every Uruguayan rugby player who walked over a mountain to find salvation, there are leagues of others who took matters into their own hands and died days before rescue. We may celebrate the Shackletons; we would learn more from the schmucks. If you're lost and someone is looking, sit down and wait. But I get it. You might think you're a patient person until you realize that you could die before finding what it is you're looking for. Rescue. Meaning. True love. It's hard enough to wait for a bus.

There were times I was tempted to swim.

I decided to follow the seal's suggestion and pay more attention to the ice. I shelved the pacing of the edge—it was an unreliable measure that exposed me to uninvited conversation—and instead turned my focus to the axes. With the sun the sky's sole star, as adrift as I was, I had no celestial marker of north or south. In its place, I decided to use the qamutik to create new cardinal directions of Bow, Starboard, Stern, and Port. The tent was pitched to Stern, the breathing hole to Bow. The pants had gone over to Starboard, Simeonie to Port. I pried four more cross pieces from the deck of the sled and pounded them in at the compass points like survey stakes. Each was two harpoon-lengths in from the edge, which I assumed was a safe buffer and an easy measure to judge any attrition of the ice. And then I paced. Four times on each segment to average out my uneven gait. Although I recorded some of my work in the journal, I made the majority of my markings on the stakes themselves. Radial distances from qamutik to edge, chords from stake to stake. I surveyed and sectioned that featureless floe with Cartesian zeal. The sun followed me like a dog.

When I was done, I sat back on the qamutik dizzy with hunger and exertion. I figured I had earned a meal and cracked open the can of mackerel. The smell brought back the seal's breathy threat. Around me, much was unchanged—drifting sea smoke, the same shiftless sun, a secretive sea. Still, with the stakes standing straight at the edges and a yarn-fenced camp at its center, I had imposed some order onto the ice. Like Selkirk, I had turned my attention inland and beavered my way back to sanity. I knew summer would eventually scuttle this ship and reduce all my effort to flotsam. No matter. At that moment, the island was mine. I sopped out the tin with an extra piece of bread and headed to the hole.

By habit, I turned away from the glare before dropping my pants and mooned the sun. In addition to saving my eyes, I figured the light on my ass was good for a daily dose of Vitamin D. The mackerel can twinkled in its new place on the line. Behind it, the tent sighed in the breeze. I felt vulnerable facing away from the water and decided not to linger. I did my business and rose out of my squat. As I did, my shadow stretched out in front of me.

Scattered thoughts lay before me like parts on a tinker's bench. It was by habit that I had oriented my ass to the sun. I had done the same on each previous visit to hole. But when I was accosted by that seal in mid-squat I had been facing the sea. On this trip to the loo I was facing the camp. It was then I realized the sun had been steadily circling the hole the entire time. With it ducking in and out of inconstant clouds over the featureless floe, it had seemed to be floating free. But by defining directions and planting stakes I had captured it. I had turned the blank space of my island into the face of a clock, my shadow its single hand.

The qamutik, my compass, would be my sundial. I rigged a slot into the center of the sled and planted the harpoon. Its shadow crossed the deck on the starboard side of stern. It flickered as a low cloud slid by, then set. The mark stayed true.

I had harnessed the sun.

CHAPTER 35

With time on my side the days became easier. My first task was to set up a schedule. I was down to four cans of fish, a half bag of bread, ten oranges, and an onion. I continued to ignore the flour and jerky. I placed the pile of oranges at the bow and left the remainder of the food in the kitchen at the rear. The harpoon would impose discipline, dispensing food like a prison guard. When the shadow was astern I'd have my main meal. *Fish and brewis* as the Newfoundlanders call it. Twelve hours later when the shadow crossed the bow, I'd treat myself to an orange. If I were still afloat when the fish ran out I would cut back to an all-orange diet. If nothing else, I'd at least be safe from scurvy.

Once I had allotted bow and stern to mealtimes, my next decision was to define day and night. Ever since I had left darkness behind in Winnipeg, the normal cycle of sleep—as steady as the ocean surf—had stilled, with each wakening less certain than the one before it, and each sleep less deep. It attenuated, like an echo. I knew I needed to regiment my routine if I were to temper insanity. It seemed reasonable that sleep should follow the bigger meal, so I decided that when the sun was in starboard I would go to bed. I'd do the bulk of my work on the other side of the clock, while the sun went around Sim's side.

I checked the time. The harpoon's shadow had moved almost twenty degrees since dinner. It was getting late. I placed a boot to mark the spot and settled into the tent for bed.

Sandwiched between skins and settled by the knowledge I could now keep time, I fell fast into sleep. I woke a number of times. First to the sound of the tent in the stiffening breeze, later with the urge to pee. It was a suggestion at first, easily ignorable. Later, a little more insistent, but still deferrable. Finally, an ultimatum. The bladder is a predictable negotiator.

I stumbled out of the creamy dimness of the tent and into the sharp white light of sun on snow. I took five blind steps, tripped over the wire, regained some vision, veered right and pulled to a stop when I thought I was far enough to not overly befoul my camp. The sun, which typically penetrated the cloud with all the intensity of gravy through gauze, was unusually confident. Into that light, I unleashed a stream of sparks, which I watched through a single, half-open eye. It was a beautiful sight. I restowed myself and walked back past the qamutik towards the tent. The shadow of the harpoon fell across the sled at a spot almost exactly opposite the boot.

I must have slept in.

It was my first real day on the floe and already I had missed breakfast and was late for work. I rooted around in the tent for my snow goggles, then grabbed an orange and set off on patrol. It was incredible, really—eleven hours of sleep and still I was tired. I figured I must have been on the ice significantly longer than I had thought. A week maybe. I had been depriving myself of sleep for days. Now that I could stick to the clock I would be more diligent.

I measured the ice and made my marks. Little had changed in the twenty-four hours since my last survey. The distances were much the same. The wind, which had shifted around Bow overnight, settled that morning before dying out. The water stilled. To one side of the ice, a vault of gray clouds shut out the sky and inched towards the sun. My island's surface was itself unchanged—pools of turquoise bounded by white, a Bahamas caye rendered in ice. On the line between Starboard and Stern I found a crack that gave me some concern, but I wasn't able to convince myself that it was either new or ominous. Certainly the ice on either side seemed solid enough. I made a note and moved on.

And so it went. I went about my tasks with the mindlessness of a shop worker, an eye more to the end of the shift than the job to be done. It was liberating. Time eased away. In the early afternoon when the sun had passed the Starboard stake, I decided to take a break. I took a Coke to the edge and sat on the hummock that contained the rope. I hadn't lingered at this spot since Sim's drowning. On that occasion, I had sat soaking wet and wailed into the wind until my eyes froze shut. This time, I had a bit more control. I was, temporarily at least, comfortable. The cardboard goggles shielded my eyes from the sun and the seals from my sight. I had food and shelter. I was warm. I had time.

And so I cried for Sim.

It was more a weeping than a wailing. It wasn't the unleashed grief of acute loss or the terror that death, whetted, was coming back for me. Those emotions I felt on the outside, like an aura or a sweat. This sadness came from inside—the deep sorrow felt for a friend. I know that no one believes I am capable of feeling such an emotion, nor will anyone care that I do. I recognize that the prevailing view is the wrong person got off that ice. But allow me a moment to mourn that man. I liked Sim. I would have liked to have had him as a friend.

The combination of crying and cold was a purgative for my nose, and before long my moustache was overloaded with snot. The arms of my Gore-Tex jacket were completely non-absorbent and my sweater had no sleeves. In the absence of anything more useful, I scraped up a fistful of snow and scrubbed my face. I blew my nose.

Out of the silence came its echo.

Then, an echo of that echo.

The sound, a sibilant puff, was coming from the left, off the water and onto the ice. It was cyclic but arrhythmic, in a meter that made no sense. A scattered set, then silence.

I waited and watched the sea.

It happened again, to the right of where I had been watching. In the stillness that followed, I projected the sound's path forward and focused on the spot where I thought it might next occur. After a minute, there was another puff—now a "psssht"—louder and closer. It seemed to have come from the site of a small wave. Above it, a little cloud of mist dropped into the sea. I watched as the surface of the water broke on either side. Two marbled melons, smooth as polished granite, rolled out of the sea. A blast of air blew from both, the same sibilant sound slightly offset. As those two descended, a row of three more followed. The first broke the surface with its tusk.

There were six, maybe more. The narwhal were coming vaguely towards me, traveling on a tangent to the ice. They would go under for a minute or two and then reappear closer, expected but not predictable. At times, they would lift their tusks clear of the water when they came up as if to show them off—*do you believe in us now?*—but most of the time they would just barely break the surface with their blowholes. On their closest pass, I could have skipped a stone between them. The alien sound of their spouting became more intimate up close. More human. A breath.

They had to have known I was there, but as I watched them pass all but one ignored me. The last slowed at the surface as its pod-mates dove. It rolled a single eye out of the water, then stopped. We were alone. We *saw* each other, that whale and I, but said nothing. The narwhal shut its eye as if to sleep and dropped back into the sea.

CHAPTER 36

Day two, post-sundial, was much the same as day one. I had spent part of the previous evening constructing a cardboard sleep mask out of the back end of the Coke box, identical to my goggles but without the slits. With it I was able to sleep more consistently. I had also made a point of moving the head of my bed to the door of the tent so that when I awoke during the night I could pull back a door flap and check the time without having to get completely up. Still, I struggled out of bed when the shadow struck Bow. I am not a morning person.

Now that I knew how much time was passing, I was able to estimate a rate of attrition. My initial pacing showed minimal change in the dimensions of the ice; it was noticeable but not bad for a twenty-four-hour period. The seal's warning aside, I was confident that in current conditions the ice would easily last as long as the food. Harder to measure, however, was the perseverance of whatever search and rescue group had been tasked to find me, or my own patience in waiting for them. I expected these might dissipate faster than the ice.

I passed much of the day at the edge. I watched for any sign of a boat along the horizon, and for animals nearer to shore. All the while I listened for any sound outside those in my own head. The only interruption was a distant plane, forty-thousand feet and a world away. That part of the Arctic is often overflown by passenger jets—usually on flights between Europe and the west (Vancouver, SFO, LAX...), occasionally on flights between Asia and the east (Toronto, JFK, DC...). On either route, that segment is in the insensate middle of a long journey, when all systems, mechanical and mental, have been put on auto-pilot. Shades down, eye-masks on; a fitful sleep in economy, a business-class buzz up front. The planes sneak ahead of their sound as if they are trying not to disturb anybody. Whenever I heard a plane, I would stop and stare skyward. I had the vague idea that I might be able to use their trajectory to deduce my own position. But with high haze and sunburned eyes, most of the time I couldn't even find the plane. I was as blind to their business as they were to mine.

When the sun dipped over Bow I retreated back to camp. I ate half a tin of sardines and a single piece of bread. I was hardly hungry, but I knew I had to stick to my schedule. A loss of appetite can be as much a portent of doom as a loss of food itself.

Days three and four were complicated by cloud. By any other measure, the weather was fine. The clouds stayed separate, clumped like curdled cream, and provided needed respite from the glare. They did, however, disrupt my ability to tell time. For most of the day the sun cast not so much a shadow as a suggestion. It would hint at the time, tease and trick me. Every once in a while when I was at work on the ice it would sneak out from behind a cloud and surprise me with my own shadow. I'd chase it back to the qamutik so I could reset the boot before the sun left me again. Seals showed up intermittently and heckled me from the sea.

On the plus side, the oysters were delicious.

Day five stood still. When I woke, the walls of the tent hung limp on the frame. The air was cool and close. I opened the flap to an inanimate world. There was no wind, no sun, just a heavy, low ceiling of gray cloud. Light seeped into it like a stain. I walked in silence to the water. The sea was inert, still to the horizon.

I tried to do my chores. With effort I could determine the quadrant of the sky that contained the sun, but not once was I able to see it directly and at no point did I get a clear measure of the time. There were no shadows. For an extended period I lost all sense of the sun's location. I had marked the last place I thought it to be and distracted myself with busy work, all the while waiting for a weakness in the sky that might let some light leak through. When the sun did return for a brief visit after an absence that felt like hours, it had scarcely moved.

I spent much of day five tracing the labyrinth of lines that scored the surface of the floe. It was less the meditative meandering of a yoga retreat, and more the mad pacing of a caged bear. I stopped at the crack between Starboard and Stern. I remembered it as a snake's tongue, a long fissure that forked just as it ended. Now it was more bird's foot. A talon. The original two branches were thicker and longer than they had been previously and were now joined by a third thumbing back towards the sea. The main crack was more muscular too—a water-filled gap that could now fit my arm.

I followed the fissure to the edge. The ice tilted under my approach, then reset. Little waves dispersed from under the ice, as inconsequential as puffs of air. I lay down and peered over the side to get a sense of the seriousness of the crack. It looked to be full thickness, but the sides didn't move independently. Satisfied with the ice's solidity, I rolled onto my back and stared at a ceiling of cloud. I held my breath and emptied my brain. Everything settled into nothing again.

The wind picked up on day six. The harpoon's shadow marked time with the tremulous hand of an old man. The sky had broken, collapsing like the ceiling of a ruined church and leaving my floe afloat among the rubble of low clouds.

After eating an orange, I spent some time at the hole. While I had been able to impose the discipline of the clock on many of my bodily systems, my colon was recalcitrant. With the wind and sun astern, I kept an eye forward and captained my ship from a squat. The ice ahead of me was bare. The Bow stake seemed to be missing. I shelved my efforts at the hole and assembled myself for a walk to investigate.

The water was rough, the ice wet and smooth. I had hoped the stake had simply blown over, but it was gone. And with the ice resurfaced as if by a Zamboni, I was unable to identify even the spot where it had stood. I couldn't be sure that the ice the marker had been hammered into was still there. I had counted steps from the hole, but the number did me no good, as my earlier marks had all been made on the stake.

I checked the others. Port was strong. Starboard was loose, like a tooth. The approach to Stern was treacherous. Waves crested over the edge and spilled onto the ice. The movement of the floe, the dampened bob of a moored boat to which I had become accustomed, was exaggerated by the back-and-forth slosh of bilge water. I stepped towards the stake and the ice sank. The puddle I was in began to fill. I retreated.

The floe was battered but still strong. Like a solo sailor in a stiffening wind, I needed to get to work. My first task would be the replacement of the missing marker. After that, I needed to devise a backup system for tracking the ice. The edge itself didn't seem safe. I pulled two more crossbars off the qamutik. I prepared one to be my new Bow marker. The other I split like kindling. I tugged the Coleman stove out from under a heap and began to set it up. There is something to be said for ancient technology—my grandfather could have started that stove, yet it always seems I'm only a week away from not being able to operate my own phone. I didn't prime the stove well and soaked the burner in gas. As a result it choked out a sooty, foot-high flame. It was perfect. I charred a half-dozen sticks and shut it down.

My plan was simple. I used the sooty stakes to mark yardage. Once every ten paces, plus or minus depending on the dryness of the ice, I'd pull a pencil from my quiver and charcoal a line onto the frozen surface. The floe had possessed the clean lines of a cricket pitch, the pure and peaceful surface of a simple game. I turned it into a gridiron. While I was at it, I began to annotate the ice.

I settled back into camp when the sun's shadow was well past Stern. It had been a difficult day and I had earned both food and rest. I ate the last of the sardines. Tomorrow, I realized, I would need to choose between opening the brisling or eating an onion.

Day seven. The wind lightened and the clouds, like kites, drifted down to touch the sea. Fog wandered across the water and over the ice. The sun flickered like a fluorescent bulb. It had been a week since I had started keeping time, possibly two since I had been set adrift. Any search underway should have been well into its second week. And yet, nothing. I didn't know what resources Brisebois and the Rangers would have at their disposal. Snowmobiles for sure, not that those would be doing them any good. Boats, I suppose, if they had dragged some over the ice. If the outpost Mountie had been feeling resourceful, he might have seconded a helicopter from some resource camp, assuming their summer exploration seasons had started up. But if there was aerial support involved it was a long way away. I had yet to see even a bird.

The fact that Canada has kept itself together is a sign of either the kindness of its neighbors or a worldwide lack of interest in what that place has to offer. Certainly, they don't put up much of a defense. The world's longest coastline and, as far as I can tell, the country seems to rely on the honor system. Once, an Arctic cruise ship I was speaking on got hemmed in by pack ice. Our captain radioed for help, summoning out of the mist a Chinese icebreaker. The Canadian Coast Guard, for their part, faxed him a form. We laughed about it on the bridge as we followed the crimson flag out of Lancaster Sound. We thanked the foreigners with a blast of the horn, but inside we raised a toast to the nonchalance of our absentee hosts.

It's easy to admire a pacifist until you're depending on him for your life.

Since my discovery of the sundial, I had been happy that time was simply passing. I knew I was going to have to wait, and keeping track of the hours reduced the torture of the otherwise endless day. But as the days bled together, I became increasingly aware there would be a point at which the likelihood of rescue would peak and the effort of those still looking would begin to wane. I worried that point had already passed. My best hope was that someone had found our tracks and would follow them to the wreck of Simeonie's machine. If they found that, they could find me.

A fugitive shadow signaled Stern. Earlier in the day I had set out the tin of brisling. I returned it to the bin unopened and went to bed.

CHAPTER 37

It was the start of my second week of recorded time—day eight—and it was cold. I sat shivering on the qamutik and waited for the sun to show. But the sky was crowded, busy with low cloud and fog. The sun was distracted. I watched it as a suspicious man might watch a lover. I had arrived in the Arctic in mid-June and we were now just past the solstice. Soon, the sun would start to drift away; it would grow distant and turn cold. The signs would be subtle at first, then certain. I knew this. I had been through it before.

I left the sun alone to flirt among the clouds and turned my attention to the sea. The water's surface was smooth that day, but the ocean itself was alive. Swells rolled like bodies beneath a sheet. My camp heaved as each wave, invisible, passed beneath the ice. I ate an orange, hoping the queasiness I was beginning to feel might settle down with food. It did not. I considered going back to bed—my mother used to reassure me that you can't vomit in your sleep (a lie of course, though hers were forgivable). I opted instead to try and walk it off, as one does when drunk. I tossed the peels into the hole as I passed, a little shit-potpourri, and weaved my way to the edge. I decided to check on my marks.

My new stake at Bow stood strong. Immovable, actually. I leaned on it like a cane and settled my stomach with a belch. At Port, the marker looked loose and a little too close to the sea. I stopped a few feet short and watched water washing over the surface between the stake and the edge. I wanted to measure that space as it looked like my ice might have shrunk, but instead I stood swaying, and stared. The slosh of the water and the heave of the ice were discordant, out of phase and perpendicular in plane. It was hypnotic. Perhaps emetic. I took a knee to make a note, then stashed my journal, steadied myself, and stood. Another belch, this one bilious. I swallowed and staggered towards Stern.

In fair weather, a quarter turn of the floe was little more than a hundred and twenty paces. On my earlier peregrinations, the section between Port and Stern had been nondescript, a quiet march as I counted my way up towards or away from the place of Simeonie's death. On day eight, with every third step going sideways, I quit counting before I was halfway done. The fog was blowing in off the water, and the Stern stake, my target, began to fade in and out of view. I considered aborting the trip at that point, retreating to the tent and to bed, but was worried about the possible attrition in the ice. I needed to get the survey done while conditions were good. Diligence, like appetite, is an attribute of survivors.

When I arrived at Stern, the entire area was slick from the previous storm's surge. The stake stood at an angle, its bottom half encased in new ice. Some of my charcoal marks were visible beneath the clear surface, distorted and uninterpretable, misrepresentations preserved under glass. I tried to mark the space with new observations, but couldn't get the soot to set into the fresh ice. In the effort, I spent a moment too long staring down. I looked up to an unhinged world, vertiginous like when you stand too fast. Except I wasn't standing. I was on my hands and a hip, legs together and to the side like a merman hauled out for a rest.

I barfed.

In all my research, I have never read the account of a starving man who has vomited. Perhaps my affliction was uncommon. Or possibly all the pages on which it had been documented were subsequently eaten. If so, I suspect it would have been done out of an equal combination of hunger and shame. I'm not proud about what happened next, but what can I say? Along with little bits of orange, I had lost a precious amount of fish.

By the time I left Stern, the fog had thickened. I stepped away from the stake and stained ice, shutting them off from sight as surely as if I had left a room. Above me was a thin wisp of fast-moving mist. Above that, blue sky. In every other direction were walls of white. Unable to see my camp or any marks—really, unable to see anything but the ice beneath my feet—I navigated by ear towards the Starboard stake. To my right was the resonant emptiness of ocean, deep and still. To my left, the thin, tinny silence of the ice. With the sounds centered, swells passed under me from behind my right shoulder. Like an ocean sailor, I trimmed my sails and set a course into the fog.

I picked up the bird's foot crack and followed it into the cloud. I could tell I was getting closer to the edge. Sounds of water began to emerge from the white noise. Along with the distant sound of surf, there was a closer, quieter noise. A persistent, pitchy tinkle of water flowing, or ice dissolving. It got louder as I walked. It was punctuated by occasional dyspeptic rumbles—borborygmic bass-beats that I could feel beneath my feet. There was a creak. I stopped. Then, a groan. I wanted to retreat, but standing in fog and surrounded by the sounds of water I was no longer confident about which way to go. The swells had changed as well, with a bit of a wobble added to the ever-present heave. I turned and started to follow the crack back.

Although I was in retreat, the movement in the ice continued to increase. The sounds became louder. I hurried. With a lengthened gait, my limp was exaggerated and my balance was even more compromised. I moved like a man being pursued down the corridor of a moving train. I got to the fork and saw, too late, a branch angled acutely across my path. I tried to stop but started to slide. I jumped, clearing the crack, but botched the landing. My right leg slipped out sideways to the full extent of some previously anonymous groin muscle. Making the sound of a mortally wounded goat, I fell to my knees, then onto my shoulder. I rolled onto my back and came to a rest. Everything hurt.

I lay on the ice and itemized my injuries. My shoulder, already sore from the crash of Simeonie's machine, was definitely hurting. My knees throbbed. From deep in my groin came an intimate ache. I was hungry and nauseated. I was cold. I was seasick. I wasn't homesick, for what that's worth. There was nowhere really that I wanted to be. I just didn't want to be there.

I have told the stories of people who pulled themselves out of plane wrecks, fell off of mountains, were carried over waterfalls, all of whom were able to get up, brush themselves off, and go home. I once met a solo ocean kayaker who had been attacked by a shark and carried on to finish her crossing.

I had tripped over a crack. I was ready to give up.

I fell asleep on my back on the ice. I may owe my mother an apology—the death of countless drummers notwithstanding, I did not vomit in my sleep that day. In fact, when I woke I did feel slightly less queasy. The mist had thinned and the movement of the ice had settled somewhat. Through gaps in the fog, I watched a plane cross the sky from my right, its four engines etching a contrail across a pale blue sky. It passed directly overhead, heading to the horizon on my left. It flew behind a cloud and I fell asleep again. It was a temporary relapse, the kind of sleep that comes at you in little waves after a deeper sleep. Echoes of unconsciousness. When I woke I didn't know for certain how long I had been out, but it felt like it had only been a matter of minutes. In that time another broken bank of fog had moved in, and was partially obscuring the sky. It cleared just as I succumbed to another nap.

That sleep was brief, fitful. I didn't have full control over my thoughts, but at the same time I wasn't free to dream. As I had nodded off, I had thought I'd seen the contrail appear out of the cloud. It was still centered overhead, but instead of a horizontal line halving the sky, this one ran on an oblique from my right foot to my left shoulder. A slash.

I dreamt a Dali dream of deformed clocks.

I woke. Another bank of fog had moved onto the floe. I watched it wash over me, unsure of whether the movement of the contrail had been part of the dream. It was possible, I thought, that the whole thing, plane included, had been part of a larger dream. I was alert, but stayed still, flat on my back and eyes fixed to the sky. When the mist moved again the plane was gone. The contrail, however, was still there. It was real. But this time it was on an angle between my left foot and right shoulder. A backslash.

I sat up.

Patches of fog lingered over parts of the floe. In the distance in front of me, the camp emerged from out of a cloud. To my left, Stern's sheen of new ice was only a few steps away, the stake a couple of meters beyond that. The Starboard marker, the one I had gotten lost looking for, stood tall and clear a long way off to my right.

"What's the matter, sailor boy?"

I turned. Ten feet behind me was the edge. A few feet off that, sitting on its own piece of ice, was a seal.

"What time is it?" I asked.

"Summertime!" the seal said.

"How long have I been lying here?"

"You mean since you fell down? That was nice, by the way. Very graceful."

"How long ago did that happen?"

"Dunno," the seal said. "Twenty minutes, maybe?"

"Twenty minutes?"

"Max."

Another seal hauled itself over the far side of the little floe. "What's happening?" it asked.

"Not sure," the first seal said. "He fell down."

"He seems agitated. Did he hit his head?"

"Don't think so. He was acting weird before he fell down."

I had been holding my head in concentration, my eyes in my hands. When I looked up, the seals' ice seemed a little to the left of where I had first seen it.

"Am I spinning?" I asked.

"Do you feel like you're spinning?" the seal said. "Maybe you should lie back down."

"Not me," I said. "My ice. Is this floe spinning?"

"Oh that," the seal said. "Yeah, it's spinning."

"Like a record, baby," the other seal said.

I struggled to my feet. Without a goodbye to the seals, I started to jog towards the camp. I heard them calling out behind me, a nondescript barking out of which I could make no words. I didn't care. My focus was on the qamutik.

When I had set off that morning I had, as always, left a boot to mark the time. On my return, the harpoon's shadow was clear and confident, a clean dark line across the qamutik and onto the ice. It was an hour behind the boot.

For eight days I had been using that shadow to mark the passage of time. To dole out food. To measure hope. I watched it now with a more critical eye. I noticed for the first time that it moved with each passing swell. A little wobble. A tell. The harpoon was fixed on the sled, the sled on the ice. The construction was sound, but the concept was flawed. It wasn't the sun that was unmoored and unpredictable. It was the ice. And me.

I thought I might be able to calibrate my machine, that maybe whatever current was spinning my ice was doing it at a steady rate. I broke open an orange and started marking the minutes with segments. If it were only the sun that was moving, the shadow would travel clockwise three-hundred-sixty degrees every twenty-four hours. Fifteen degrees an hour. A quarter degree per minute. It was imperceptibly slow, and well within the margin of error introduced by the shadow's movement on the swell. Still, I needed to measure it. I considered closing my eyes and counting through the minutes but I was too agitated to settle my mind for such a meditative chore. Instead, I placed a segment on the shadow and paced my way to the Bow stake. I shortened my steps and slowed my tempo. One hundred and eighty steps to the stake and back at one beat per second. A dirge. On my return, the shadow was a hint off the orange and towards the boot. I placed another segment and walked to Stern. Another three-minute march. The shadow had moved again.

I continued to pace from Bow to Stern and back again, stopping on each pass of the qamutik to mark the shadow. The two seals had drifted towards Starboard and were joined on the little floe by a coterie of their kin. On occasion, a new arrival would pass near the marks on its way around my ice to join them, but they said nothing and seemed to be giving me wide berth. Like a ceremonial guard at Lenin's tomb, I ignored them, counted steps, and carried on. For almost an hour (by my measure) I paced the ice and did a forensic accounting of the previous eight days. If my clock were wrong, how off might it be? Was I on the ice longer or shorter than I had led myself to believe? There had been days when time seemed frozen and others that simply slipped away. But that must have been perception. Or boredom. Or weather. After a while, I had sixteen segments lined up neatly behind the shadow. They were evenly spaced and marked a steady progress back towards the boot. I relaxed a little. The clock was keeping time. I even allowed myself the luxury of eating the first two slices of orange I had placed. But I kept my apparatus intact—I'm a scientist, of sorts— and continued to collect data.

It was at the twentieth segment that things started to fall apart. I placed it, reluctantly, between numbers seventeen and eighteen. The twenty-first was set back closer to ten. I walked faster, following a route now flagged with orange peels. Even so, the next segment went into the empty space left behind from those I had eaten. It was as if I had wound the sundial like a spring and now, in recoil, it was accelerating backwards in time. It wasn't keeping time. It wasn't rotating at a constant, correctable rate. It wasn't even spinning in a consistent direction. I hadn't built a clock, I had built a whirligig.

I was trembling. Not from cold or fear, but anger. It was a shiver that mustered itself into a shake. Then a scream. I ripped the harpoon out of its anchor in the center of the qamutik and lifted it over my head. Its shadow, released, skirted across the ice like an unleashed dog. The shadow stopped a few meters away and waited for my next move. The sun was behind me, at Port. So I stalked the shadow. Pursued it. Slowly at first, then with increasing pace. I chased it towards the Starboard edge, raising the harpoon high on my approach like an Olympian.

The seals saw me coming and scattered off their floe. I wasn't aiming for them. I couldn't have hit that ice had I tried. I heaved the harpoon into the empty water well to the left of them. It pierced the sea without so much as a splash, a pin pushed into butter.

And then it stopped.

I'd had no idea that seal was there.

CHAPTER 38

A bright crimson stain spread like a ballgown across the surface of the water. I had never seen blood in the ocean before. I would have assumed it would have been more muted. Maroon maybe. Or dilute. It's not. If anything, it was brighter. Redder. More alive.

After its sudden stop, the harpoon had rolled over and slipped under the surface. The seals were off their floe and for a moment I was alone. Sea smoke whispered around the periphery of the scene. The ice rose and fell with my breath. A finger of blood seeped out of the slick and reached towards my feet.

Bubbles broke out of the clean water to my right. Through it, a seal surfaced. As its face broke the water, the silence was pierced with a gasp—a sharp, stridorous rasp. The first panicked breath of someone released from the clasp of death.

"You hit me!" it screamed.

"Oh shit, oh shit, oh shit!" I ran down the edge to the spot closest to the seal. "I am so sorry. Are you OK?"

"No, I am not OK." The seal made a wet, guttural noise. A half-swallowed scream. "You harpooned me, asshole."

Two seals popped out of the water next to their injured colleague. A secondary slick of blood, smaller than the first, began to form around the group.

"I didn't mean to hit you," I pleaded. "I had no idea you were there."

One of the first responders broke off from its ministrations. "You hurled a harpoon into the ocean and just happened to hit a seal? You expect us to believe that? You're such a prick."

"It's true," I muttered. The seal had already turned back to help its friend. As I paced my patch of ice, they managed to get the wounded one to settle down. With its breathing calmed, it looked less on the verge of death. They coaxed it onto its back, then rolled it to one side. The seal lifted its flipper and revealed underneath a short gash. Fat extruded out of the fur-lined hole. Blood ran down its side and oozed into the water.

A fourth seal emerged, saw the wound and looked like it was going to be sick. It swam around the far side and busied itself away from the group.

"Is your friend going to be OK?" I addressed my question to an empty patch of water to the side of the seals. I couldn't watch.

They didn't respond, but I could hear them reassuring the injured seal. *It's just a flesh wound. The bleeding has almost stopped.* The pool of blood continued to grow. Behind them, a dozen heads bobbed in silent vigil. One of them was holding the shaft of the harpoon sideways in its mouth. Out of that group, a single seal swam forward. It checked on the wounded one and spoke quietly with the medics. Then it looked at me and, without breaking eye contact, swam directly towards my ice. I recognized it more by demeanor than appearance. It was their leader.

The convulsing I had been feeling a few minutes before had settled into a quivering. From rage into fear. To shame. The seal, for its part, was as calm as the sea.

"Is it going to die?" I asked.

"No."

"I am so sorry. I honestly didn't mean to hurt anyone. I was just throwing the harpoon away."

"I don't care."

"You have to believe me," I said. "I wouldn't do that on purpose. I don't even hunt."

"You think that matters? Do you think that because you're sitting up there eating fish out of a can that you're somehow absolved of all this?" The seal rose a little higher out of the water and puffed out its chest as a target. "You want a seal? Take me."

I looked down at my feet.

"Oh, yeah. That's right," it said. "You're not a hunter. So then, what exactly are you, Guy?"

"I just wanted to see The Edge." I heard the pathetic whine in my voice.

The seal stared at me.

"Schmuck."

It turned and swam back to its injured friend. After a brief conversation, the wounded one tipped up its nose and went under, accompanied by its helpers. The leader barked some orders at the bystanders and the crowd began to disperse. When it was just me and the leader left, the seal took one last long look at me, then dove.

The two pools of blood merged and dissolved into the sea. The harpoon shaft, abandoned, floated on the surface to the side of the

270

seals' smaller ice. I was exhausted, alone and utterly lost. I sat at the edge, too frightened to cry.

I stayed at the water for what felt like hours. The harpoon drifted away until it became an uncertain speck. An abstraction. I held it in my view until it was extinguished. The little floe continued its journey towards Bow, orbiting my larger ice like a moon. Or was it? I had no idea which was moving, it or me. Or both. I felt like a lesser astronomer in Copernicus' court—my old, solipsistic understanding of space and time had been disproven, and I hadn't a clue of how to make sense of anything without it.

Eventually I got cold and stiff. I peeled myself off the ice and limped back to camp. The orange segments were scattered on the qamutik, fragments of a shattered clock. I gathered them up and put them in a pile next to my remaining food. I didn't know if it was time to eat, I couldn't tell if I was even hungry, but I allotted myself a single segment. It was mealy and juiceless, barely more satisfying than eating the peel. In the time I had left them out, they had been desiccated by the dry, arctic wind. I had three oranges left—each of them taken apart in my attempt to calibrate the clock. My food stores were now down to twenty-eight separated segments of orange, the equally arid piece of caribou, one can of brisling, and the onion. Plus flour, should it come to that. It crossed my mind that I could end up being the first Arctic explorer to subsist on Play-Doh.

I retreated to the tent. The canvas walls lay limp like the empty sails of a becalmed boat. The light inside throbbed as banks of fog moved over the ice. I tried to sleep but couldn't quiet my mind. Whenever I'd close my eyes, my thoughts, along with the motion of ice, would amplify. A heaving, nauseating cycle of seals and shadows and Sim. I undressed and swaddled myself in caribou skins in the hope I might be able to induce a proper sleep, a dreamless state. Instead, all I was able to achieve was a warm, sweaty fug that smelled of death. I did eventually fall asleep, sometime after I had given up trying. Still, it did me no good. I woke with a start, unsure of how much time had passed. I dressed and exited the tent.

All around my ice, the sea smoldered with fog. The satellite floe drifted in the distance off Port. I thought I saw an animal on the floe, but before I could confirm what it was, a wisp of fog wiped the surface clean. Another bank of fog moved aside off Stern revealing a similar floe fifty meters off that edge. From behind that, I saw a splash. In the mist, I thought I could make out another hunk of ice.

I started towards Stern. I was halfway there when I realized I had forgotten to count steps. No matter. Step-counts were going to be of limited use without a measure of time. The rate of attrition was no longer relevant, only the result. I was in a three-way race: rescue versus starvation versus drowning. Starvation and drowning were making good progress. I wasn't sure rescue was even in the running.

I came to a crack that lay perpendicular across my path. I looked back to make sure I was on course—there hadn't been a fracture across that radian before. It looked to peter out a short ways to my right, so I followed it left. Partway between Starboard and Stern, the crack connected into the bird's foot fissure, a grotesque extension of what had been that crack's little toe. Beyond that spot, the ice was unrecognizable. A sizeable section was missing entirely. Another appeared to be attached but was moving independently of the main floe. As I watched, I heard a distant groan coming from the direction of Starboard. It coursed towards me, a low growl that I could feel in my feet, passing through the main fissure just to my left. There was a pop. The ice I was on heaved up like a released cork.

I hopped over the fissure and watched as the entire segment peeled away.

"Jesus Christ," I muttered. I saw a shadow drop off the edge near the Starboard stake. I ran towards it, arcing towards camp to avoid the heaving ice and turbulent water at the newly-hewn edge.

"What the fuck are you fat freaks up to?" I screamed at an empty ocean. I saw no actual seals, just shapes and shadows. Suggestions.

Still. I knew they were there.

CHAPTER 39

I fired up the stove and pried off several more staves from Simeonie's qamutik. I kept the flame burning constantly as I walked the ice and etched the inside edge of every crack and fissure I could find. I recognize now that it was not a wise use of fuel. Regardless, I tattooed the face of the floe, then sketched its likeness into my journal. I thought of it as a code book at the time, as if hidden in the cracks might be the solution to my demise. I patrolled the ice, monitoring and marking my territory like some sad Russian general at the end of the Soviet Empire, watching powerlessly as bits of my domain kept breaking away.

The weather remained calm and foggy. Moist and close. Other ice pans and bergy bits moved in to join my floe and its armada of breakaway ice. We were all moving somewhere together. At one point, all the pieces hove together and the sea came to a stop. I stood at the edge of my floe and looked out over a larger confederation of ice, a semi-solid consolidation that stretched into the fog and out of sight. It shifted and creaked, twitched like a sleeping dog, but stayed in place. I sensed there was something a little ways farther out, hidden by the mist. Something more substantial. With the way the ice had gathered together I wondered if we had come aground, or had gotten caught up on the shore-fast ice. Either way, I realized, it might be an escape.

I stepped onto the first free segment. It shifted a bit, but stayed true. The second was more sketchy, but with a couple of hops I was able to cross it on to the third, more solid, piece of ice. I looked back to the camp. I could see it clearly—there was no fog in the way—but it looked strangely small. I recognized I was farther from camp than I had been since we were set adrift.

I continued out onto the ice pans. The navigation was complicated, as each piece made contact with multiple others, all slotting together like cells in a honeycomb. There were any number of paths forward, most of which ended at a wobbly piece of ice or a watery gap that was too large to leap. I backtracked regularly, both to find a safe way forward and to reassure myself I could still get back to the main floe. The only landmark that ever appeared out of the fog was the camp itself. The ice otherwise remained undefined and infinite. If there were land or shore-fast ice within reach, it was a lot farther than I was willing to venture. I gave up and turned back to camp.

I started back with confidence. The route I had taken had seemed easy enough and the fog was never so thick as to completely obscure my view of the camp. Even so, I ended up on a wobbly segment within the first few hops and had to back up, realign, and resume. That next line led to a lead that I couldn't jump. The third to a berg-sized pocket of slush. None looked like the route I had taken out. I bumped along the ice, parallel to the main floe but unable to find a route forward, like a housefly flying against glass. I saw one possible route, the only entry to which involved an uncomfortably long jump. It too was a dead-end. I jogged back to the start to get over the lead before it widened any further.

"Lost?"

A seal had popped up in an open patch between floes. I chose to ignore it, diverting instead to a path heading in the opposite direction. I crossed two more ice pans and came to another wide lead. Another seal was waiting for me there.

"I wouldn't jump this if I were you. What with your gimpy leg and all."

"Fuck off," I said.

I turned right. I sped up. The camp remained fixed in the distance.

A seal emerged in a narrow lead just as I was about to jump. I veered left down a narrow corridor of ice that rolled like a log. I leapt off and landed on a circular floe, then stopped. The ice rotated like a turntable. I saw seals in every direction.

It was like a funhouse at a carnival, except it wasn't fun.

I weaved, hopped, and wobbled my way back towards my own ice. The seals, like carnies, barked at me every time I passed within earshot. To avoid them, I took risks that were entirely out of character. Twice I ran across semi-sunken bergs, ankle-deep in seawater and a whim away from being flipped under the ice. Ava's qamiqs saved me. You can say what you want about seals; if nothing else, they are waterproof.

I leapt the final lead, a meter-wide gap right at the Starboard stake. I landed on my floe and was comforted when it didn't give. It didn't sag. There was no slosh of water displaced or surge of ice unloaded. Just the faintest dampening, a father's hug, and a little ripple in the water off the edge. I was back on solid ground.

The movement of the ice started back up. Whatever we had been hung up on had been displaced and the conglomeration began to disperse. My floe began to move free of the crowd. I walked back from the water towards the camp. After my foray onto the strange, unoccupied ice I realized what a mess I had made of my own island. A sagging tent and shattered sled squatted in a rabble of trash, surrounded by a thin circle of yarn. Just outside that was my bedazzled shitter, afloat with the peels I hadn't managed to flush. The rest of the ice was scratched, stained, and tagged, vandalized like an abandoned railcar. If the floe were to survive and I were not, my death would be well-documented in annotations of urine and soot.

I sat down for dinner. I was still saving the brisling, so opted for a bit of the caribou and some onion. The latter I peeled and ate like an apple. My eyes watered. I sighted a small floe off Bow. Contrary to the movement of all the other ice, this floe was moving towards me. Like it was powered. Deliberate. I blinked away my onion tears and watched. As it approached, an animal hauled out onto its far side.

"Go away!" I yelled.

I expected to hear a contemptuous bark, the seal's retort. Instead, the animal was silent. Its ice moved closer.

I scanned from Port to Starboard. There were no other seals within sight. They had left with the ice. Just the one creature coming to bother me, and at dinnertime no less.

"Leave me alone," I shouted. "I'm eating."

The animal's floe bumped into my edge.

The gaff was lying on the ice by my feet. I grabbed it as I got up. I had no intention of harming the thing, I just wanted it to go away. I wanted to dispel it, like a dream. But after the incident with the harpoon, I thought it wise to carry protection.

The animal had its back towards me and was looking out to sea. As I walked towards its floe I spoke aloud, shooing it as one might a raccoon. The closer I got, the more its seal-like shape morphed into something else, something much larger.

I slowed to a stop at the edge of my island. The animal turned to face me. Two huge white tusks hung below an old-timey moustache. It had the weathered face of a sad cowboy.

"You might want to put down that gaff, son," it said. "That kind of shit ain't going to work on me."

CHAPTER 40

"The time has come," the walrus said, "to talk of many things." Its voice was soft and oddly high-pitched for such a sizeable beast. I didn't know what walruses were supposed to sound like, but I wasn't sure this one was well. It paused to clear its throat, which in turn triggered a paroxysm of coughing.

I waited for the fit to settle. "Are you OK?" I asked.

"Just shut up for a second," it wheezed. It cleared its throat again. Its voiced loosened, the walrus lost a little of the Brando impersonation. "Seriously, I'm getting too old for this."

"How old are you?"

"Thirty-nine."

"That's old?"

"That's ancient. Unless you're a Bowhead. Those things live forever. Anyhow, we need to talk. I'm not sure you've been getting the message."

"Look," I said. "If you're here on behalf of the seals, I really don't know what else to say."

"I don't speak for the seals. I'm here for Sedna."

"Sedna?"

"You've heard of her?"

"I have."

"So you know the whole backstory?"

"I do."

"Are you sure? I know you're not from around here. I need to make sure you're up to speed with who we're talking about before we get to the nitty-gritty."

"I know her story. Drowned by her father, morphed into a mermaid-type creature, fingers turned into all the animals of the sea. All-powerful. Maybe a bit fickle."

"Vengeful."

"That too."

"Have you seen her?" the walrus asked. "A picture or a carving maybe?"

I thought about my Sedna, stashed in the drawer of a hotel room I might never again see. Her breasts. Her mons. Her braids. Powerful hands concealing her face in a gesture not of fear, but of rage.

"I have a carving."

"And how did that carving make you feel?"

"Weak."

"Alright then," the walrus said. "This is good. It'll save us some time. One thing though."

"What's that?"

"Don't ever call her a mermaid."

The walrus invited me to sit. I hooked my gaff into the side of the little island to hold our floes together, then sat cross-legged on my side of the gap. Standing, I had a small height advantage over the animal; sitting, I realized how tiny I was. The walrus was size of a small car but showed no inclination to threaten or intimidate me. In fact, it seemed fatigued even with the task of talking to me. The walrus said it was an emissary, sent by Sedna to collect my side of the story and to represent her concerns. It approached the job with the wearied air of someone nearing retirement.

I talked. For ages. More than I had talked since leaving Winnipeg. I told the walrus of my own backstory, the impetus for a trip to The Edge, the wreck of Simeonie's machine, and my suspicions about a possible shoulder injury. I began to describe the situation surrounding Sim's drowning and started to sob. The walrus hushed me. *It's OK,* it said. *We know this part. Go on.* I talked about my failed sundial, about how I was afraid I was running out of food and out of time. I told it about my troubles with the seals, that I honestly never meant to harm anyone. I asked if it were possible that they had been deliberately taunting me. *Well, they are seals,* it said.

When I was finished, the walrus sat in silence for a minute.

"Well," it said. "Sounds like you've had quite the adventure."

"I have."

"I mean it. Part of me admires your gumption."

"Thank you."

"You never belonged here. You really never should have come. But you tried. I respect that. Don't ever let anyone tell you that you didn't try."

"That means a lot to me, sir."

"Which is why it's difficult for me to have to ask you to leave."

"What?"

"You're going to have to go."

"But, why?"

"Why?" The walrus chuckled. "Well, let's see now—where should I start? You yourself just recounted a whole litany of offenses: careless use of a weapon, wounding a seal, defecating in a breathing hole—I mean, honestly, son, what were you thinking with that one? Take a look around you; take a good look at what you've done to this ice and ask yourself why. You're a mess, my friend. Sedna wants you gone."

"Can she do that? Can she just kick me off my floe?"

"Well now, the rules are clear as they pertain to the water and to the land, but ice . . . ice is a gray zone. By convention, Sedna doesn't claim dominion over shore-fast ice. You, however, are adrift. It's her call, son. Please don't challenge her on this. She'll crush your little island in a second."

"Where am I supposed to go?"

"That's up to you," the walrus said. "But I'd stay out of the water if I were you."

The walrus asked for Simeonie's gun. A sign of goodwill, it said. Detente. I asked if in exchange Sedna might grant me some time. *Not time,* the walrus said. *Mercy. Maybe.* I limped back to camp, grabbed the rifle and rooted around for any boxes of ammunition. The ten-round magazine that was in the gun was down to a single shot after our assault on the gingerbread snowman. I knew a professional guide must have brought more ammunition with him, but it certainly wasn't anywhere to be found. Perhaps if it had been in Sim's pocket when he went under, Sedna would already have it.

I shouldered the gun and turned back to Bow. When I arrived, the walrus was gone, its ice abandoned. The animal's island drifted offshore, my gaff still hooked to its side, marking it like a signature. A swell lifted the little floe, spun it slightly, then carried on across the open water towards my edge. My stomach heaved as the wave passed beneath me.

282

"Hello?" I called out. "Are you still around?"

There was no answer. Just the intestinal sounds of water under ice.

"I've got the gun if you want it." I lifted the weapon to show the sea.

The little floe rode up and over another swell. I braced myself as the wave approached my island. This one was larger than the last and I stumbled as it passed. When the ice settled, I steadied myself and stepped closer to the edge. I wondered where the animal had gone. It made no sense for the walrus to have left without the rifle.

In the distance, I saw a wave rise from the surface of the water. Others gathered from either side. They joined together into a single line that extended across the horizon, an army gathering at the front. To the right, the top of the swell curled into a break—a ragged white gash crossing a previously smooth sea. An ocean baring its teeth. The wave rose up behind the walrus's little island like a beast. It hurled the ice pan into the air, then swallowed it from sight. The sea rose in front of me.

I turned to run. I heard the crash of the water hitting the edge, the growl of the ice as it was pried from the sea. I was in a full sprint when the wave passed under me. For a moment, I gained speed, running, as I was, downhill. The ground heaved up. My knees buckled. I stumbled, then fell. I could hear a sound on the other side of the floe. I could feel it vibrate through my hands and into my core. It was the wail of a banshee.

From all fours I watched the wave cross through the floe. As it passed the camp, the tent stretched and stood erect, its ropes strained. Anchors popped. The breathing hole blew like a geyser. The tent fell like a soufflé. The swell continued to Bow and exited the far edge. Like a man regaining composure after a rage, it reassembled itself into its liquid form and traveled off to sea. The island, stilled, continued to moan.

I stayed where I had fallen, fearful another wave might be coming. As the movement of sea settled, the sounds of protest within the ice soothed. In the calm that followed, my shaking was uncontrollable. Whether the rogue wave was a warning shot or an attempt to knock me off the floe was irrelevant. Sedna had shown her hand. My time on the ice was nearing its end.

After a time, it began to seem like the imminent danger might have passed. I got up to assess the damage. The camp was intact, though the tent was down. The orange peels were out of the hole, splattered across the ice like snot on a screen. It was difficult to tell if there was any new wreckage around the qamutik and scattered provisions—the pre-swell state already had the markings of disaster— but it didn't look good. Farther away, I could see light glinting off the flooded surface of the aft ice. The Stern stake was missing. Offshore, the walrus's floe was shattered into pieces. The gaff was gone.

I reassembled my meager pantry, now reduced to the one can of brisling, a bag of flour and a gnawed-upon onion, and stowed it beside the stove. I crawled inside the collapsed tent and retrieved the caribou skins plus a few personal effects, which I then laid on top of the canvas. As I worked, swells crossed the island at intervals. None so strong as the first, but each enough to shove me to the side. Bullies in a crowd. I stumbled, but stood my ground. I gave no thought to re-erecting the tent. I was fatigued and it was futile. Instead, I crawled atop the pile of cloth and fur and lay down.

The ice continued its complaint; groans and creaks, random in direction and pitch, echoed by the sounds of my own gut. It was a private conversation, conspiring and mutinous. I lay atop the skins, face to the sky, and watched the sun spinning through the fog on its circuit around the island. I felt like I had taken up residence in one of the Frenchman's time-lapse shots of the endless Arctic night.

I closed my eyes.

CHAPTER 41

I slept poorly, weary and without rest. I burrowed into the skins attempting to keep warm, spooning one skin, smothering myself with another. A frost had formed on the folds of canvas I had heaped around me, so that every time I stirred, ice crystals would fall into my intimate spaces and melt. Cold subbed in for sleep. I gave in and got up.

The wind had increased and fog had once again moved over much of the floe. The ice, quieted, muttered to the sky as it passed. Offshore, the sea's smooth swells had shattered into whitecaps. I could feel an increase in the movement of the floe. The nausea no longer bothered me—I was too tired to vomit—but I could tell we were on the move. I had lost the gaff and thrown away the harpoon, so I picked up the rifle and went for a walk. I didn't count steps.

The Port stake had laid claim to its own little island, a lifeboat-sized berg tethered to the main floe by a length of thawed rope. It tugged at the line as though it wanted to be free. I was tempted to jump aboard, to abandon my camp and set off on a new adventure. A fresh start. I could set sail, like William Bligh, or take up oars, like Henry Hudson. Or, more likely, I would be smashed by Sedna and swallowed by the sea. I left the little lifeboat tied up at Port and walked to Stern. The ice at that end was awash in seawater and slush. The Stern stake was gone and the charcoal marks I had made earlier were smeared across the surface like tear-tracked mascara. I skirted around the sketchy ice and followed a new shore, the dry side of the former bird's foot crack, to Starboard. There, just short of the stake I found a fresh fault—a clean crack, clear across my island. It coursed across the floe to the opposite edge at the far side of Bow.

The gap by the stake was two meters wide and looked to be growing. I followed the lead to its end, a spot at the old edge where the two floes still touched. Water wormed its way into the space and was prying the pieces apart. I realized I was minutes away from losing a third of my remaining ice. There was nothing for me to do but choose sides. I stepped over the gap and looked back at my camp, at my mess. The ruins of my failed adventure. Then, with as hard a force as I could muster, I jumped back to my side and pushed the treasonous ice out to sea.

With my camp no longer centered on the floe and the floe no longer round, the rotation of the ice became noticeable and irregular. It was syncopated, lurching, as if mocking my gait. The waves buffeted the edge, adding a horizontal shudder to the eternal heave and spin. As I staggered back towards the qamutik, a new queasiness rose inside me. I wondered if it could be in part due to fear, but I felt none. I felt nothing, really. Just the emptiness and fatigue that comes with defeat.

The noise of the water faded behind me, replaced by a cyclic sucking sound that rose from the direction of the camp. As I approached, I saw that seawater had flooded over the ice from behind the tinseled tripwire, floating the scattered peels. I stopped and watched the water as it was drawn back into the hole, vacuumed in from under the sea. The peels disappeared, the pipe went dry. The sound paused, then turned, and started back up the hole. Seawater, absent the oranges, was regurgitated onto the ice. A pause, a sigh, and the ocean inhaled again.

It was the deep, wet respirations of an edematous death. It was the end of my ice.

I put the gun down beside the qamutik. I retrieved my notebook and pen from the duffel and took the tin of brisling from the kitchen, then climbed onto the bed of skins. Putting the fish aside, I opened the journal. I kept the penned capped.

I had made a career of reading and recounting the diaries of dead adventurers. Some were easy, linear accounts—logbooks really—where death was noted factually. *Geoffrey is gone. Godspeed. Boots a good fit for Daniel.* Others are circular, explosive. Insane. Professionally, I always preferred the former. I could add emotion to those stories myself, in the same way one completes a coloring book. A few simple crayons, always staying within the lines, and story would be true. Complete. Consistent. The latter type of journal comes infused with its own emotion. There is nothing for me to add to those. There is a lot that is hard to ignore.

The most difficult journal I've ever tried to make sense of was that of Donald Crowhurst, the solo sailor who entered a round-the-world race in 1968 only to drift about the South Atlantic while his competitors circled the globe. He falsified position reports, faked a faulty generator to avoid having to maintain radio contact and waited for months for the others to round the Horn. His plan, it seems, was simply to rejoin the field—not to win the race, just to finish—ideally far enough back that no one would ever notice his deception. And while he waited, he went mad. To be sure, Crowhurst had been a little cuckoo before he ever cast off. Still, he had built himself into a trap that had no way out. In the end, he stepped off the back of his boat somewhere in the Sargasso Sea, leaving his logs and his journals (and his family) behind. His last words—*It is finished. It is finished. IT IS THE MERCY*—have achieved some fame, but that may be only because they are among the few in his journal that make even a whiff of sense.

I tried to form a story out of Crowhurst's diary. It was like building a castle out of dry sand. Amazingly, much of what he wrote he himself had crossed out—a single strikethrough that left the redacted ramblings fully legible. I ended up giving up on what he wrote and concentrated instead on what he erased. It's a strategy I recommend. When reading the ramblings of a lunatic, it's usually more informative to focus on the bits that he himself thought best to leave out.

I selected four pages from my journal and tore them out, then opened the can of brisling. My plan had been to make a sandwich, but the paper made for shitty bread. Instead, I opted for a wrap. Four sheets of paper, each rolled tight around a single fish. Four oily joints. One last, lousy supper. It is worth noting that even in the depths of suicidal despair I was still able to feel disappointment. Brisling, as it turns out, is just a fancy word for sardine.

I ate, then tossed the tin and remaining fish into the shithole siphon. The ice gurgled and sucked them inside. It exhaled a froth of seawater and foam.

I uncapped the pen.

The only empty pages I could find in my notebook were non-contiguous and nowhere near the end. I couldn't date my entry. There was no temporal notation or orderly flow to allow a future reader to find my last words. I suppose I could have titled it, used all-caps and an underscore for emphasis, perhaps. Instead, I just doodled a little star. It's at the top of page twenty-two of what had been a forty-page notebook.

Under it, in the middle of an otherwise blank page, this:

I have not need to prolong the game.

My final words, a quote. Donald Crowhurst.

CHAPTER 42

A trigger warning. If you're a middle-aged asshole who has ever contemplated suicide, this next part gets heavy.

I sat on the side of the qamutik and looked out over the abbreviated ice separating me from the Port edge. The stake was now gone, as were the ropes. I had traveled untold miles from the time Simeonie had drowned, spinning like a top ever since. Still, to me, that was the place he had died. If I stepped over that edge and dropped into that sea, I might find him. I could hand him the gun. I could ask him to do this for me.

I had one bullet. One shot. One chance to get this right. A non-fatal gunshot wound would have been beyond stupid.

I removed my qamiqs and rolled off my socks. For the first time since sometime in Iviliiq, I freed my toes. They were white and soft. I wiggled them and they waved back. They seemed naive, somehow. Innocent. For a moment I felt selfish for what I was about to have them do. Then I thought of Sedna, her fingers floating free in the sea, her face a silver moon swollen with sea salt and scorn.

I slipped the pen through the trigger guard and grabbed it with both big toes. I wrapped my hands around the barrel, sat up, and looked to sea. Then, like a musician mouthing a clarinet, I took the muzzle between my lips. It was cold and tasted of iron. I removed it and tucked it under my chin instead, the cool metal snugged into the warmth of my beard.

I held the position like a yoga pose, eyes ahead and unfocused. Smoke washed across the silent sea. I could see the whitecaps and spray and knew there must be wind, but could no longer hear or feel it. The scene slowed. The heave and spin of the floe was drawn out of the ice and came up inside me. Movement was sucked into my body like seawater at the siphon, until it was only me that rocked. I was alone, my body afloat. I entered a state of calm where the only matters of significance outside my mind were my toes, distant and ready.

They tensed.

Or maybe they flinched. Regardless, they dropped the pen. I leaned forward to pick it up and clocked my chin on the muzzle. I swore and put the gun aside. Frankly, I'm surprised it didn't go off. I was rubbing the sore spot under my beard and mustering the courage for another attempt when I saw movement at the edge. A block of white, a berg below the surface. But instead of cleaving off my ice and floating free, it was coming out of the water. It was coming for me. I watched as two huge paws reached from the ocean and grabbed onto the side of the floe.

The beast heaved itself out of the water and stood sixty paces away. Water flowed from its coat and pooled onto the ice as it transitioned from an aquatic to a terrestrial state—liquid muscle freezing, forming. On Ava's wall I had seen Yves' photograph of the same scene. Although beautiful, the photo hadn't done it justice. His was artistic. This was mystic. Besides which, my bear was bigger.

The animal shook off the remaining water, completing its transformation and, amazingly, making itself larger still. It turned towards me. Two charcoal eyes and a black nose punctuated a wall of white, an emoticon communicating nothing. The face of an assassin. It didn't seem surprised to see me there.

:•

"Hello," I said.

The bear snorted a response. It stepped out of its puddle, then rose on hind legs, nosing the sky for a scent.

I cleared my throat. Still, my voice squeaked. "If you're looking for a seal they just left."

The bear, standing, looked straight at me. It hadn't come for a seal. I reached for the gun. The beast dropped down onto four legs, then started towards me.

I've heard that when faced with a bear, you should make yourself look bigger. It made sense back home among the black bears when I was growing up. I'm not so sure it's much use with bears for whom "bigger" is little more than upsizing from a small to a medium meal. In any case, I stood up. I raised my arms above my head, the rifle held out in one. The animal snorted again and continued on. I backed up onto the broken qamutik, making myself one whole foot taller.

The bear stayed its course.

It was halfway between the edge and the camp, thirty meters, max. It was in no hurry—just a steady slow pace with a slight meandering on and off the straight line to me. As the bear approached, I could hear its breath: heavy, long pulls of air that whistled as they drew through the nose and into the lungs of the beast. They weren't labored, just large. If anything, the animal seemed relaxed. It thrummed like a machine at idle.

I picked up one of the qamiqs with my free hand and threw it onto the ice to the left of the bear. The animal ignored it.

"Stop!" I yelled. "I'll shoot!"

I raised the gun. I shut my twitching eye and took sight.

I looked through the gun's iron sight at the bear's blank face. I wanted the bear to show something, anything. Menace, maybe. Intent. I begged it to speak—every other fucking animal seemed to have had something to say. The bear stayed mute. I raised the sight a foot over its head. I would have fired a warning, but had only the single bullet.

I aimed the gun, closed my good eye, and fired.

The noise was louder than the last time I had shot. Either my ears hadn't healed from target practice or they had become attuned to the relative silence of being at sea. In either case, the blast echoed inside my head and extinguished all other sound. In my haste to fire, I had failed to position the rifle properly—sorry Sim—and the recoil drove the butt into my shoulder and pivoted me off balance. I stepped backwards and felt my right foot drop between two of the sled's surviving slats. I twisted towards the ice and fell.

I was on my front, feet up and behind me. My right foot was twisted, injured, and trapped. I tried to scramble forward, towards the fallen tent, but the ruined qamutik refused to release me. I could hear nothing but the screaming deafness that had overtaken my ears. I wriggled to my side; I wanted to get a look back towards the bear, but all I could see was the scattered shit of a hobo camp. I lowered my face to the ice and waited.

CHAPTER 43

For what seemed like weeks I had been thinking about death. I had sat with a gun in my mouth not minutes before and had been at peace. Now, trapped and wounded and waiting for a polar bear to dispatch me, I felt pure fear. The bear may have offered the only honorable end to this particular life, but I didn't care. I do not want to die.

The gun, now neutered, lay out of reach on the ice in front of me. Sim's knife was packed away in the kitchen. My foot was jammed, my shoulder throbbed. I was deaf. I was barefoot. With my face flush to the floe, I whimpered and wheezed. My breath spread over the ice in a low fog.

As time passed, my terror began to abate. I wondered if it were possible the shot had scared the beast off, and if so, for how long. I tried to get up but realized my face had become fused to the ice. I was now fixed to the floe at both ends. I peeled myself from the surface, leaving behind a patch of beard and some skin from my earlobe. With my top half freed, I was able to wiggle back and wrestle my foot loose. I swung myself around and sat up. Barefoot and bedraggled, I looked around the ice. There was no sign of the bear.

It was a strange feeling, being alive at that moment. There was no sense of excitement. No celebration. Just a queasy sort of relief. I suspect it's like being released from death row or discharged from the

ICU—*OK now, get dressed. You're good to go.* I gathered my socks from the side of the qamutik, along with the one of the qamiqs. I put them on while keeping an eye out over the floe, then hopped out to get the qamiq I had thrown. When I stooped over it I noticed the drops of blood. Single at first, then sets, in a trail leading left. They were bright red on the white snow. In my monotone world of muted grays, whites, and bluish greens, they stood out like highlights on a hand-tinted photograph.

I retrieved the knife, the only weapon I had left.

I followed the blood track from where it started partway to the Port edge. It deked towards Stern, then disappeared around the back side of the fallen tent. The drops were scattered at first, then closer and thicker. Either the animal had slowed down or the bleeding had sped up. Or both. The trail wavered as it went around the tent. I followed it out the other side, then stopped. The blood carried on towards the Starboard edge to a white hummock a few meters short of shore. It was the body of the bear. A red line traced across the ice from the beast to my feet, connecting us like a thread.

I walked towards the body. Offshore, a seal strained out of the water, then dove below the surface. The bear was on its side, facing me. As I approached, I could see the fur of its chest stained pink. Its face was blank, unmoving, with eyes open. I slowed, but kept moving forward. I was less than two body lengths away when it blinked. When it reopened its eyes, I was standing still a few steps farther back. We were less than ten meters apart.

The bear was still breathing. Not the deep, resonant breaths I had heard when it first climbed onto the ice, but a faint, whispering wheeze. The sound of a soul departing. The animal watched me. It closed its eyes in slow blinks, each blink looking to be its last, each time forcing its eyes open again. It was looking at my knife.

I backed away and sat down on the snow. I watched.

I waited.

The fog climbed up from the ice, the clouds reached down. The sky became a squall. Sleet carried across the surface of the water and lashed over the floe. The wind rose and erased the sound of the animal's breaths. With its bloodied coat matted with ice and washed in rain, I couldn't see it if was breathing. I could only watch it as it stared at me, asking me to finish what I had begun.

I was wet and my beard was frozen when I realized the bear had stopped blinking. Snow had begun to settle onto it, covering its blood-stained body like a tarp. I was stiff and cold, as immobile as the bear. But of the two of us, it was me that cracked the rime and rose from the surface. I crossed through the sleet that separated us and knelt by the body of the beast. It was no longer warm, the pooled blood no longer fresh. I stroked its massive head and sank my hand into its coat. Deep inside, close to the skin, I could feel a hint of heat. An ember of life. I lay down next to the animal, curled up into it as one might a mate, and slept.

The storm increased. Clouds and fog rolled over my island and out to sea. Through small breaks, the sun scanned the surface like a searchlight. The sounds of wind and waves rose, stitching themselves into the residual ringing of my ears to create a quilt of deafness and white noise. I could feel vibrations coming through the ice—voices of the ocean, muted and low, arguing on the underside of the floe. I lay awake beside the bear, my left hand over its massive paw. In my right

I held the knife. There was a crack, and a shudder. With that, I got up. The ice heaved and shoved me back to my knees.

A few meters away, waves were breaching the edge like the gunwale of a foundering boat. Seawater pooled on the surface. Rivulets formed into fingers that reached for the body of the bear. I leaned into the beast. It didn't budge. I tried to roll it, but it was heavy and stiff and frozen to the ice. A skim of water came around the animal's head and onto the bloodstained snow. Reanimated, the congealed blood began to flow. It diffused into the water and drew back towards the sea. It moved through a lacework of channels, a capillary network suffusing the surface of the floe. The ice blushed— pinked, like a baby on its first breath.

I am not a hunter. I have not prepared animals to feed a family or to make a rug. I had a single goal at that moment. In retrospect, I'd like to say that mine was a measured response, that I acted as I did because I knew the presence of one dead bear would attract others. They are, after all, carnivores who will cannibalize the bodies of their kin. But at that moment, while I was certain others were coming, it wasn't bears I was worried about. That animal was a sentinel, sent by Sedna. I had to get rid of its body before anybody realized what I had done.

I knelt before the beast like a priest at the altar, the knife held between my hands as in prayer. I released my left hand, ran it through the fur of the bear's bloody chest until I found the bullet hole. I slid a finger inside and pulled back the skin, then inserted the knife. I sliced from the chest to the groin in one long, deep gash. I gagged on the smell of shit and seal. I could taste blood.

I pulled the entrails away from the carcass and over the ice, then set to dismembering the body. I started with a hind foot. It took me a while to understand the anatomy—the foot itself was the size of a briefcase—but once I figured out how to hold it and where to cut, its removal was quick. A slice through the Achilles tendon and around the ankle mortise and I was able to pop the thing off like a shoe. I heaved it onto the ice. Three other feet followed, then I started on the legs. It was hard work butchering that bear, and it was complicated by rolling ice and hands frozen in blood. Every once in a while, I would stop and try to move what remained of the body. It felt like I had hundreds of pounds of parts pulled aside, and still I couldn't shift what was left.

I decided to take a break. I was exhausted and hungry and less than halfway done with the job. I stacked the limbs like firewood and lined up the feet on the ice. I gathered up the stomach along with an armload of intestines and staggered towards the water's edge. The shore was undulating, the floe no longer moving as a single piece of solid ice. Seawater flowed over the surface. To my left, a small crack had opened up, into which an adjacent pool was draining. In one arm, I held a heap of omentum against my chest. I lowered myself to the ground and shimmied to the edge, the intestines stretching out behind me. Waves surged onto the ice and reached under my body. The floe heaved up from behind and pitched me forward. The ocean was conspiring to pull me in. I held firm and pushed the entrails over the side, watching as they sank straight down, trailing a cloud of blood. The intestines, following, slipped through my hands like rope. I squeezed slightly, felt the weight of the gut slow in my grip, then let go.

I returned to the carcass and sliced off a piece of liver. I sat aside the bear. Blood ran over my fingers and through my beard. The liver on my tongue was soft and warm, but tasted of iron. It tasted like the gun.

Offshore, a gallery of seals bobbed in the surf, watching me in horror.

CHAPTER 44

I continued to disassemble the bear. I didn't feel safe at the edge of the floe, so I dragged most of the organs to the breathing hole. The ice surrounding my shitter was wet and ragged; the hole itself had grown. A mouth, opening. It gasped and frothed like the maw of a mangy dog. I stood a few feet back and heaved bits of bear into the hole. It accepted most of my offerings. Some it spat back. I left those pieces on the ice where they lay.

Between the Starboard edge and the camp, the floe was strewn with body parts and stained with blood. Far from covering up a crime scene, I had turned a single shot into the site of a massacre. The knife, my arm, my chest—no doubt my face—were all smeared with the blood of the bear. Footprints mapped a path in red from the carcass to the camp to the edge of the ice. To me. Offshore, seals had begun to arrive and had surrounded the floe. Behind every wave, a face. But when I tried to focus on one, another wave would come and wipe the spot clean. I couldn't tell how many there were, dozens maybe? More? If I kept my eyes off the ocean, I could try to ignore them. Still, within the noise inside my head, I could hear their voices. Distant and unintelligible. Barking. Taunting.

I turned my back to the sea and started to peel off the hide. I hummed to drown out the seals. At one point I was certain I heard the walrus—*She's coming, my son*, it said, *I'm sorry*—but when I turned, the animal was nowhere to be seen. I pulled my hat over my ears and doubled down on dissecting the bear. Another sound began to assemble inside the tinny hiss of my injured ears. It was constant, like my tinnitus, but lower pitched, more a buzzing than a ringing. It rose to the edge of certainty. I stopped sawing at the bear, convinced for at least a moment that I was hearing something new, something real. The sound receded, slipped back into the crowd of noise and was extinguished. The voices of the seals rose up again.

I got back to work.

A while later the buzzing came back. It was louder and this time had direction. It was coming from behind me. I tried to ignore it. I had just entered the chest cavity by using Simeonie's knife to saw between ribs, then prying them apart with the barrel of the gun. I reached inside the cavity and pulled out the beast's massive heart. The buzzing became loud enough that it started to break apart into separate sounds. The drone became a whirr, and a rattle. A collection of tones, assembled. It was loud. It was mechanical.

I turned towards Stern. I held the heart against my chest and looked towards the sky. The noise was coming through low clouds, loud enough now that it started snuffing out other sounds. I stared at the space where it seemed to be coming from, above the water, in the clouds just offshore. It came over my ice so loud and close that I flinched. As it roared overhead, I saw for a moment the belly of a plane. It disappeared back into the cloud beyond Bow. The sound carried out to sea.

It was a search plane. It had military markings and was flying only a hundred or so feet above the water. But even then, it was in the clouds. If this were a random scan of the area there was no guarantee they would have seen me, and no good reason to believe they wouldn't move on. I could hear the plane circling around towards Starboard. I had to make sure I would be spotted. I dropped the heart and ran to the qamutik. I grabbed a jerrycan and began to douse the sled in gasoline. I dropped the first can on its side and left it to empty, then, using Sim's knife like a bayonet, stabbed the second. Gas bled out both sides.

I heard the plane getting closer. Offshore, seals began shouting. I picked up the first jerrycan and dribbled a line of fuel away from the sled and filled a small pool, then threw the empty back on the pile. I dug through my clothes for the lighter, then squatted by the puddle and spun its little wheel. My thumb was too cold and too numb to get the lighter to spark. The plane passed somewhere off Starboard and the sound began to recede. I switched hands, then used both thumbs. Finally, a little flame. I lowered it to the gas. The fire flashed across the ice and climbed onto the sled. The qamutik exploded into flames.

The noise of the fire drowned out any ability I had to hear the plane. With no point of reference, I scanned the sky. I doubted I was going to be able to locate it, as the clouds were close and fog continued to cross the sea. I just had to hope they would be able to pick my plume out of a crowded sky. The qamutik burned well, with a high bright flame. It was, however, burning clean. I needed more smoke. I ran to the fallen tent and dragged the canvas and the caribou skins back towards the fire. I started with a skin. A thick, foul cloud rose from the fire. It smelled of singed hair and death. I bathed in the heat of a funeral pyre.

A cloud of steam rose from the far end of the qamutik, followed by another just to its left. I poked an unburnt end of the skin deeper into the flames, then circled around to check on the steam's source. There was a hiss and the sled slumped forward. I found the front end of the qamutik resting in a pool of water. A fissure had formed from there to the breathing hole; another began to open towards the edge of the floe. The fire was melting through the ice, an accomplice to my extirpation. A hoarse wail rose underneath me. It was followed by a thunderous crack. I looked towards Bow and saw the two sides of my floe moving independently on the swells, like flail segments in a fractured chest. Ahead of me, a bus-sized segment at the edge cleaved off and turtled.

My island was being torn apart.

I ran to the bear, falling twice as the ice heaved under me. Away from the fire, I could hear the plane somewhere off in the fog to my left. I scrambled towards the edge. There was a group of seals just offshore. I called for them. I needed their help. *There's a plane!* I screamed. *I just need a little more time. Please!*

The seals parted, then dove. Bubbles rose out of the black sea between them, tracing a line on the surface that was coming for me.

It was her.

It was a shadow at first, then a shape. It was human, to a point. Feminine. Strong. She moved through the water at speed. I saw a flash of her great green tail. I wanted to escape but knew I had nowhere left to go. So I stood, knife in hand. And waited.

She surfaced. Her hands reached out of a surge of bubbles at the water's edge and grabbed onto the side of my ice. They tensed as she readied to haul herself out. I had one opportunity to buy myself more time. One chance to survive. I raised Simeonie's knife high and

304

brought it down full force, a cleaver across her knuckles. Then, with a foot to the forehead, I pushed her back to sea.

Fingers, like baby carrots, lay scattered on my ice. I scraped them over the edge with the side of the knife, and ran.

PART FOUR

CHAPTER 45

They found me hiding under the hide of the bear. From beneath the bloody skin I saw two feet approaching. I felt an enormous sense of relief. Of gratitude. As I started to crawl out, one foot planted in front of me. The other carried straight into my gut. The man stepped on my arm, then kicked Simeonie's knife across the ice.

"Where's the other guy?" he shouted.

"Sim?"

"Angalaarjuk—your guide—where is he?"

He had me on my front, a knee pressed against my back. Water dripped off him and onto the side of my face.

"He drowned," I said. "His machine. He sank trying to cross the water."

"Are you sure?"

I didn't answer. I mean, seriously, what kind of question is that?

The man pulled my hands behind my back and bound them, then dragged me a few feet from the carcass and left me on the ice. I watched him walk back towards the water. Two other people were at the edge of the floe, both women. They were dressed in similar diving gear; fins and tanks were piled by their side. One was standing, sobbing; the other on one knee in front of her, tending to the weeping one's hands. They looked like they were cradling an injured bird.

I'd like to say that the Search and Rescue technicians were kind—they did, after all, rescue me—but the bulk of their empathy was directed towards their wounded colleague. I watched their ministrations while lying on my side on the ice. They seemed to have a remarkable amount of equipment for a trio who had just jumped out of a plane and swum onto an ice floe. At one point the man left his colleagues' side to don his scuba equipment. He stepped off the edge as easily as one might step outside a house. I suspect he was looking for the fingers. The woman left her injured partner and went to the qamutik. She dragged the canvas tent over the burning wreck and smothered the flame. Snuffed it, like a candle.

The swimmer came back over the edge closer to the bear and removed his gear. He walked past me on his way back to the wounded woman.

"Any luck?" I asked.

"Fuck off," he said.

They continued their work, gathering up equipment and intermittently checking on their colleague. The man set about flagging a spot on the open ice for the helicopter. The woman came to me. She sat me up and covered my shoulders with a blanket.

"How are you doing?" she asked.

"OK, I guess," I said. I looked past her to the water. A single seal watched from a distance. "How's your friend?"

"We got the bleeding stopped. She's in a bit of pain, but not too bad. Mainly she's just stunned. Do you mind if I ask why you did it?"

She looked sympathetic. Possibly even understanding. I didn't know where to begin.

"I thought she was someone else."

310

We could hear the helicopter before we could see it, a dot in the distance coming in low. The woman gave me instructions, her voice rising in volume until she was shouting over the wet, slapping sound of the rotors.

"It's not going to be able to land," she shouted. "The ice won't support it. We're going to have to climb in while it hovers."

"Can you loosen my handcuffs?" I yelled. "They're a bit tight."

"They're zip-ties," she said. "You can't loosen them. You have to cut them."

"Can you cut them, then?"

"No."

She hauled me to my feet. With a hand to the back of my neck she bent me forward and drove me towards the helicopter. It hovered a few feet off the ice, whipping water off the surface and into my face. The injured woman was already on board and the man was heaving tanks up and into an open door. When we arrived into the confusion of noise and wind, he grabbed me like a duffel bag and threw me inside.

The helicopter lifted off and tilted forward. It arced away from the floe and over the open ocean. My world of white was replaced with a wash of greens and grays. The woman slipped a headset over my ears, muting the sound of the rotors. She fitted herself with her own and brought the microphone down to her mouth. I watched her speak. Her voice came from inside my own head.

"We're going to be about an hour to Iviliiq," she said. "Let me know if you feel like you're going to be sick."

I tried to answer. I formed the words, felt my mouth make them, but heard nothing. The woman reached to my ear and lowered the microphone. She gave me a thumbs up.

"Thanks," I said.

"Are you hungry?" she asked.

"A bit." I wondered how much blood I had in my beard. "I barely had enough food for the first week."

"The first week?" she asked, reaching under her seat.

"Yeah."

She handed me a juice box. She looked confused.

"How long do you think you've been gone?"

CHAPTER 46

We came in low over Iviliiq, executing an aerial version of the ground tour Sim had taken me on when I first arrived. The place looked bigger somehow, busier. The flags at the hamlet office were flying at half-mast and a crowd of snowmobiles was gathered in front of Ava's house. The pilot hovered over the airport while positioning himself to land. The little blue shipping container that served as a terminal building was dwarfed by a Canadian Forces Hercules aircraft. As we maneuvered, I noticed a large number of vehicles parked in front of the airport. Brisebois' RCMP truck was among them.

After we landed, the woman led her wounded colleague directly to the Hercules. The man stayed on board to assemble their gear, tossing the bags onto the gravel outside the door. Another man in military garb came over to transfer them to the plane. He stopped to lean inside the helicopter, to look at me. He shook his head, picked up the bags, and left.

With the gear offloaded the only thing remaining in the helicopter was me. My hands were still bound and I was belted in. They had left the headset on me after the flight. It continued to cancel all external sounds but intensified the noise inside my head. While the scene outside was on mute, I buzzed like a broken amp. I watched the man climb back onboard. He unbelted me, then removed the headset. I was relieved. The world was quieter without it.

"Get up," he said.

"Am I coming with you?"

"No." He gestured out the door. Brisebois was standing outside. "You're going with him."

We stood on the apron, the Mountie and the military man a few feet away conferring with each other. I swayed, on solid land but feeling at sea. Brisebois watched me throughout. When they finished talking, both men came over. The Mountie took my elbow, the other moved behind. I heard a snip and felt the pressure on my wrists release. I turned to thank the man, but he was already on his way to the plane. Brisebois led me in the opposite direction.

"Am I under arrest?" I asked.

"Not yet," Brisebois said. "I'm taking you to the health center. I don't think you ought to be out in the community right now."

He led me away from the terminal building and directly to his truck. He opened the back door, the one to the kennel-sized prisoners' compartment. I squeezed myself inside, noticing this time there was nothing on the front seat. Our trip to the nursing station was short, but indirect. I didn't know whether Brisebois was trying to avoid onlookers or if he was taking me on a perp parade. In either case, everyone we passed stared at me through the window of my cage. For what it's worth, he did avoid Ava's place.

At the health center, Brisebois pulled his truck directly into the garage. A nurse was waiting by the inside door. She led me down a hall into an examining room, bypassing the public parts of the building. The Mountie followed a few steps behind and stopped outside the door. When we were alone in the room, the nurse took my blood pressure and temperature, made a few other measurements and interrogated me on my physical state, all the while making notes in a thin beige chart. When she was confident I wasn't acutely unstable, she handed me a gown and a garbage bag.

"Put your clothes in the bag," she said. "I suggest you take a shower. You can put on the gown when you're done. The doctor will be in shortly."

She left, closing the door behind her. I was alone, again.

I began stripping off my clothes. As I laid them out, I got a sense of how others had seen me. It was a slow-motion reveal of the invisible man. My hat and gloves, along with my Coke-box sunglasses were already gone, lost somewhere around the time I had boarded the helicopter. My jacket—the high-end Gore-Tex number that had been quite a hit in Telluride—was bloody and badly torn. The cable-knit sweater vest was heavy and wet, with bits of flesh clinging to the wool like lint. The qamiqs looked surprisingly clean and were somehow dry. Still, they reeked of death. The jeans, stiff with blood, maintained their shape when I tossed them on the floor. My underclothes, consisting of layers of long underwear, shirts, and socks, had been protected from the elements and sealed from the slaughter. They had, however, been bathed in terror and sweat.

I set the qamiqs aside and, after removing my journal from the pocket of the jacket, bundled everything else into the garbage bag. I tied off the top and placed the bag and boots next to the door. I walked naked into the bathroom and adjusted the shower faucet to the exact right temperature, just on the warm side of hot. I stepped in, then leaned back to soak my head. Water ran over my face and through my beard, then continued out over my shoulders and down my arms. Blood dripped from my fingers. The pool I was standing in turned red.

Warm and dry, I sat swaying on the edge of the bed. There was a draft on my ass. Through the door, I could hear the nurse speaking with a man in the hallway.

"His vitals are good?" he asked.

"Fine," she said.

"No sign of hypothermia?"

"None at all."

"And how is he cognitively?"

"Seems OK. A bit disoriented as to time, but otherwise nothing too out of the ordinary."

The door opened. The doctor came in first, followed by the nurse. He had the same beard as me—a certified northern adventurer—though his was a bit better groomed.

"Jesus," he said. "What's that smell?"

The nurse motioned towards the garbage bag and qamiqs. She retrieved them and left the room, closing the door behind her again.

The doctor sat down and asked me to tell him my story. I recounted it much as I have written it here. When I was done, he probed me about my past medical history (minimal) and drug use (none). Following this, he conducted a half-assed physical exam. He listened to my heart and lungs much like one listens to an irritating child, with no expectation they would tell him anything of interest. He spent a few moments torturing my left eye with his light.

"Alright then," he said. "I've just got to make a couple of calls."

And then he left.

The room was white and largely bare. It heaved like a boat at sea. I found that if I walked, paced really, the unsteadiness inside me would settle. The fluorescent tube cast a shadowless light. Its buzz was in harmony with the ringing of my ears.

The man had told me the day—Tuesday—and the date. He confirmed what the military woman had said on the plane. I had been gone six days, probably adrift for four. The search was into its third day. The Hercules had arrived that morning following a lead from the local search and rescue team. The crew had spotted me on the plane's first pass.

It didn't make any sense.

I looked around the room for anything that might mark the time. There was a wall calendar, but no clock. The window looked out over the bay, over an expanse of white. The sky had cleared and sunlight glinted off the surface, but I couldn't see where the sun itself was. I leaned out the window attempting to find it when the doctor walked back into the room.

"Whoa there," he said. "You might want to cover that up."

I pulled myself back into the room and turned around. I pulled the gown together over my backside.

"What time is it?" I asked.

"Two fifteen."

"AM or PM?"

"PM." He had my chart on his lap. He hadn't opened it. "Is everything OK?"

"Sure," I said.

"Do you want to sit down?" he asked.

I was standing next to the examining table. I suspect I was swaying.

"No."

"Alright then." He opened the chart. "So here's the plan. I don't think it's safe for you to stay in town right now and there's no plane until Thursday. I also don't think it's going to be good for you to be traveling on a scheduled flight. So what I'm going to do is get you on a medevac. There's one coming in about an hour to take out a sick child. They can take you along, so long as as you are stable. That should get you to Winnipeg early this evening."

"Awesome," I said. "Thanks."

"I'm not done," he said. "This is a medical flight, not a favor. Part of the deal is that you're being transferred to a higher level of care. I've discussed your case with a team down there and they'd like to get you in for a couple of days."

"Is that really necessary?"

"Yes." he made a note, then closed my chart. "Any questions?"

"Can I go the hotel and get my stuff?"

"If you're quick. I'll see if Lance will take you over."

The nurse found a robe to cover the back of my gown and lent me an abandoned pair of sneakers from the front entrance. Brisebois drove me to the hotel. I wasn't sure why I needed a police escort, but at least it saved me from having to walk through town in pajamas. He waited in the common area while I headed to my room. I noticed someone had boarded up the broken window in the time I had been gone. I wondered if they were going to add that to my bill.

My room was much as I had left it—a metaphoric crime scene, made more literal by the cop waiting downstairs. I changed my clothes and put on my shoes. I started gathering up my gear when I realized I had left my duffel bag on the ice. The only luggage I had was the rucksack I had taken as a carry-on when I arrived. I looked at the heap of possessions assembled on the bed. I pocketed my wallet and slid the computer inside the bag. I swaddled Sedna in a sweater and shoved her in beside. Everything else I left where it lay.

I came back down the stairs.

"Got everything you need?" Brisebois asked.

"Yup." I walked past him out of the hotel. I let myself into his truck.

The medical plane was of a similar size to the scheduled flight I had taken up—a two-engine turbo-prop with the dimensions of a cigar tube. There were two pilots, a nurse, and a mother and child. Everyone but the child ignored me. We stopped once, for fuel, in Churchill, Manitoba. The child, who was on oxygen and had a nasty cough, stayed onboard. I bummed a cigarette off the mother and stepped outside for a smoke. I noticed my vertigo, which had all but disappeared while on the plane, came back as soon as I stood on solid land.

We arrived in Winnipeg in the early evening. I stepped from the plane and was hit with the heat of the summer sun, still high in the western sky. It was confident, intense. It seemed of a kind with the trickster sun of the Arctic, but not the same. A cousin maybe.

There were two ambulances waiting. As one crew bundled the mother and child into their rig, I asked the driver of the second if there were a bathroom I could use. She pointed to a low building that straddled the fence separating the airport from the city.

"Through that door. Washroom is to the right."

I walked in off the tarmac, and out onto the street.

CHAPTER 47

I t's mid-winter now and the rain is constant. Occasionally when it snows, I'll sit on the deck of this boat and watch the flakes fall onto the water and dissolve into the sea. I live in a world of grays and greens. The sun, for the most part, leaves me alone.

My journey from Winnipeg was uneventful. Their airport conveniently contains a bus station, apparently in the service of a clientele either too drunk or too poor to be allowed aboard a plane. I caught a coach labeled Saskatchewan. It wasn't where I wanted to go, but it was in the right direction. I continued from there into Alberta. Once in the Rockies, I tried my hand at hitchhiking, but found that long waits at the roadside would induce the sea-legged swoon that had been so soothed by the bus. The resultant rocking, combined with my general countenance, was not conducive to getting people to stop. So it was back on the bus, and on to Vancouver. From there I caught a ferry to Victoria and then another to Seattle. Once here, I cashed out (as opposed to selling out, see Ch. 2), bought a sailboat named *Gnomon*, and settled in to write my opus.

I leave the *Gnomon* occasionally, usually on my weekly trip to the dispensary. I'm fine on the dock but as soon as I exit the tall iron gate and make my way up the pier, the movement begins again. It's subtle at first—a bit of a shift, the sense that I'm adrift—then steadily increases. By the time I hit 36th Street, the sidewalk will be heaving like a skiff in a storm. There's a doctor in town who has been quite helpful with medications and forms, but it's the boat that keeps me sane. The condition is called *mal de debarquement*, in case you're curious. It turns out it's the reason Franklin went back to sea.

Today I made a special trip, off the boat and into town. I'm well aware that away from the *Gnomon* I appear more hobo than hermit. I'm all damp wool and wild beard. I sway when I stand and have a tendency to stare into the middle distance. I have found it helpful if I construct a false horizon out of objects on the street—mailboxes, parked cars, people—and fixate on it to dampen the movement. It's disconcerting to some, though by local standards I don't think I'm all that strange.

The clerk at the post office must have seen me as I approached today. She probably watched as I weaved my way across the street. When I entered the door she was already placing the parcel on the desk. I went through the formality of presenting my identification; she pretended to check it. The driver's license is expired. Revoked, actually.

"This one's a heavy one," she said.

I lifted it off the desk. Its weight helped anchor me.

The walk from the post office back to the boat is downhill, direct. The grade grants me speed, accentuating the limp and attenuating the stagger. The rain increased. Water washed over the road and collected against the curb. It ran along beside me like a dog. I left it in a pond-sized puddle at the end of the street and crossed to the gates of the marina.

As I came down the ramp, I paused to see if anyone was around. The only sound, aside from the rain, was the jangle of rigging and the quarrel of gulls. I was alone. I stepped onto the dock and relaxed my gait. Afloat again, my unsteadiness eased. I walked down the dock, past all the tarped and silent boats, and turned in to the *Gnomon's* berth. Across the water on the opposite slip, a sea lion had hauled out beside the *Intrepid*.

"Morning, Guy," it said. "Whatcha get today?"

"Nothing," I said. I stepped up on the deck.

"Looks pretty special," it said. "Can I see?"

I ignored it and climbed down the companionway into the cabin, sealing the hatch behind. The rain pattered at the door. I could hear, muted, the sea lion barking outside. I cleared the dishes off the table and set the parcel atop the crumbs.

Under the packing and through a ream of bubble wrap, I got my first glimpse of her. Smooth gray granite, streaked green—the characteristic soapstone of Cape Dorset. I didn't know the carver. I didn't care. I pulled her out of the box, felt the cool heft of her in my hands, then turned her slowly to ensure she had survived the trip intact. Her braids, her breasts, her tail. Satisfied, I looked around the cabin, at the prints and carvings that cluttered the place, for someplace to put her. For a spot to set her among her kin.

Epilogue

Announcer: Welcome to *In-Sight*, CBC's premier panel discussion of the stories behind the news. Hosted by Monica Burtynsky.

MB: Good evening. I'm Monica Burtynsky and this is *In-Sight*. On tonight's show we revisit last month's tragic events in Iviliiq, Nunavut, when a celebrated local guide was killed and a Canadian Armed Forces search and rescue technician was brutally maimed after a would-be adventurer went... *Over the Edge*.

(theme music, title sequence — *In-Sight: Over the Edge*)

MB: I am joined by Corporal Lance Brisebois of the RCMP in our Iqaluit studio, and by the internationally-renowned wilderness photographer Yves Fortin, joining us from Paris. Corporal Brisebois, Monsieur Fortin, welcome to *In-Sight*.

LB: My pleasure, Monica.

YF: Bonjour, hello.

MB: Monsieur Fortin, I'd like to start with you. You have worked extensively in Nunavut and knew the guide, Simeonie Angalaarjuk, quite well. Did you ever encounter a life-threatening situation when out on the land with him?

YF: The Arctic is inherently life-threatening, Monica. But the Inuit, they are survivors. Simeonie was my guide for years and never once did I feel imperiled. This man was with him for maybe, what, two days? It is impossible for me to imagine an accident that could kill or injure Simeonie, but would not harm this buffoon. Even if it is luck that he is alive, it is the luck of the criminally stupid.

MB: But Corporal Brisebois, you have determined that this is not a criminal case?

LB: Well, Monica, that's not exactly true. As the investigating officer, I share Yves' concern. But the job of the RCMP in these situations is simply to collect the evidence and to refer the case to the Crown. The total destruction of the sled in the fire left little to no evidence to inform our investigation into the disappearance of Mr. Angalaarjuk. Other than for some vandalism at the hotel, the only item of note was the erroneous trip plan filed by the accused which, I believe, was responsible for a critical delay of search and rescue.

MB: But the film of that eventual rescue—the GoPro footage we have all seen of his attack on the Armed Forces Search and Rescue technician—was that not enough to press charges? Of assault at the very least?

325

LB: In the determination of the Crown Prosecutor, that footage almost certainly would have led to an acquittal on the grounds of mental illness.

MB: We have the footage here. For those who have not yet seen it, a word of caution. What we are about to show is both graphic and disturbing. Roll the tape.

YF: Mon dieu. I cannot watch.

(video rolls… muffled yelling, watery scream)

MB: Incredible. I am, however, happy to report that Commander Sarah Pedersen, the Search and Rescue technician whose helmet-camera recorded that attack, is recovering well after the transfer of a number of toes to her injured hands.

LB: My thoughts go out to Sarah and her family. She's a real hero.

MB: To speak to the issue of mental illness, we have on the line Dr. Clarke Winkey, a diagnostic pathographer and a leading expert in the psychiatry of adventure. Dr. Winkey, welcome to *In- Sight*.

CW: Thank you Monica, it's good to be here.

MB: Now Dr. Winkey, when you see that footage, does that look to you like the behavior of a sane man?

CW: Clearly not. The man in that video is agitated and disoriented. I suspect he is delusional. The question, however, in cases such as these, is whether the delusional state resulted from the stress of the events or if it pre-dated them, possibly even caused them.

MB: So you're saying isolation and disorientation may itself have led to the conduct? Is there historical precedent for that sort of madness?

CW: Certainly. After an extended period lost or in isolation it is possible to exhibit all manner of psychopathologic symptomatology. In the journals of the *HMS Corinthian* there are some beautiful drawings of guinea fowl that suggest the onset of ornithological hallucinations early in their second year locked in the ice.

LB: For Christ's sake, Winkey, the guy was lost for four days!

YF: Il est fou.

MB: Doctor, I understand that you knew this man professionally. Was there ever a sign of instability in your earlier encounters?

CW: He was, at that point, an academic. I know there were accusations, by myself among others, of plagiarism. Beyond that I cannot speak to the reasons for his departure from the university. What I can say, however, is that a dramatic change in career trajectory is often a harbinger of mental illness or a sign of incipient neuro-cognitive compromise.

MB: Fascinating. Corporal Brisebois, the final word to you. Is there any advice you would have for self-styled adventurers who feel drawn to the Arctic with a desire to challenge themselves either physically or spiritually?

LB: Stay home. Run a marathon or something. Seriously, ask yourself why you need this. And then, if you do come, come prepared, be willing to walk away if things go the slightest bit wrong and, for the love of God, hire a professional guide.

YF: That didn't help this idiot.

MB: No, it did not. Monsieur Fortin, in memory of your friend, we would like to show a short montage of your photos and film of Simeonie Angalaarjuk as we cut to break.

YF: Merci, Monica. Adieu, mon ami.

Author's Note – About Sedna

There are multiple versions of Sedna's story across a number of Arctic cultures. In all of them, she loses her fingers in a violent altercation with her father and then drowns. Her fingers become the mammals of the sea upon which the Inuit depend; Sedna becomes a vengeful underwater goddess who controls access to them. In the various tellings of the myth, the circumstances of Sedna's dismemberment and drowning vary. The tale told by Ava Angalaarjuk in *Compass* is my own, a fictionalized merging of many of the key aspects of the Sedna myth into a version which, as far as I know, is not one that is told in the North.

GLOSSARY OF INUIT WORDS AND NORTHERN TERMINOLOGY

A note on spelling and pronunciation: there are a number of dialects and variations in pronunciation across Inuit Nunangat—the Inuit homelands of the Canadian North—and in many areas Inuktitut syllabics are used as the primary form of written communication. For those reasons, along with the fact that Inuktitut was not originally a written language, there is a lack of standardization in the spelling of many Inuktitut words. As much as possible, words in *Compass* are consistent with current usage in central Nunavut.

Most of the letters in the Inuktitut words below are pronounced as they are in English. The letter "q" is pronounced like "k," but further back in the mouth.

Aiviq	Walrus
Amauti	Long, primarily women's jacket with built-in child-carrying compartment in back
Angakkuq	Inuit spiritual mediator, or shaman
Angakkuit	Plural of angakkuq
Arviq	Bowhead whale
Floe (English)	Sheet of solid ice afloat on water, either shore-fast or floating free
Igloo	Home made of sliced blocks of snow arranged in a dome. Literally "house"
Inuit	Indigenous people of the Canadian north. Literally "people"

Inuk	Singular of Inuit. Literally "person"
Inuksuk	Cairn of rocks used as way-finding marker, often built in the shape of a human
Inuksuit	Plural of inuksuk
Inuktitut	Language of the Inuit (also Inuktut)
Kiviak	Greenlandic food made of auks fermented inside the skin of a seal
Lead (English)	Open stretch of water separating two ice floes (pronounced *lede*)
Nanoq	Polar bear
Nattiq	Ringed seal
Nunavut	Canadian Territory created in 1999 as part of the Inuit Land Claims Agreement
Qallunaaq	Non-Inuit person (also *Kabloona*)
Qamiq	Inuit footwear, often of bearded seal sole with either ringed seal or caribou upper
Qamutik	Large, low sled, pulled by either dog team or snowmobile
Qilalugaq	Beluga whale
Sik-sik	Arctic ground squirrel
Sila	Omnipresent Inuit spirit. Also used in reference to wind or breath
Thule	Pre-Inuit culture of northern North America
Tupilak	Greenlandic shamanistic figurine, made of carved bone and sinew
Tuugaalik	Narwhal
Udjuk	Bearded seal

ACKNOWLEDGEMENTS

My wife Marla has been a long-suffering and brutally honest witness to pretty well anything I have ever attempted. From the first sentence of the first draft, she has been this novel's most critical reader and its most ardent champion. *Compass* could not exist without her.

Thanks to Jane Ryder for editorial help, inside knowledge, and support. Her insight and energy were critical to my survival through the first few forays into the world of publishing.

Finally, I am forever indebted to the folks of Naujaat, Nunavut for their hospitality over so many years. I'm always amazed at the warmth, wisdom, and humor of the people of the community and learn something amazing every time I come up. It's honestly quite humbling—an endless gift of stories and experience that, as an outsider, I am phenomenally privileged to receive.

ABOUT THE AUTHOR

Murray Lee is a doctor and teacher of medicine, splitting his time between North and South, practicing as a fly-in physician for isolated communities in the Canadian Arctic and working with actors, clinicians, and students at the University of Calgary medical school. For over fifteen years he has served as the regular visiting doctor to Naujaat, Nunavut, a traditional Inuit community on the Arctic Circle, whose people, culture, and geography greatly inform the setting and character of *Compass*. This is his debut novel.

Visit his website at BOOKSBYMURRAY.COM.

-